AVALON HIGH
CORONATION

Books by
MEG CABOT

ALL-AMERICAN GIRL

READY OR NOT: AN ALL-AMERICAN GIRL NOVEL

TEEN IDOL

AVALON HIGH

HOW TO BE POPULAR

PANTS ON FIRE

NICOLA AND THE VISCOUNT

VICTORIA AND THE ROGUE

THE BOY NEXT DOOR

BOY MEETS GIRL

EVERY BOY'S GOT ONE

SIZE 12 IS NOT FAT

SIZE 14 IS NOT FAT EITHER

QUEEN OF BABBLE

QUEEN OF BABBLE IN THE BIG CITY

The Mediator Books:

THE MEDIATOR 1: SHADOWLAND

THE MEDIATOR 2: NINTH KEY

THE MEDIATOR 3: REUNION

THE MEDIATOR 4: DARKEST HOUR

THE MEDIATOR 5: HAUNTED

THE MEDIATOR 6: TWILIGHT

The 1-800-Where-R-You Books:

WHEN LIGHTNING STRIKES

CODE NAME CASSANDRA

SAFE HOUSE

SANCTUARY

MISSING YOU

THE PRINCESS DIARIES

THE PRINCESS DIARIES, VOLUME II:
PRINCESS IN THE SPOTLIGHT

THE PRINCESS DIARIES, VOLUME III:
PRINCESS IN LOVE

THE PRINCESS DIARIES, VOLUME IV:
PRINCESS IN WAITING

VALENTINE PRINCESS: A PRINCESS DIARIES BOOK
(VOLUME IV AND A QUARTER)

THE PRINCESS DIARIES, VOLUME IV AND A HALF:
PROJECT PRINCESS

THE PRINCESS DIARIES, VOLUME V:
PRINCESS IN PINK

THE PRINCESS DIARIES, VOLUME VI:
PRINCESS IN TRAINING

THE PRINCESS PRESENT: A PRINCESS DIARIES BOOK
(VOLUME VI AND A HALF)

THE PRINCESS DIARIES, VOLUME VII:
PARTY PRINCESS

SWEET SIXTEEN PRINCESS: A PRINCESS DIARIES BOOK
(VOLUME VII AND A HALF)

THE PRINCESS DIARIES, VOLUME VIII:
PRINCESS ON THE BRINK

ILLUSTRATED BY CHESLEY MCLAREN:

PRINCESS LESSONS: A PRINCESS DIARIES BOOK

PERFECT PRINCESS: A PRINCESS DIARIES BOOK

HOLIDAY PRINCESS: A PRINCESS DIARIES BOOK

AVALON HIGH
CORONATION

VOLUME 1:
THE MERLIN PROPHECY

CREATED AND WRITTEN BY
MEG CABOT

ILLUSTRATED BY
JINKY CORONADO

HAMBURG // LONDON // LOS ANGELES // TOKYO

HarperCollins*Publishers*

Avalon High: Coronation vol. 1
Created and Written by Meg Cabot
Illustrated by Jinky Coronado

Associate Editor - Kathy Schilling
Lettering - Lucas Rivera
Cover Design - James Lee

Editor - Julie Taylor
Digital Imaging Manager - Chris Buford
Pre-Production Supervisor - Erika Terriquez
Art Director - Anne Marie Horne
Production Manager - Elisabeth Brizzi
Managing Editor - Vy Nguyen
VP of Production - Ron Klamert
Editor-in-Chief - Rob Tokar
Publisher - Mike Kiley
President and C.O.O. - John Parker
C.E.O. and Chief Creative Officer - Stuart Levy

Acknowledgments
Many, many thanks to Jinky Coronado, Laura Langlie,
Amanda Maciel, Julie Taylor, and the entire team at TokyoPop.

A  Manga

TOKYOPOP and are trademarks or registered trademarks of TOKYOPOP Inc.

TOKYOPOP Inc.
5900 Wilshire Blvd. Suite 2000
Los Angeles, CA 90036

E-mail: info@TOKYOPOP.com
Come visit us online at www.TOKYOPOP.com

Text copyright © 2007 by Meg Cabot, LLC.
Art copyright © 2007 by TOKYOPOP Inc. and HarperCollins Publishers

Library of Congress Cataloging-in-Publication Data
Cabot, Meg.
  The Merlin prophecy / by Meg Cabot. — 1st HarperTeen e
    p. cm. — (Avalon High ; bk. 1)
  ISBN 978-0-06-117707-1
  1. Graphic novels. I. Title.
PN6727.C23M47 2007   2007006987
741.5'973—dc22

3 4 5 6 7 8 9 10

❖

First Edition

For Benjamin

CHAPTER ONE

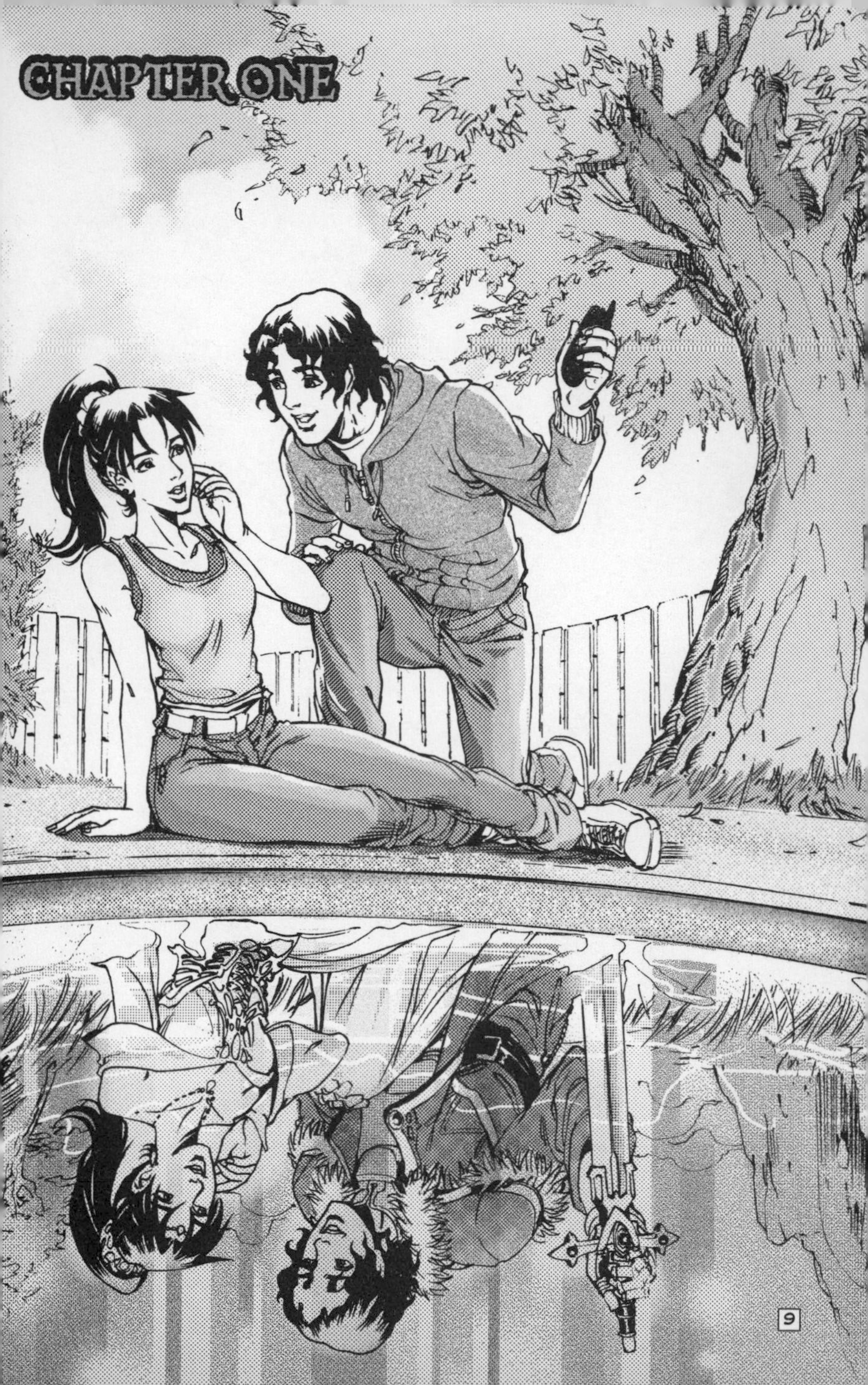

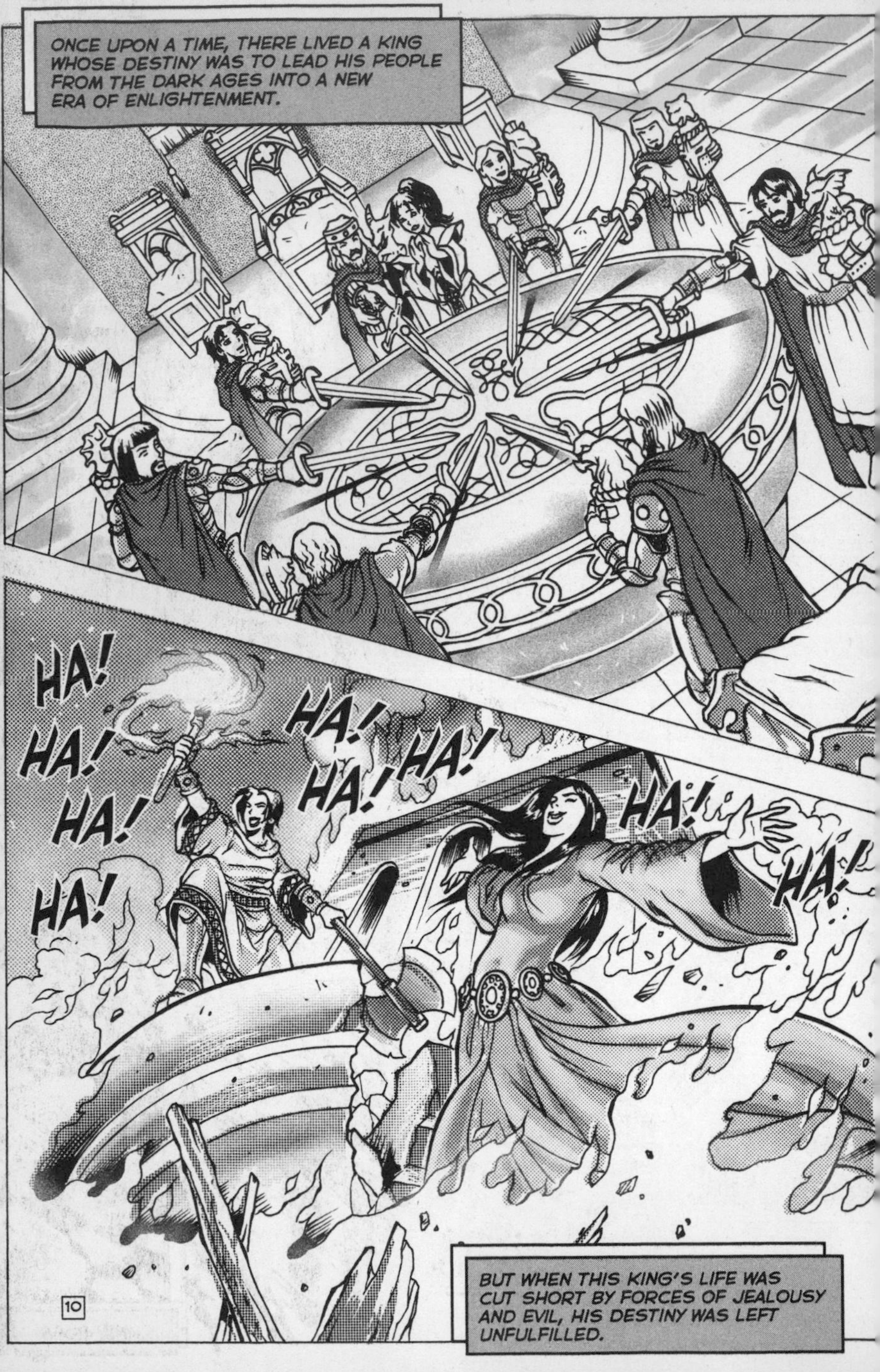
ONCE UPON A TIME, THERE LIVED A KING WHOSE DESTINY WAS TO LEAD HIS PEOPLE FROM THE DARK AGES INTO A NEW ERA OF ENLIGHTENMENT.
HA!
HA!
HA!
HA!
HA!
HA!
HA!
HA!
HA!
BUT WHEN THIS KING'S LIFE WAS CUT SHORT BY FORCES OF JEALOUSY AND EVIL, HIS DESTINY WAS LEFT UNFULFILLED.

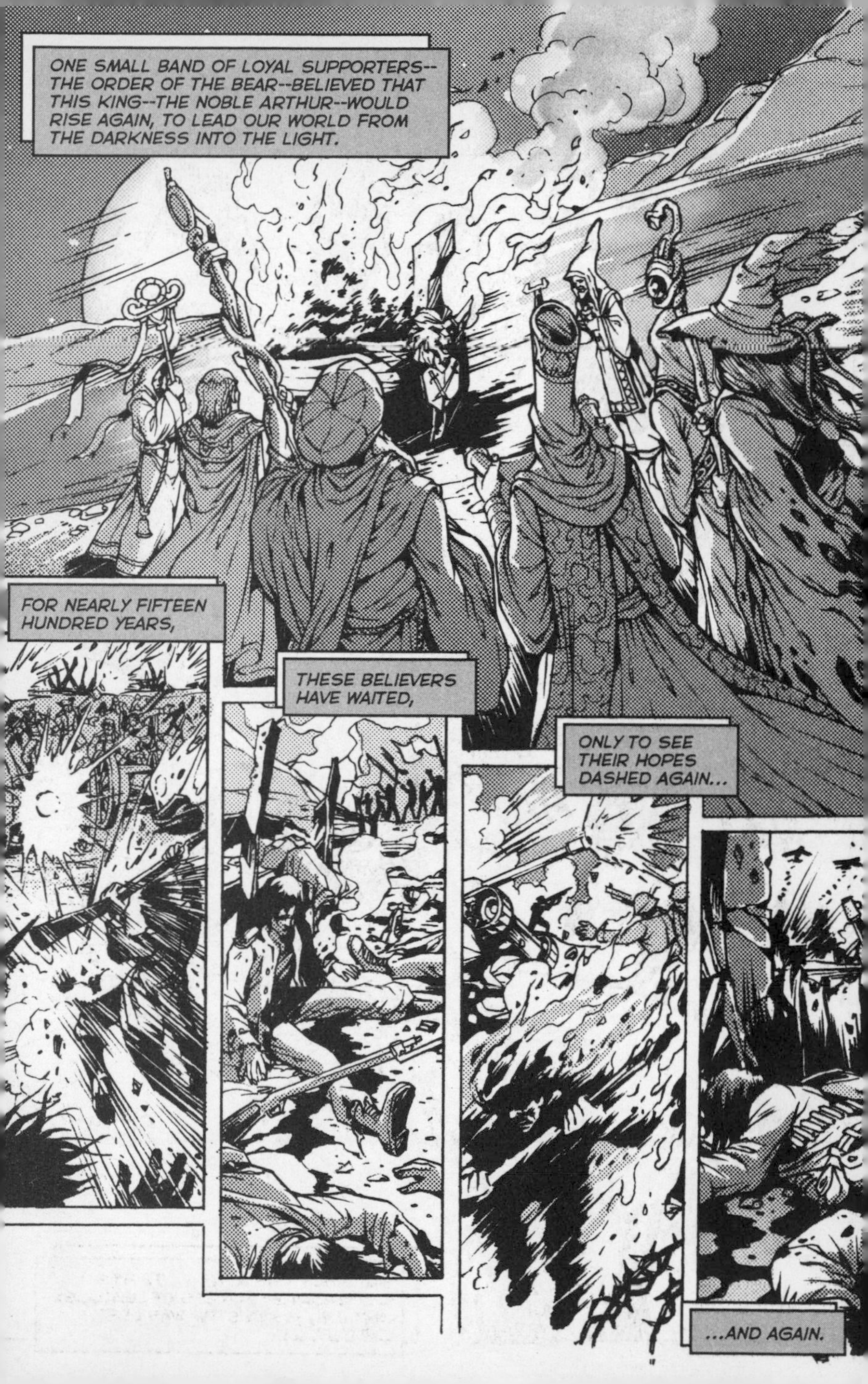
ONE SMALL BAND OF LOYAL SUPPORTERS--THE ORDER OF THE BEAR--BELIEVED THAT THIS KING--THE NOBLE ARTHUR--WOULD RISE AGAIN, TO LEAD OUR WORLD FROM THE DARKNESS INTO THE LIGHT.
FOR NEARLY FIFTEEN HUNDRED YEARS,
THESE BELIEVERS HAVE WAITED,
ONLY TO SEE THEIR HOPES DASHED AGAIN...
...AND AGAIN.

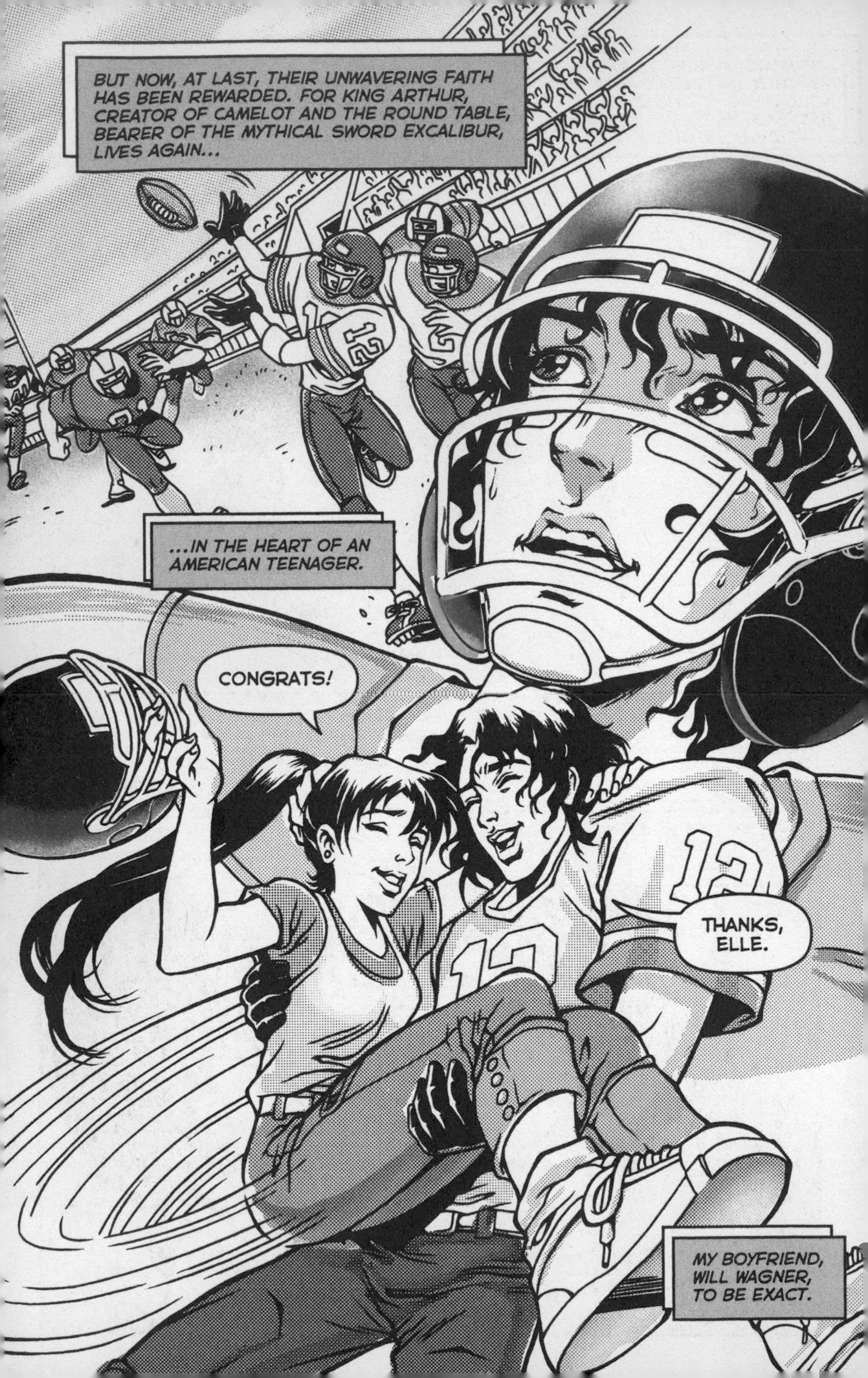
BUT NOW, AT LAST, THEIR UNWAVERING FAITH HAS BEEN REWARDED. FOR KING ARTHUR, CREATOR OF CAMELOT AND THE ROUND TABLE, BEARER OF THE MYTHICAL SWORD EXCALIBUR, LIVES AGAIN...
...IN THE HEART OF AN AMERICAN TEENAGER.
CONGRATS!
THANKS, ELLE.
MY BOYFRIEND, WILL WAGNER, TO BE EXACT.

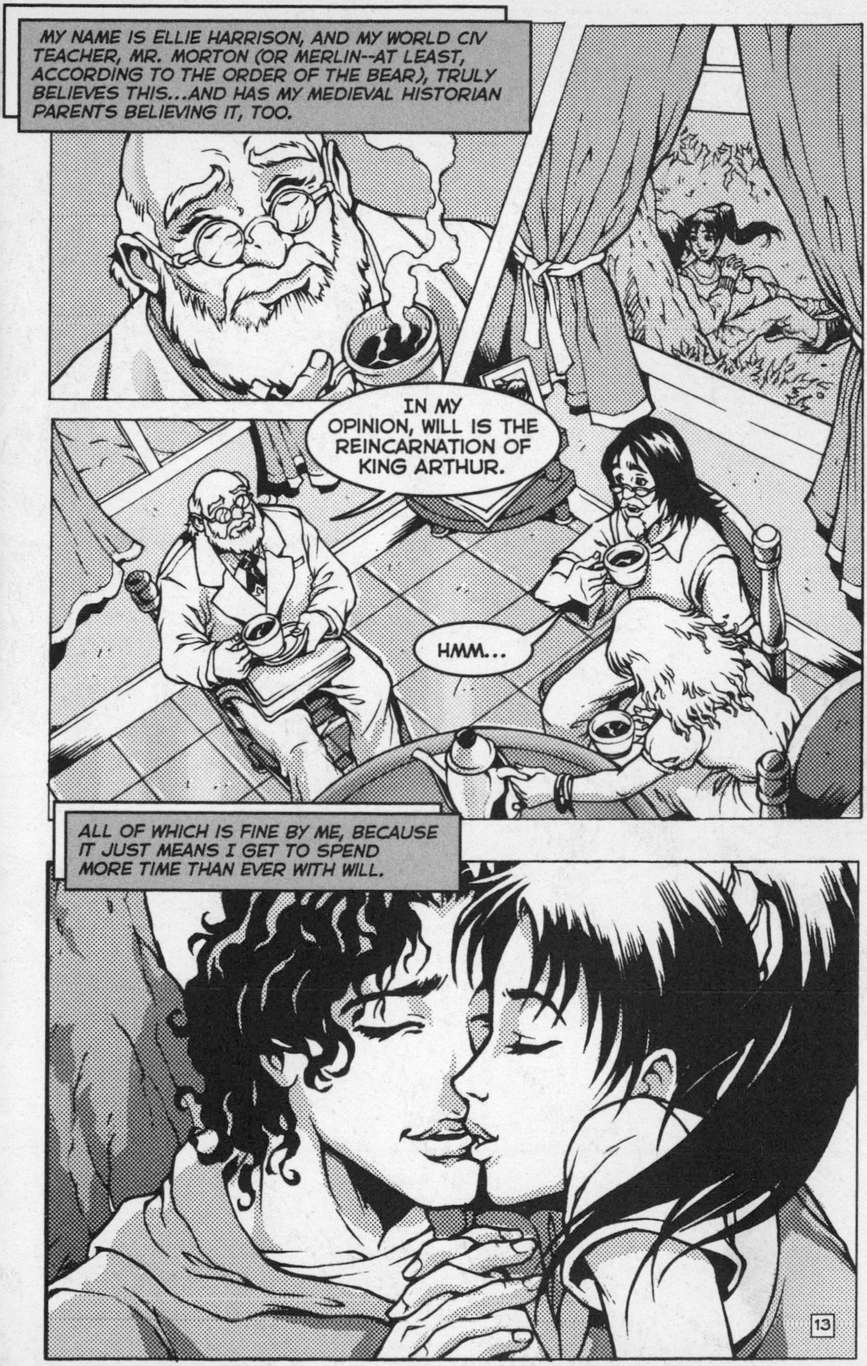
MY NAME IS ELLIE HARRISON, AND MY WORLD CIV TEACHER, MR. MORTON (OR MERLIN--AT LEAST, ACCORDING TO THE ORDER OF THE BEAR), TRULY BELIEVES THIS...AND HAS MY MEDIEVAL HISTORIAN PARENTS BELIEVING IT, TOO.
IN MY OPINION, WILL IS THE REINCARNATION OF KING ARTHUR.
HMM...
ALL OF WHICH IS FINE BY ME, BECAUSE IT JUST MEANS I GET TO SPEND MORE TIME THAN EVER WITH WILL.

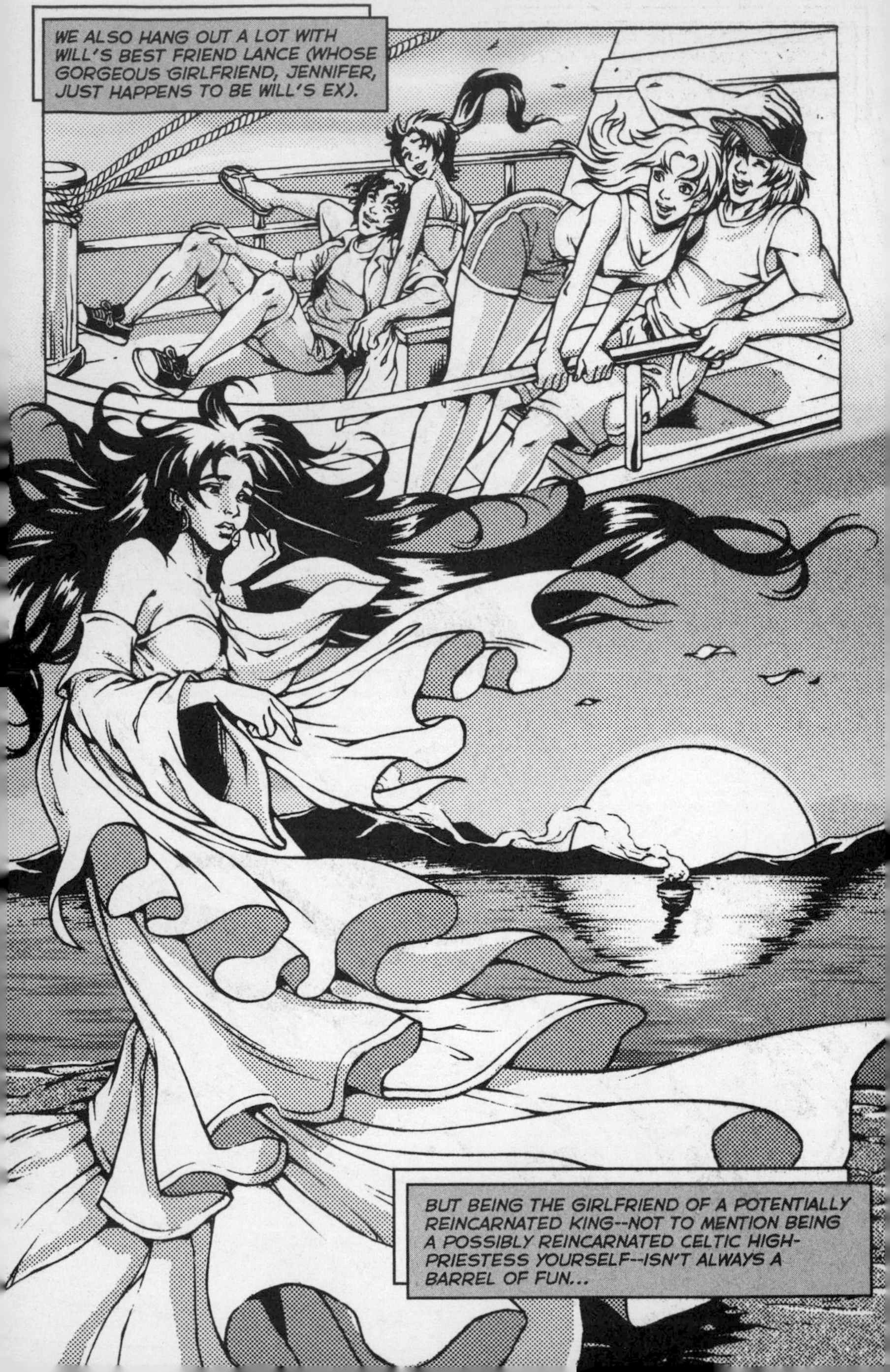
WE ALSO HANG OUT A LOT WITH WILL'S BEST FRIEND LANCE (WHOSE GORGEOUS GIRLFRIEND, JENNIFER, JUST HAPPENS TO BE WILL'S EX).
BUT BEING THE GIRLFRIEND OF A POTENTIALLY REINCARNATED KING--NOT TO MENTION BEING A POSSIBLY REINCARNATED CELTIC HIGH-PRIESTESS YOURSELF--ISN'T ALWAYS A BARREL OF FUN...

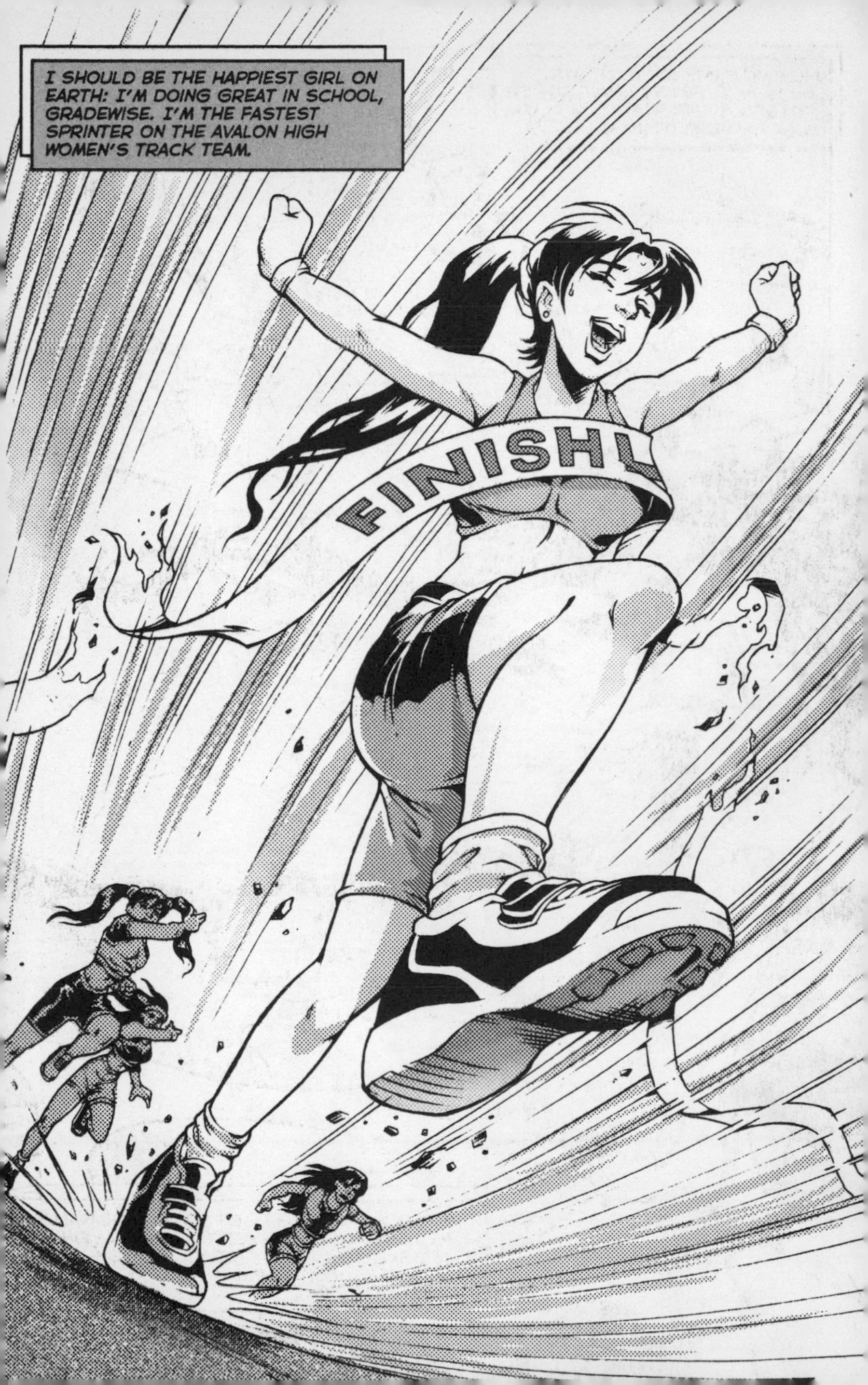
I SHOULD BE THE HAPPIEST GIRL ON EARTH: I'M DOING GREAT IN SCHOOL, GRADEWISE. I'M THE FASTEST SPRINTER ON THE AVALON HIGH WOMEN'S TRACK TEAM.
FINISH

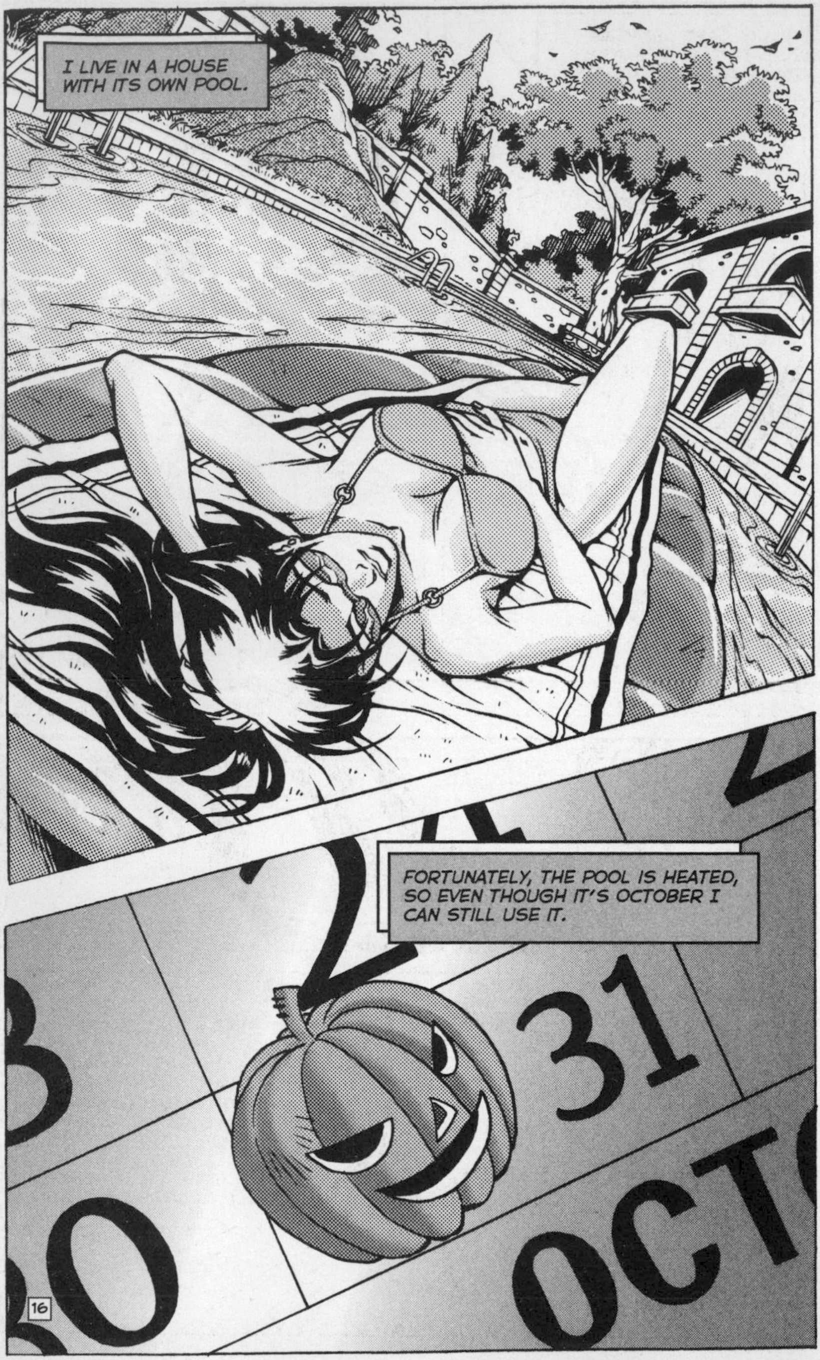
I LIVE IN A HOUSE WITH ITS OWN POOL.
FORTUNATELY, THE POOL IS HEATED, SO EVEN THOUGH IT'S OCTOBER I CAN STILL USE IT.
31

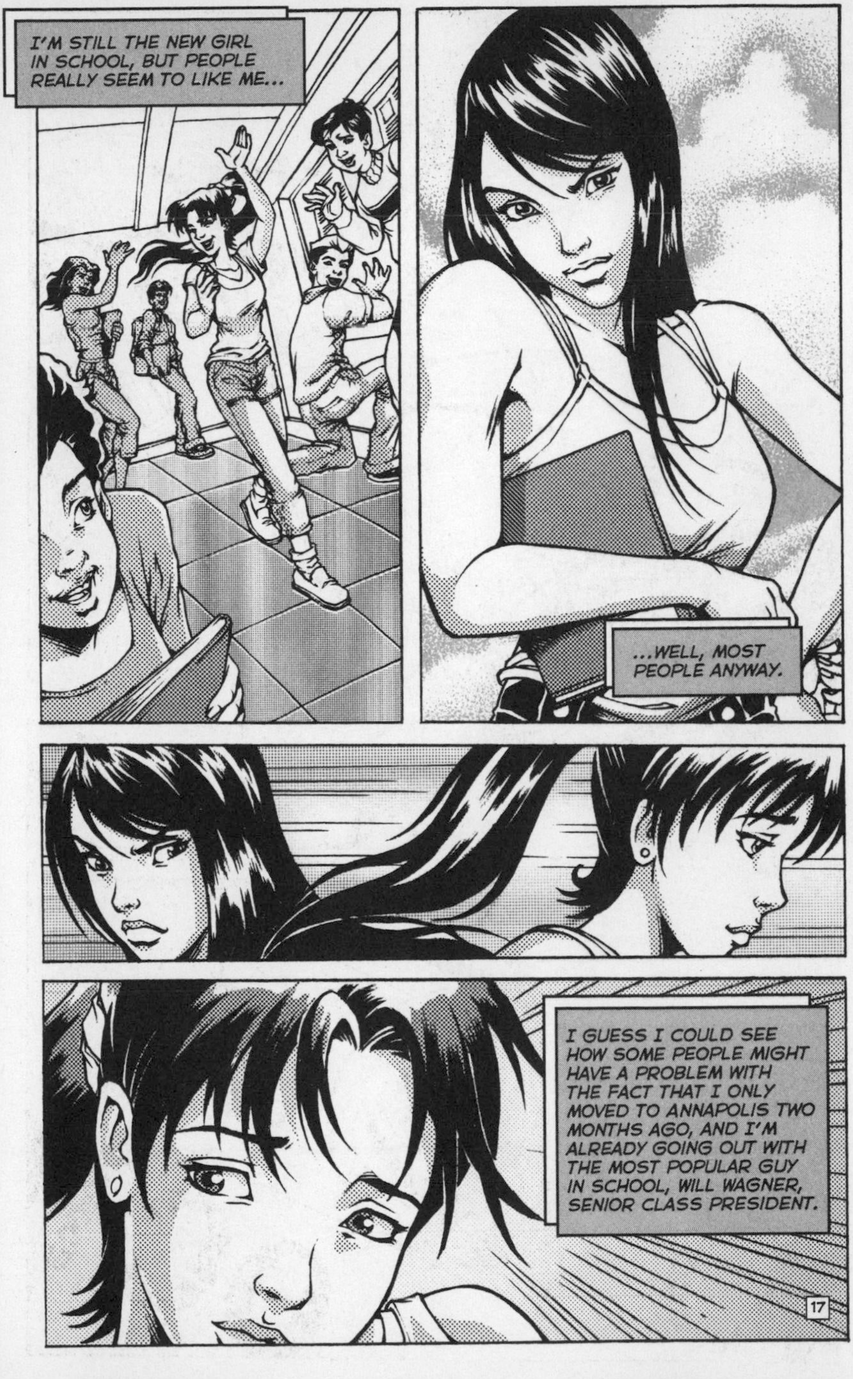
I'M STILL THE NEW GIRL IN SCHOOL, BUT PEOPLE REALLY SEEM TO LIKE ME...
...WELL, MOST PEOPLE ANYWAY.
I GUESS I COULD SEE HOW SOME PEOPLE MIGHT HAVE A PROBLEM WITH THE FACT THAT I ONLY MOVED TO ANNAPOLIS TWO MONTHS AGO, AND I'M ALREADY GOING OUT WITH THE MOST POPULAR GUY IN SCHOOL, WILL WAGNER, SENIOR CLASS PRESIDENT.

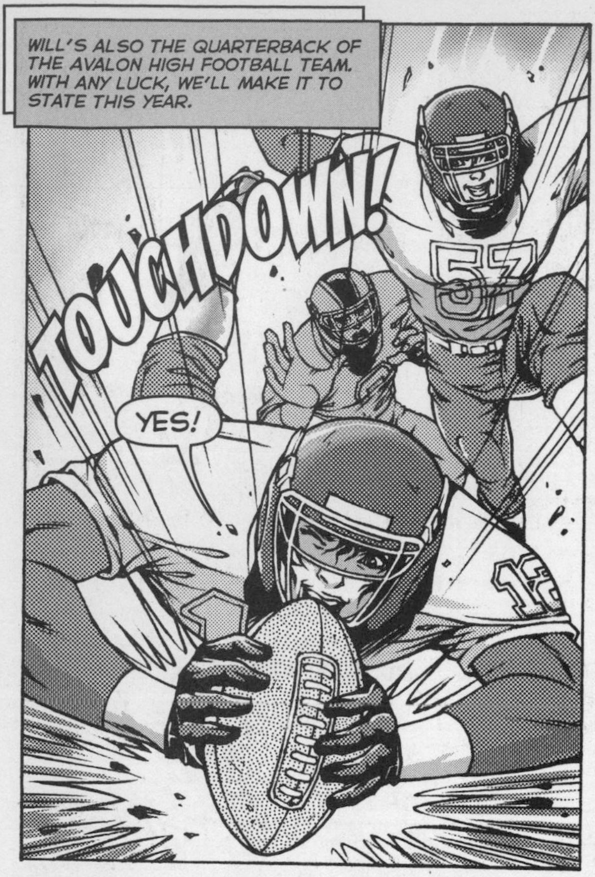
WILL'S ALSO THE QUARTERBACK OF THE AVALON HIGH FOOTBALL TEAM. WITH ANY LUCK, WE'LL MAKE IT TO STATE THIS YEAR.
TOUCHDOWN!
YES!
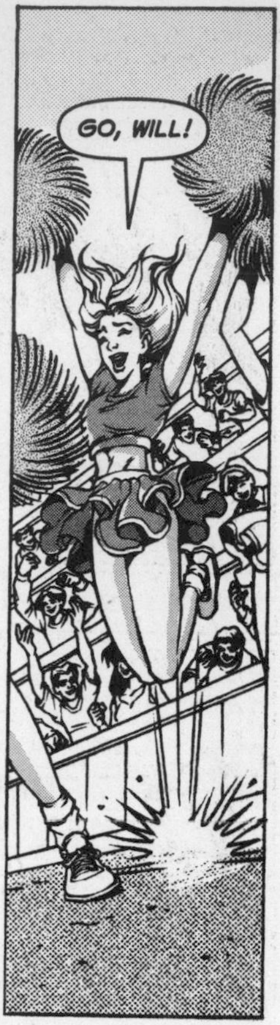
GO, WILL!
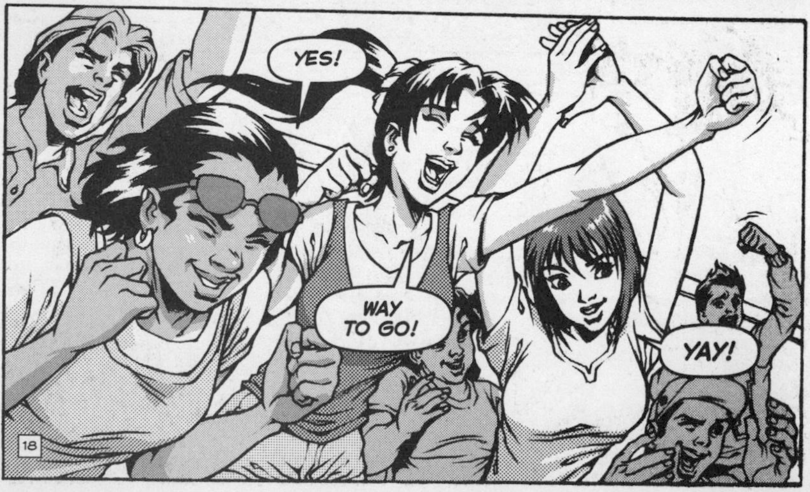
YES!
WAY TO GO!
YAY!

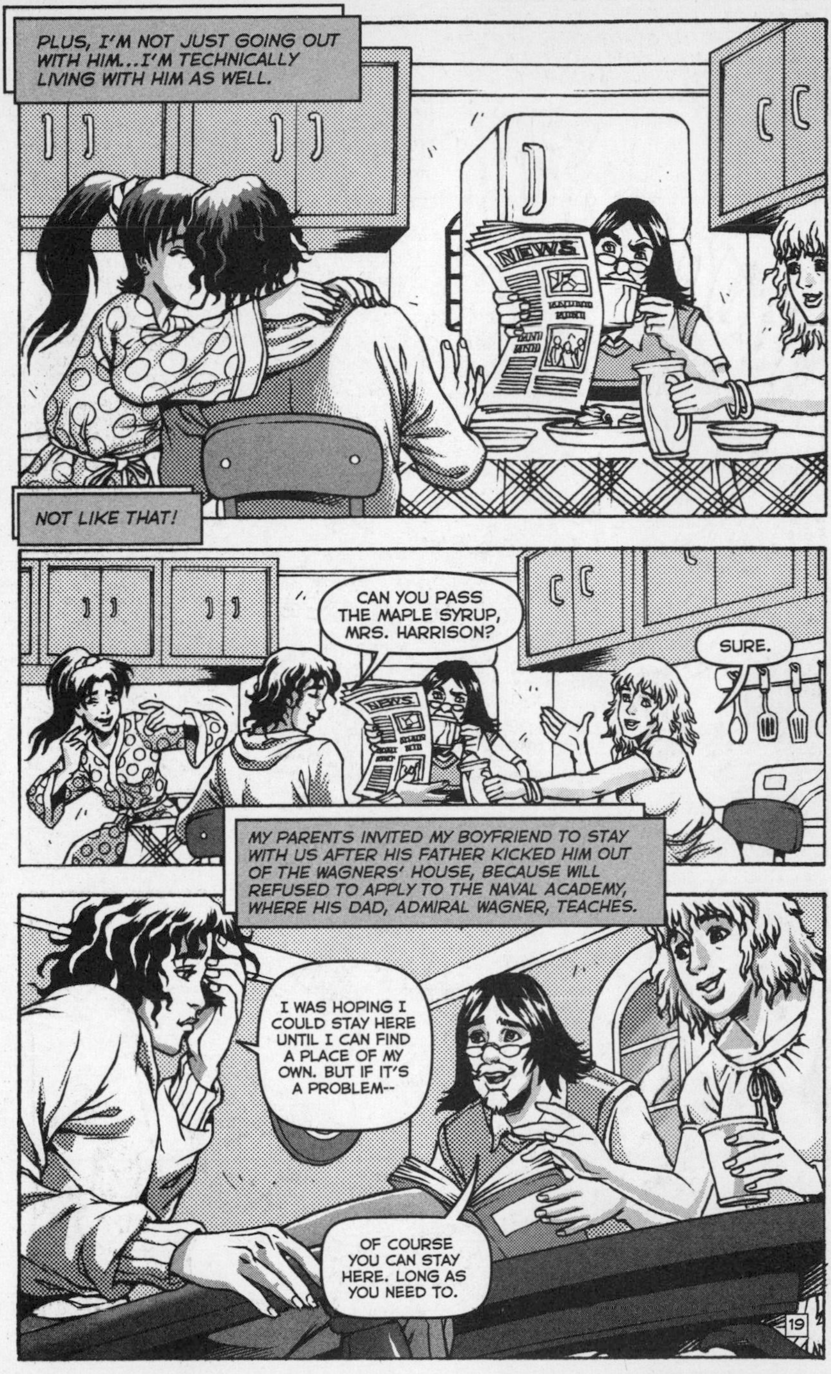
PLUS, I'M NOT JUST GOING OUT WITH HIM...I'M TECHNICALLY LIVING WITH HIM AS WELL.
NEWS
NOT LIKE THAT!
CAN YOU PASS THE MAPLE SYRUP, MRS. HARRISON?
SURE.
MY PARENTS INVITED MY BOYFRIEND TO STAY WITH US AFTER HIS FATHER KICKED HIM OUT OF THE WAGNERS' HOUSE, BECAUSE WILL REFUSED TO APPLY TO THE NAVAL ACADEMY, WHERE HIS DAD, ADMIRAL WAGNER, TEACHES.
I WAS HOPING I COULD STAY HERE UNTIL I CAN FIND A PLACE OF MY OWN. BUT IF IT'S A PROBLEM--
OF COURSE YOU CAN STAY HERE. LONG AS YOU NEED TO.

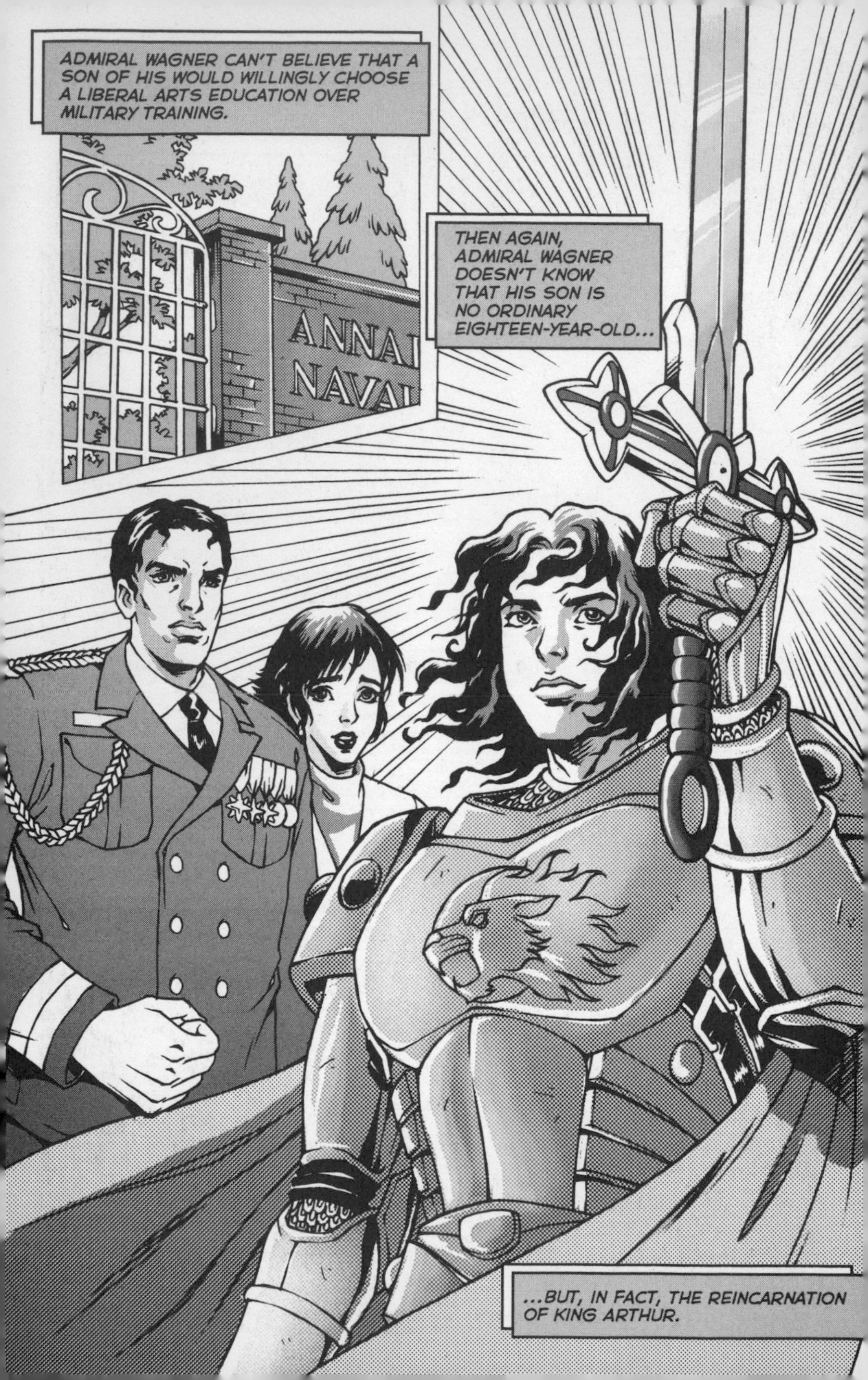
ADMIRAL WAGNER CAN'T BELIEVE THAT A SON OF HIS WOULD WILLINGLY CHOOSE A LIBERAL ARTS EDUCATION OVER MILITARY TRAINING.
THEN AGAIN, ADMIRAL WAGNER DOESN'T KNOW THAT HIS SON IS NO ORDINARY EIGHTEEN-YEAR-OLD...
...BUT, IN FACT, THE REINCARNATION OF KING ARTHUR.

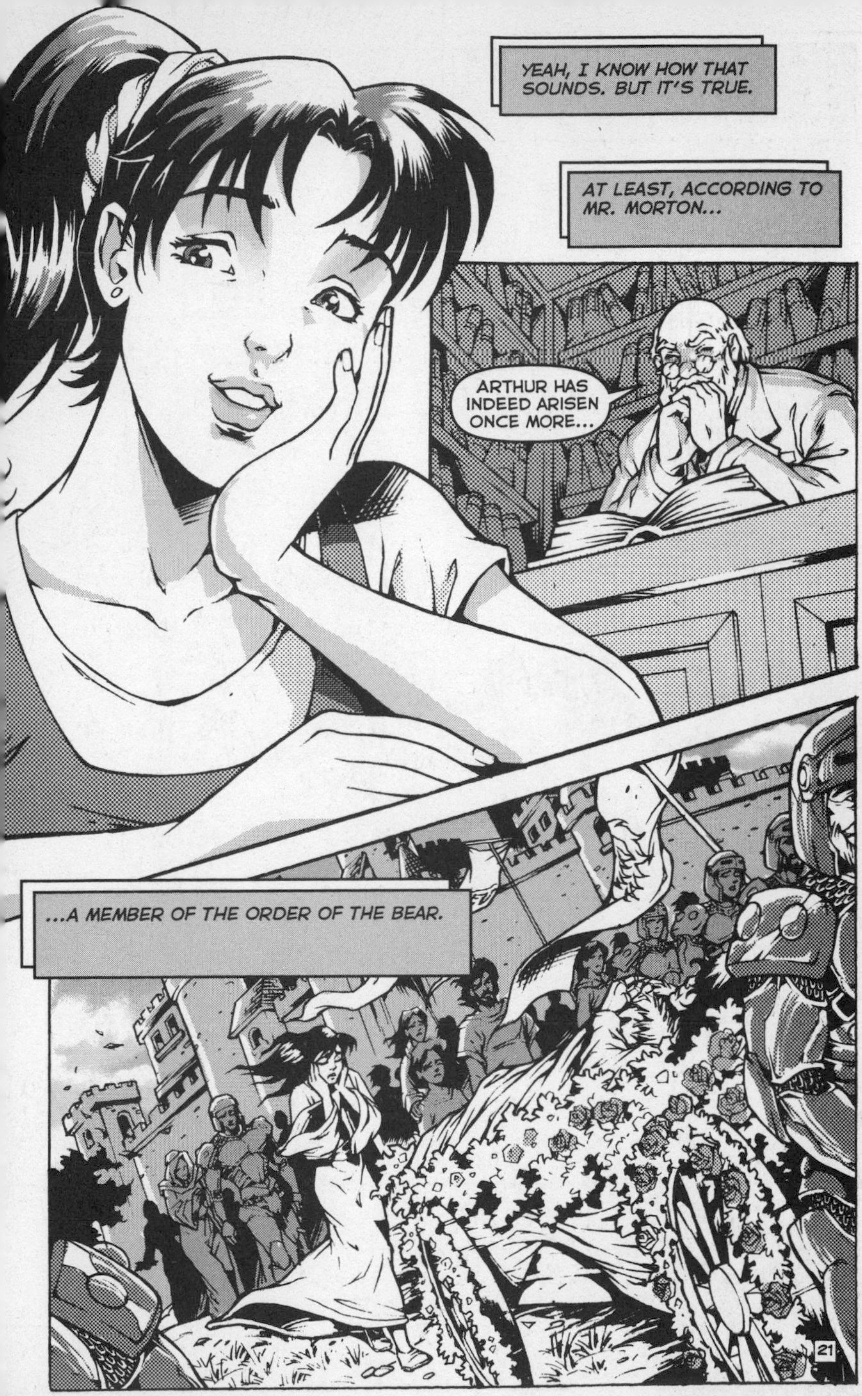
YEAH, I KNOW HOW THAT SOUNDS. BUT IT'S TRUE.
AT LEAST, ACCORDING TO MR. MORTON...
ARTHUR HAS INDEED ARISEN ONCE MORE...
...A MEMBER OF THE ORDER OF THE BEAR.

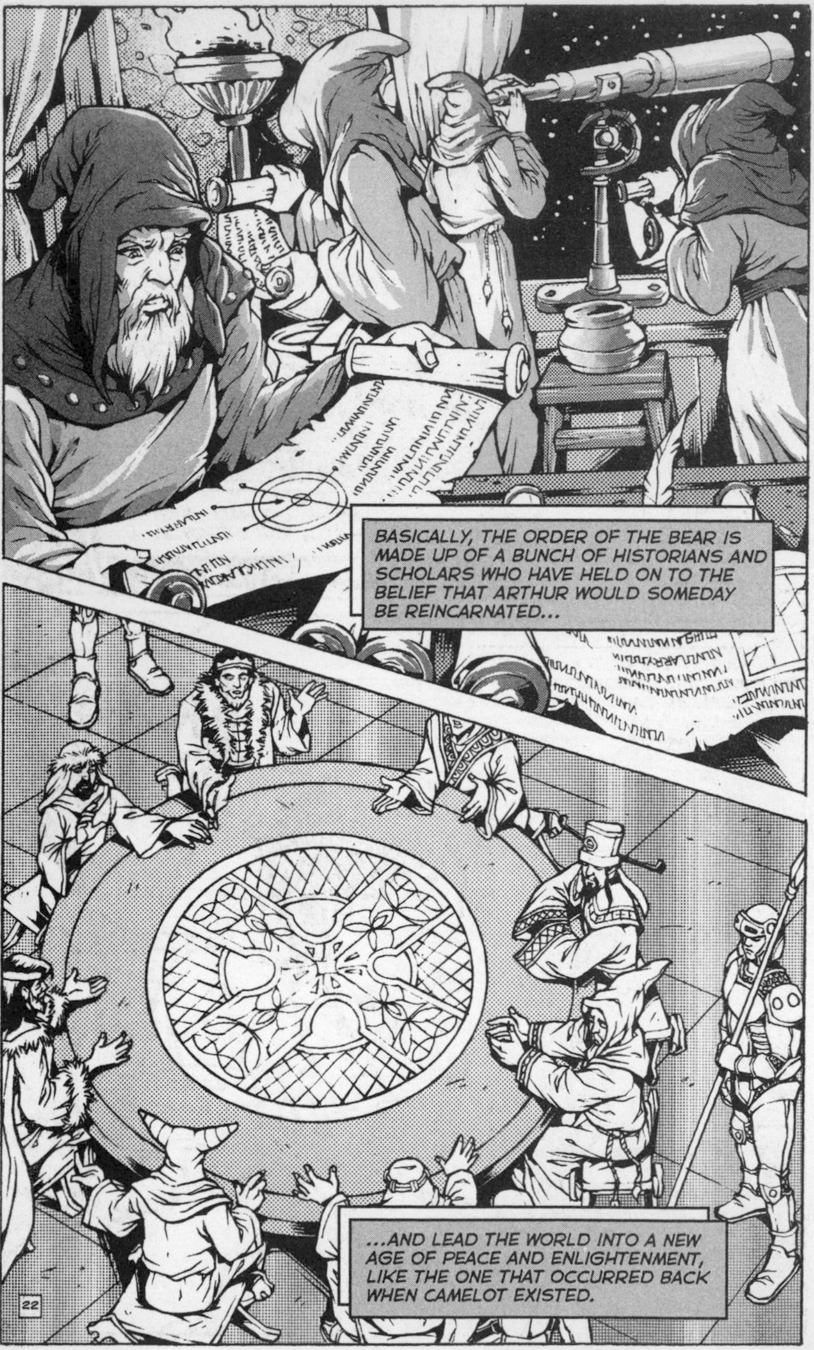
BASICALLY, THE ORDER OF THE BEAR IS MADE UP OF A BUNCH OF HISTORIANS AND SCHOLARS WHO HAVE HELD ON TO THE BELIEF THAT ARTHUR WOULD SOMEDAY BE REINCARNATED...
...AND LEAD THE WORLD INTO A NEW AGE OF PEACE AND ENLIGHTENMENT, LIKE THE ONE THAT OCCURRED BACK WHEN CAMELOT EXISTED.

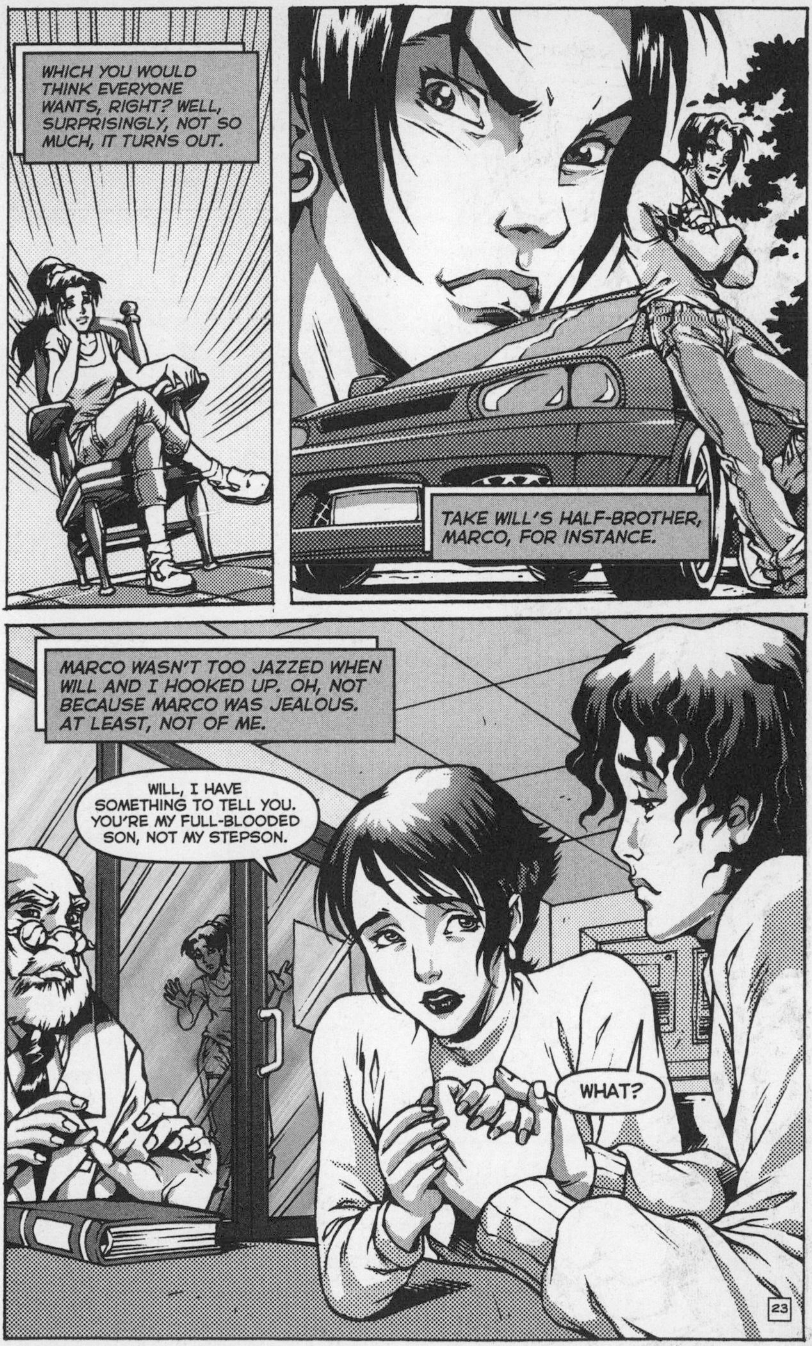
WHICH YOU WOULD THINK EVERYONE WANTS, RIGHT? WELL, SURPRISINGLY, NOT SO MUCH, IT TURNS OUT.
TAKE WILL'S HALF-BROTHER, MARCO, FOR INSTANCE.
MARCO WASN'T TOO JAZZED WHEN WILL AND I HOOKED UP. OH, NOT BECAUSE MARCO WAS JEALOUS. AT LEAST, NOT OF ME.
WILL, I HAVE SOMETHING TO TELL YOU. YOU'RE MY FULL-BLOODED SON, NOT MY STEPSON.
WHAT?

MARCO WASN'T TOO HAPPY WHEN HE FOUND OUT HIS MOM, WHO'D JUST MARRIED WILL'S DAD--IN SPITE OF THE FACT THAT THE ADMIRAL COMMANDED THE MILITARY UNIT IN WHICH HER FIRST HUSBAND, MARCO'S FATHER, WAS KILLED--WAS ACTUALLY WILL'S REAL MOM, WHOM WILL HAD ALWAYS BEEN TOLD WAS DEAD.

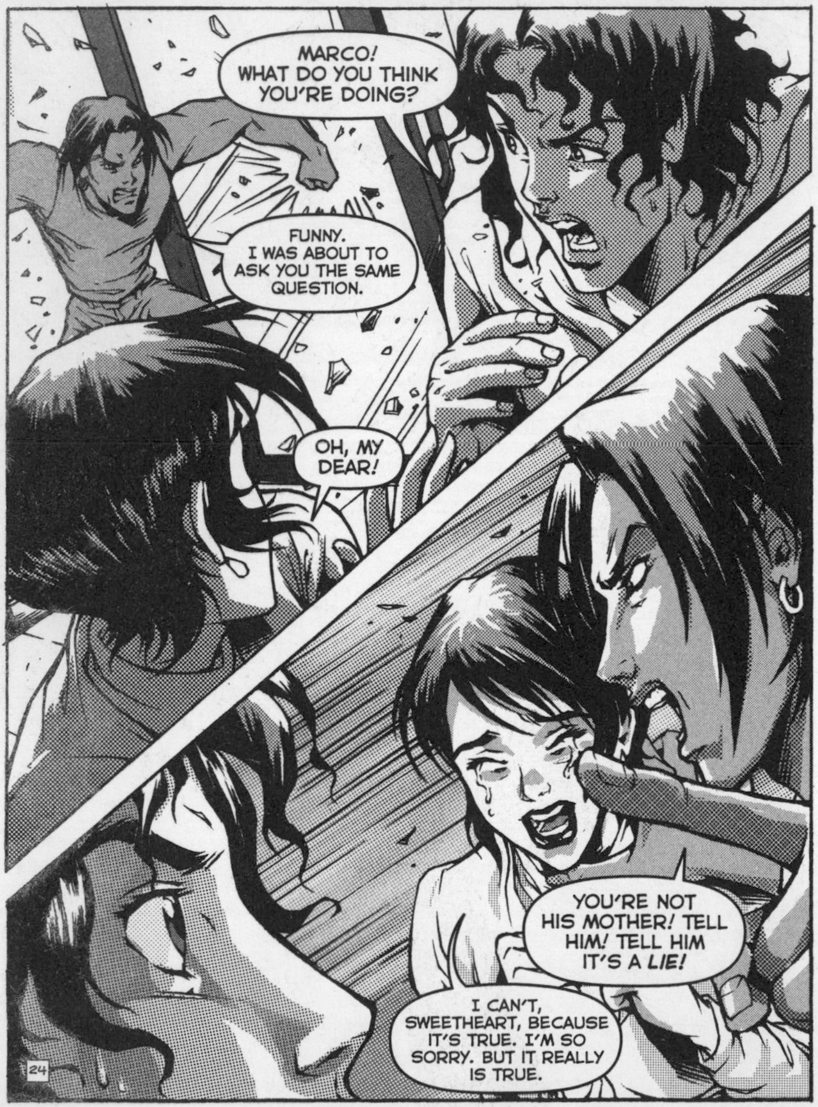
MARCO! WHAT DO YOU THINK YOU'RE DOING?
FUNNY. I WAS ABOUT TO ASK YOU THE SAME QUESTION.
OH, MY DEAR!
YOU'RE NOT HIS MOTHER! TELL HIM! TELL HIM IT'S A *LIE!*
I CAN'T, SWEETHEART, BECAUSE IT'S TRUE. I'M SO SORRY. BUT IT REALLY IS TRUE.

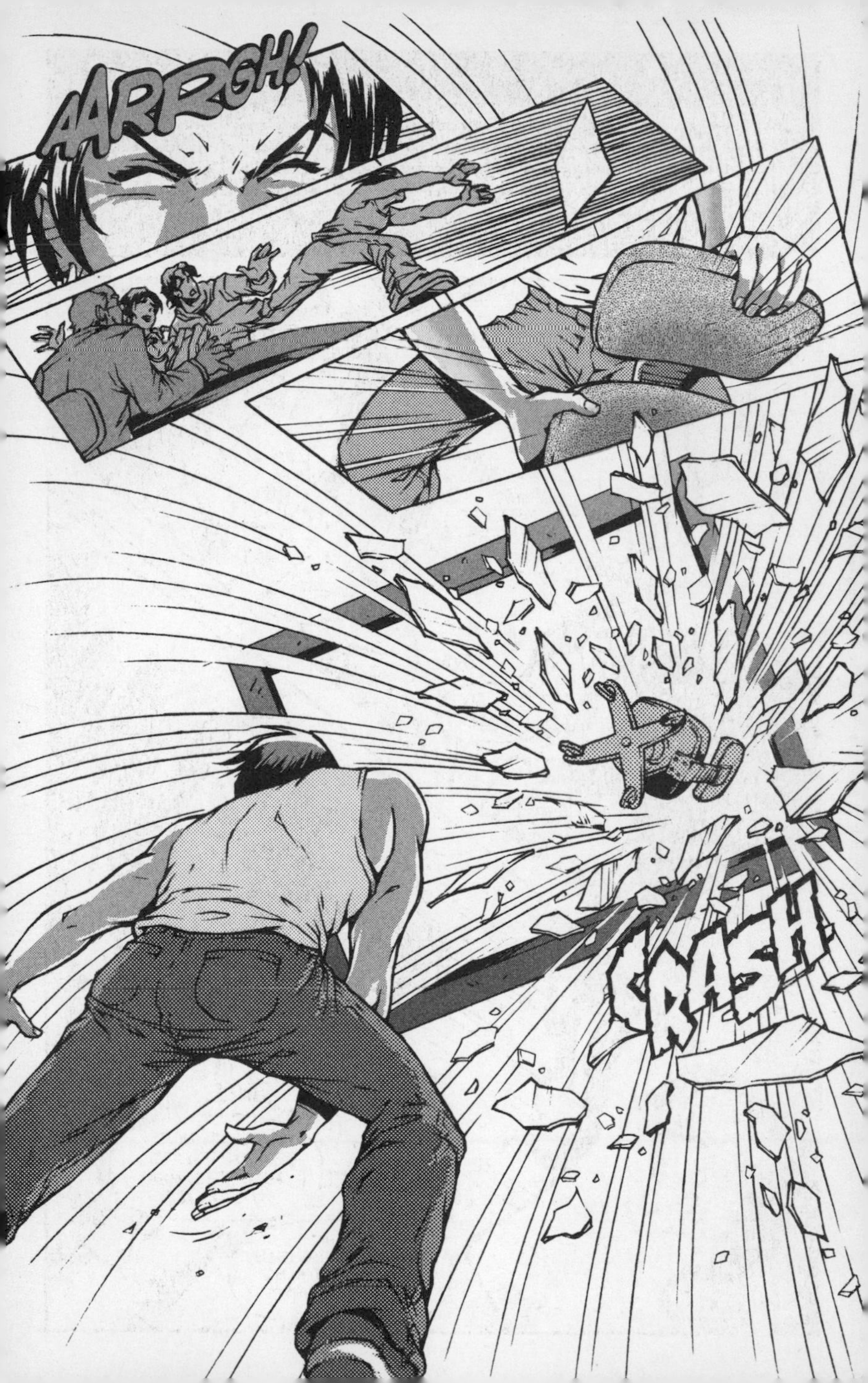
AARRGH!
CRASH

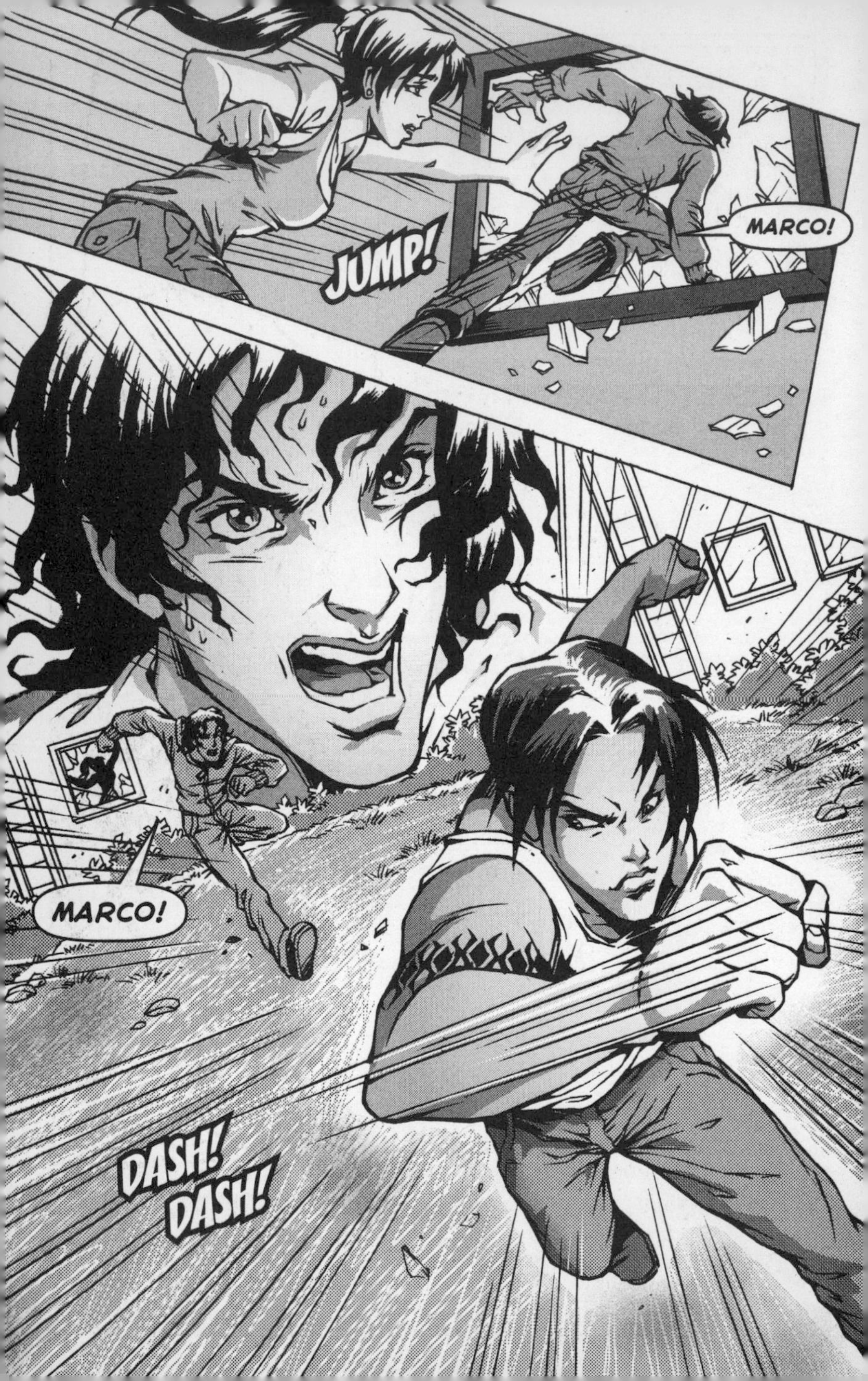
MARCO!
JUMP!
MARCO!
DASH! DASH!

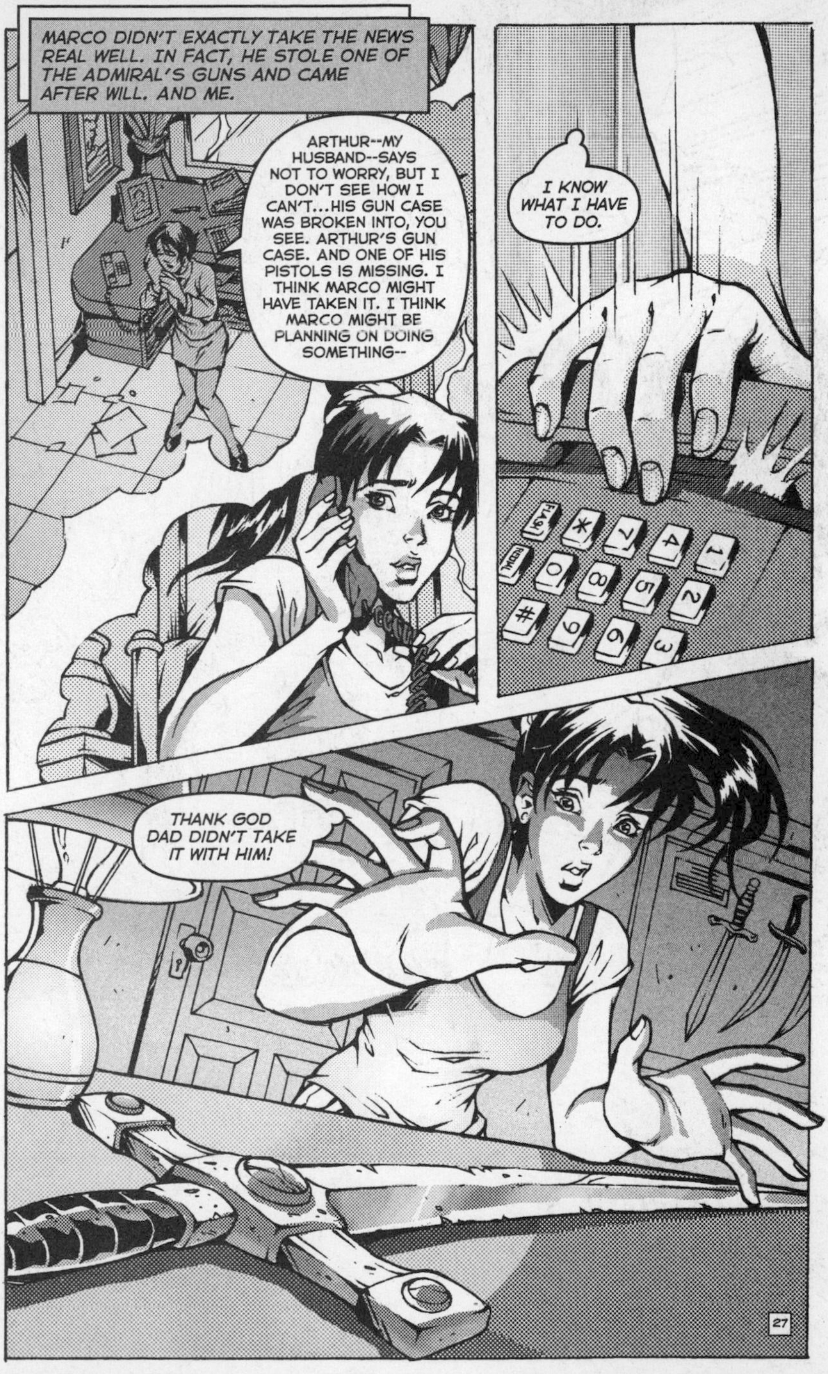
MARCO DIDN'T EXACTLY TAKE THE NEWS REAL WELL. IN FACT, HE STOLE ONE OF THE ADMIRAL'S GUNS AND CAME AFTER WILL. AND ME.
ARTHUR--MY HUSBAND--SAYS NOT TO WORRY, BUT I DON'T SEE HOW I CAN'T...HIS GUN CASE WAS BROKEN INTO, YOU SEE. ARTHUR'S GUN CASE. AND ONE OF HIS PISTOLS IS MISSING. I THINK MARCO MIGHT HAVE TAKEN IT. I THINK MARCO MIGHT BE PLANNING ON DOING SOMETHING--
I KNOW WHAT I HAVE TO DO.
THANK GOD DAD DIDN'T TAKE IT WITH HIM!

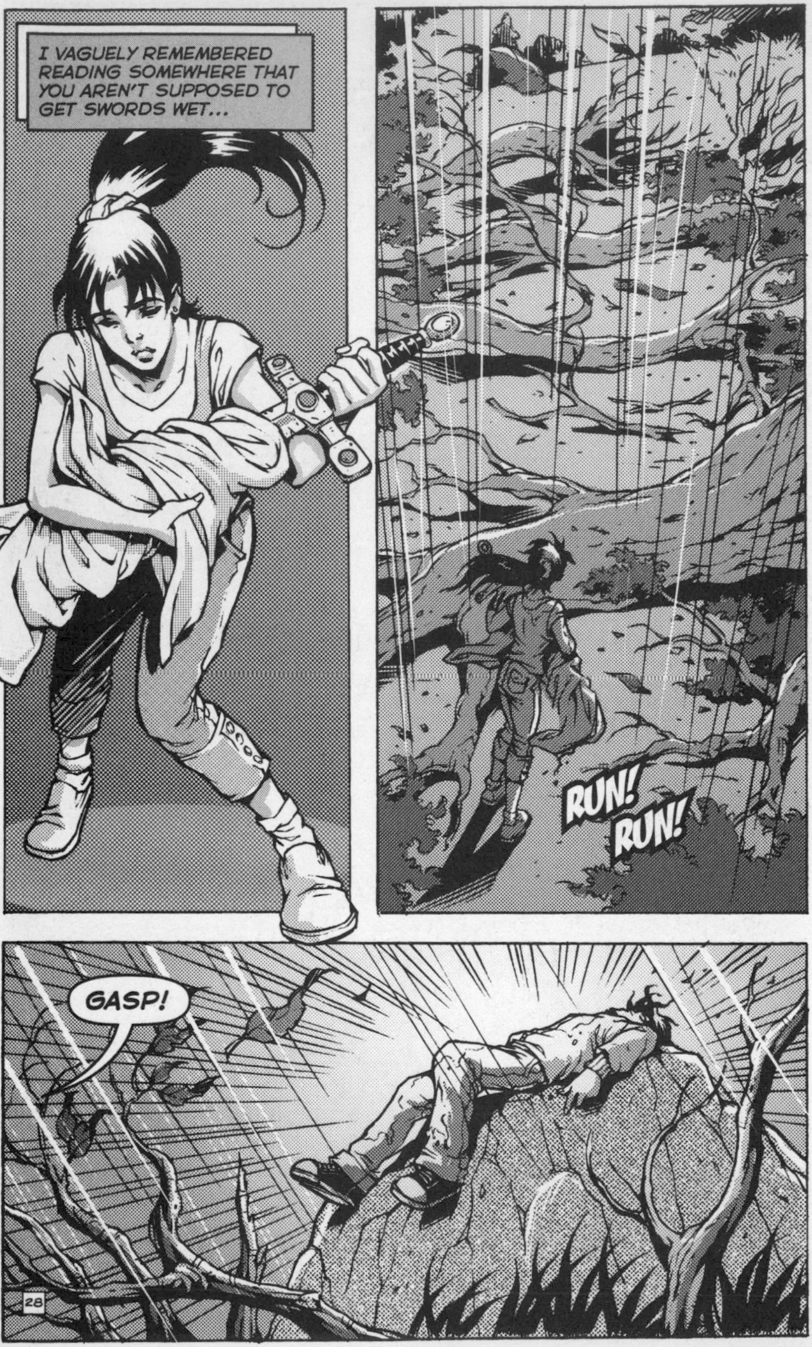
I VAGUELY REMEMBERED READING SOMEWHERE THAT YOU AREN'T SUPPOSED TO GET SWORDS WET...
RUN! RUN!
GASP!

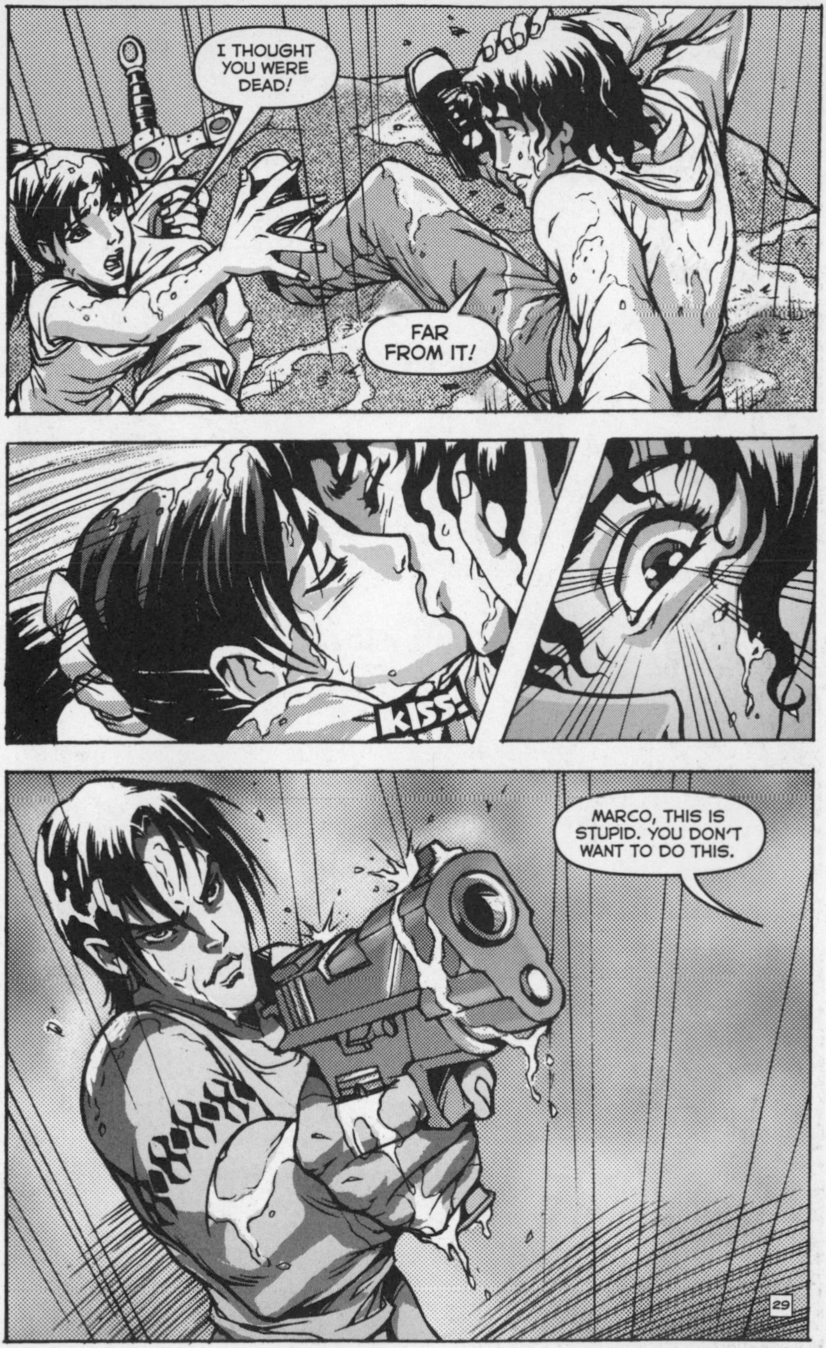
I THOUGHT YOU WERE DEAD!
FAR FROM IT!
KISS!
MARCO, THIS IS STUPID. YOU DON'T WANT TO DO THIS.

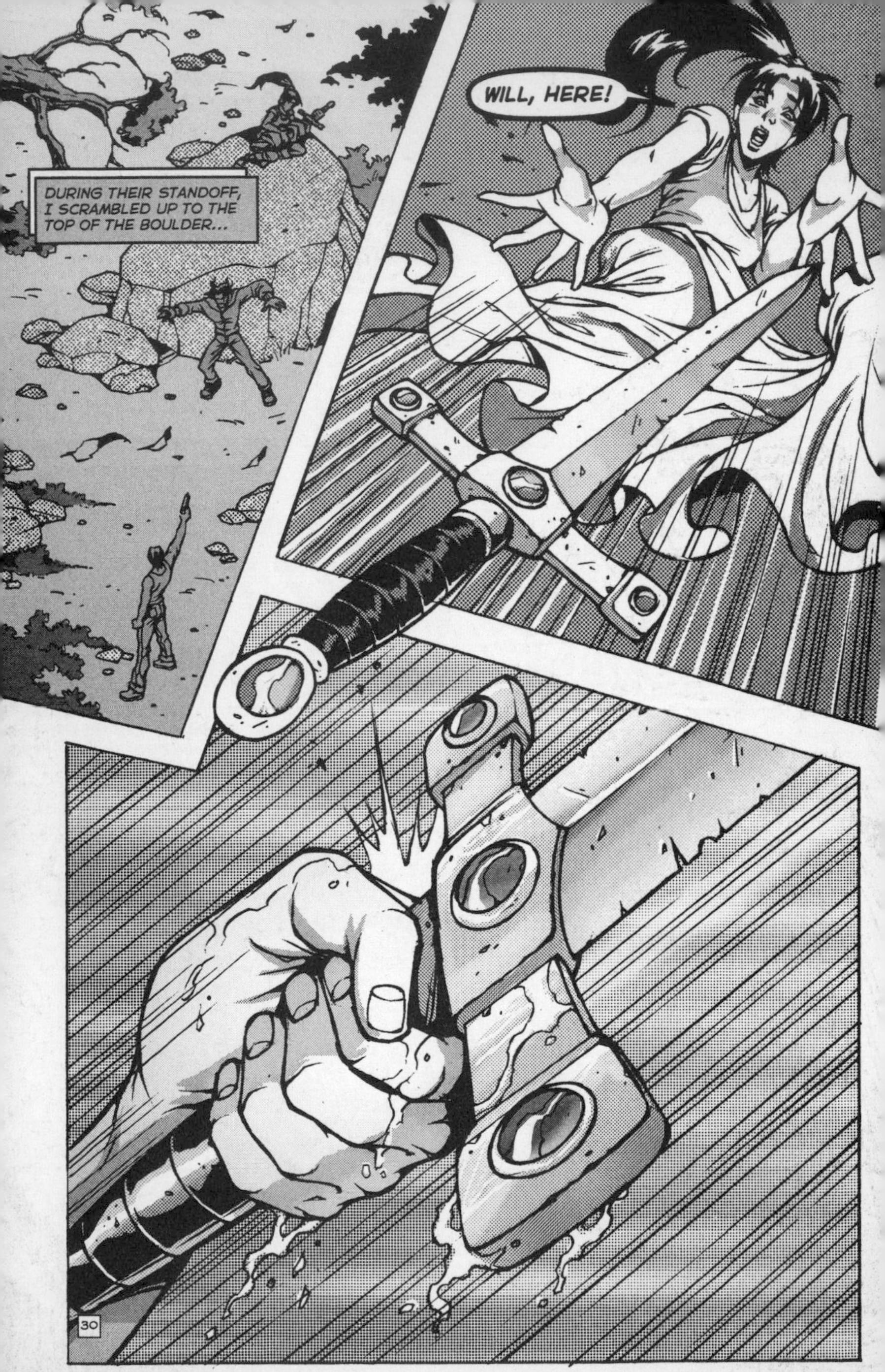
DURING THEIR STANDOFF, I SCRAMBLED UP TO THE TOP OF THE BOULDER...
WILL, HERE!

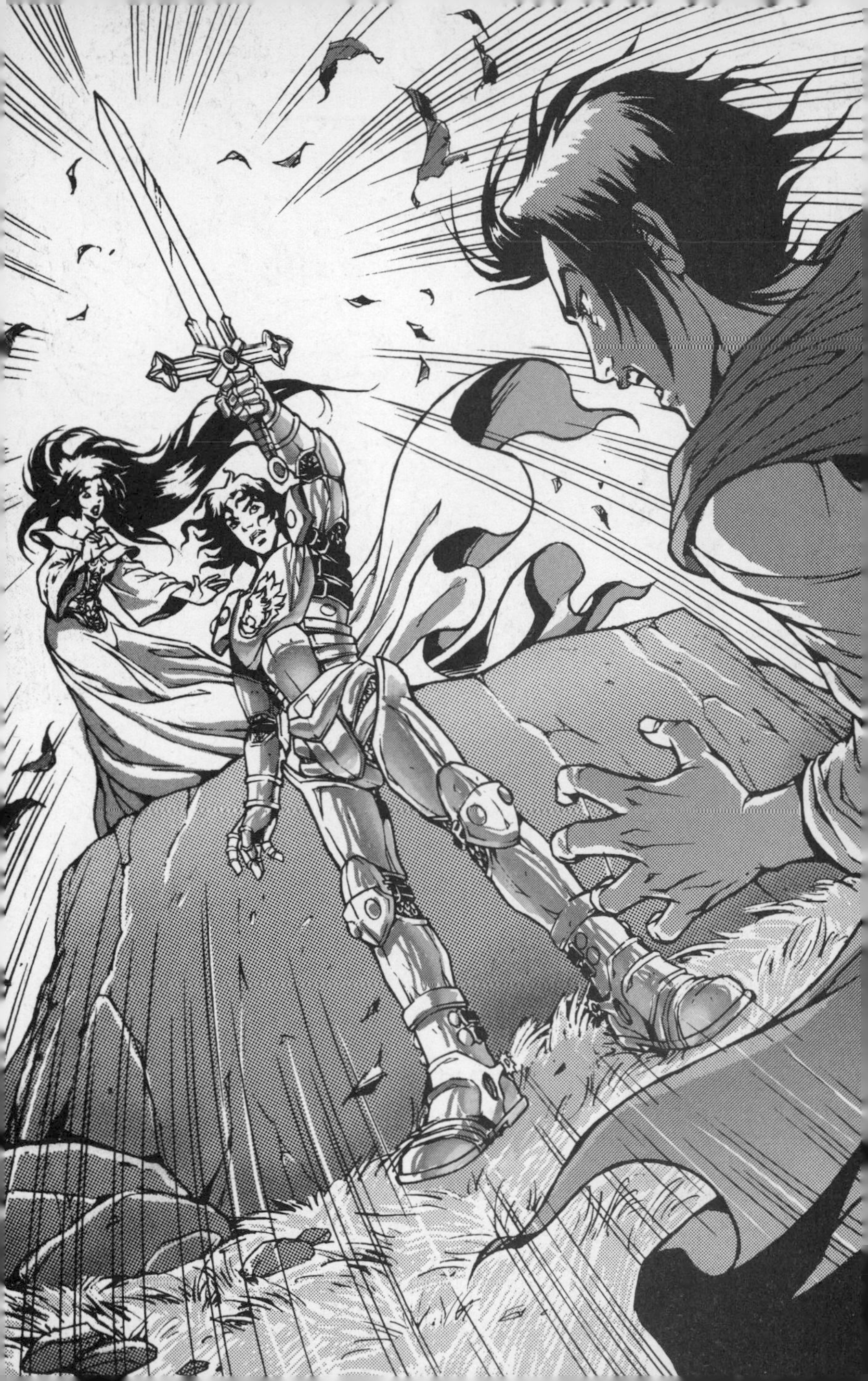

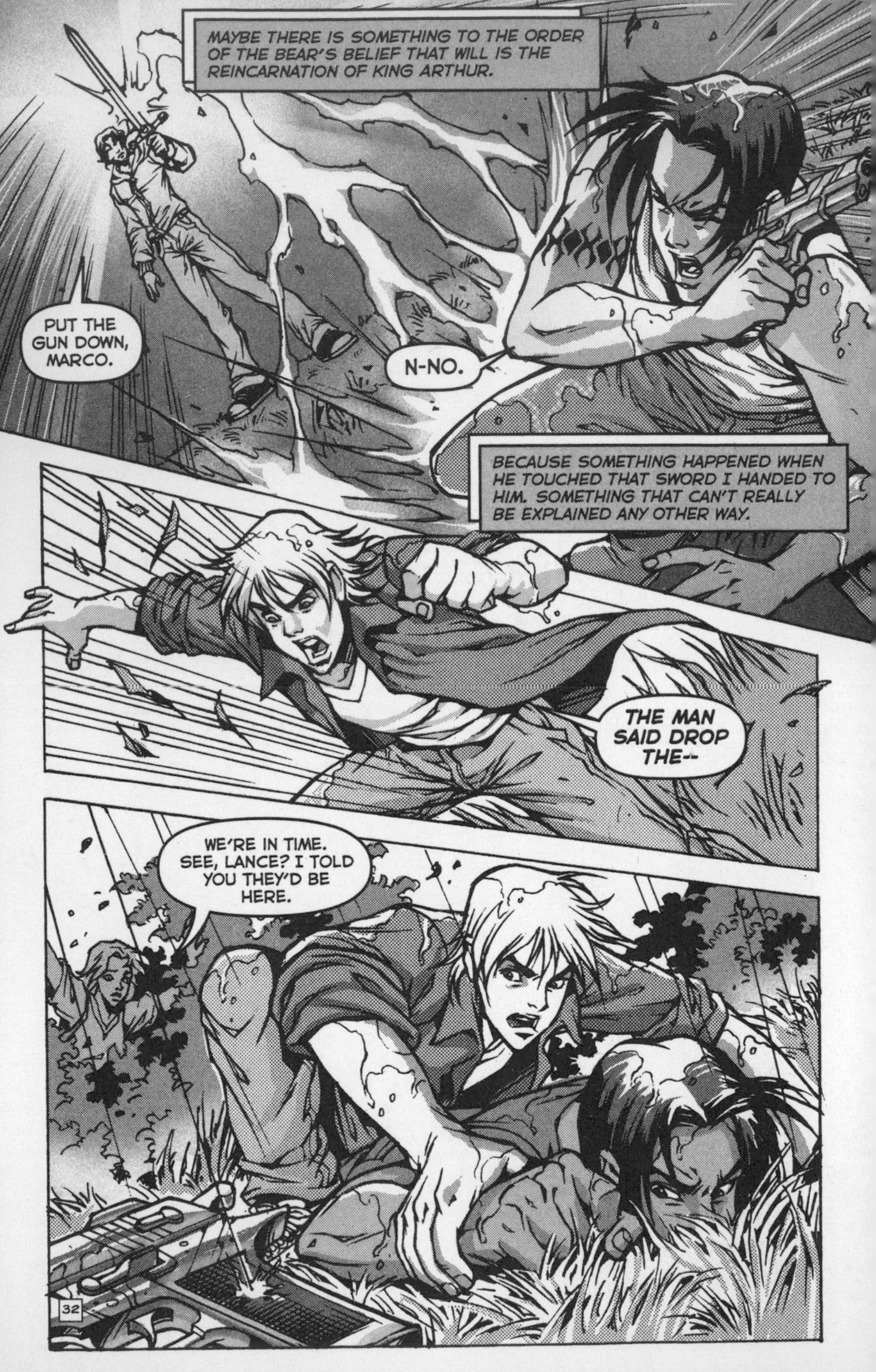
MAYBE THERE IS SOMETHING TO THE ORDER OF THE BEAR'S BELIEF THAT WILL IS THE REINCARNATION OF KING ARTHUR.
PUT THE GUN DOWN, MARCO.
N-NO.
BECAUSE SOMETHING HAPPENED WHEN HE TOUCHED THAT SWORD I HANDED TO HIM. SOMETHING THAT CAN'T REALLY BE EXPLAINED ANY OTHER WAY.
THE MAN SAID DROP THE--
WE'RE IN TIME. SEE, LANCE? I TOLD YOU THEY'D BE HERE.

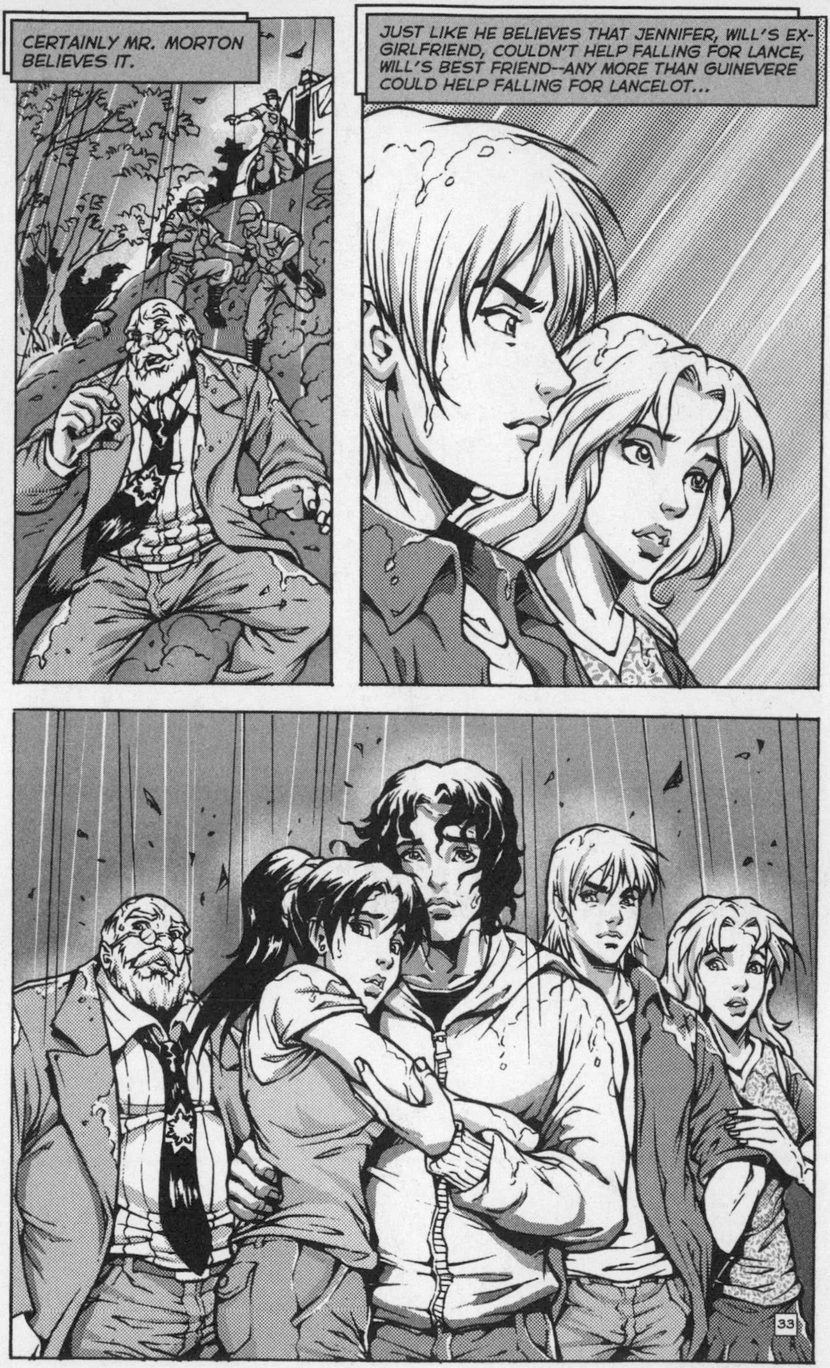
CERTAINLY MR. MORTON BELIEVES IT.
JUST LIKE HE BELIEVES THAT JENNIFER, WILL'S EX-GIRLFRIEND, COULDN'T HELP FALLING FOR LANCE, WILL'S BEST FRIEND--ANY MORE THAN GUINEVERE COULD HELP FALLING FOR LANCELOT...

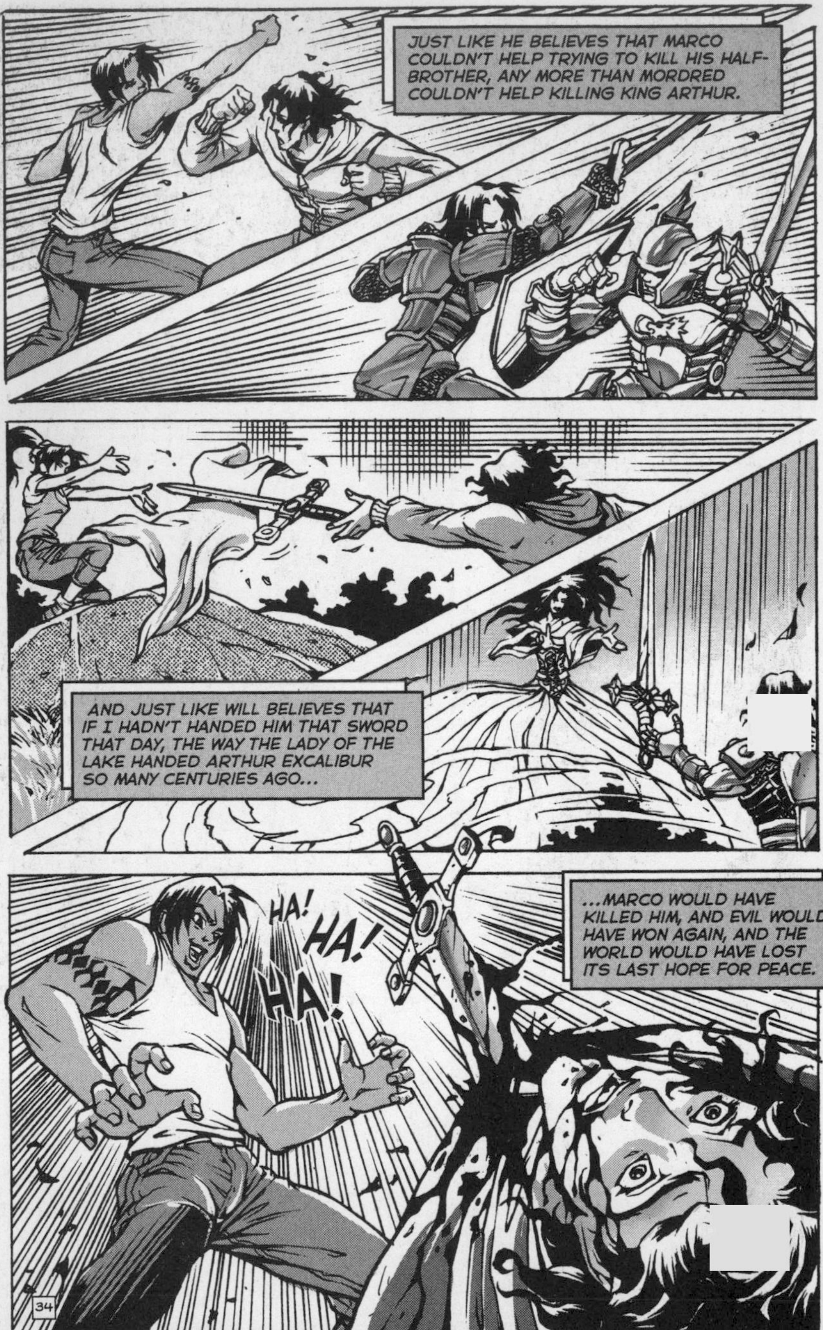
JUST LIKE HE BELIEVES THAT MARCO COULDN'T HELP TRYING TO KILL HIS HALF-BROTHER, ANY MORE THAN MORDRED COULDN'T HELP KILLING KING ARTHUR.
AND JUST LIKE WILL BELIEVES THAT IF I HADN'T HANDED HIM THAT SWORD THAT DAY, THE WAY THE LADY OF THE LAKE HANDED ARTHUR EXCALIBUR SO MANY CENTURIES AGO...
HA! HA! HA!
...MARCO WOULD HAVE KILLED HIM, AND EVIL WOULD HAVE WON AGAIN, AND THE WORLD WOULD HAVE LOST ITS LAST HOPE FOR PEACE.

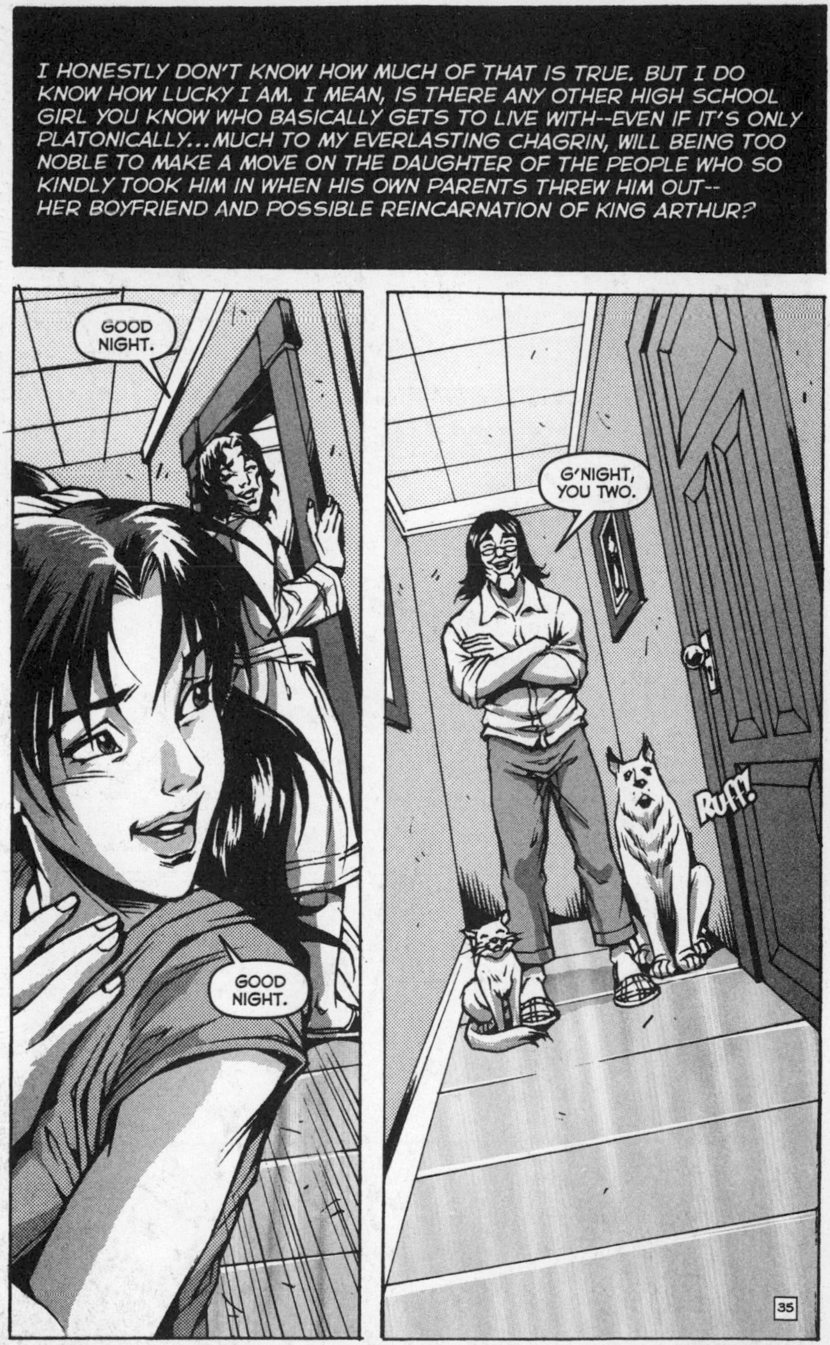
I HONESTLY DON'T KNOW HOW MUCH OF THAT IS TRUE. BUT I DO KNOW HOW LUCKY I AM. I MEAN, IS THERE ANY OTHER HIGH SCHOOL GIRL YOU KNOW WHO BASICALLY GETS TO LIVE WITH--EVEN IF IT'S ONLY PLATONICALLY...MUCH TO MY EVERLASTING CHAGRIN, WILL BEING TOO NOBLE TO MAKE A MOVE ON THE DAUGHTER OF THE PEOPLE WHO SO KINDLY TOOK HIM IN WHEN HIS OWN PARENTS THREW HIM OUT--HER BOYFRIEND AND POSSIBLE REINCARNATION OF KING ARTHUR?
GOOD NIGHT.
GOOD NIGHT.
G'NIGHT, YOU TWO.
RUFF!

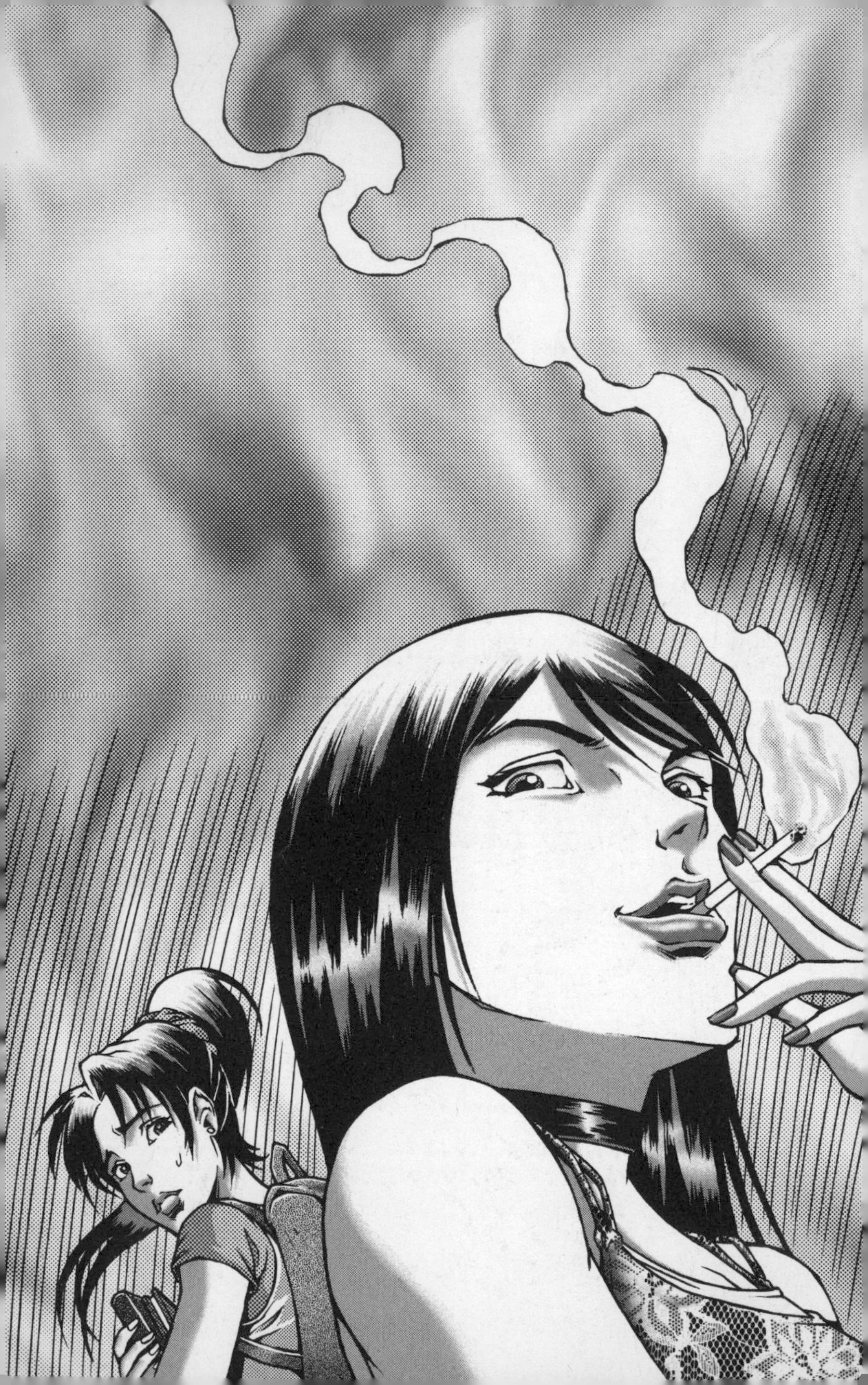

CHAPTER TWO

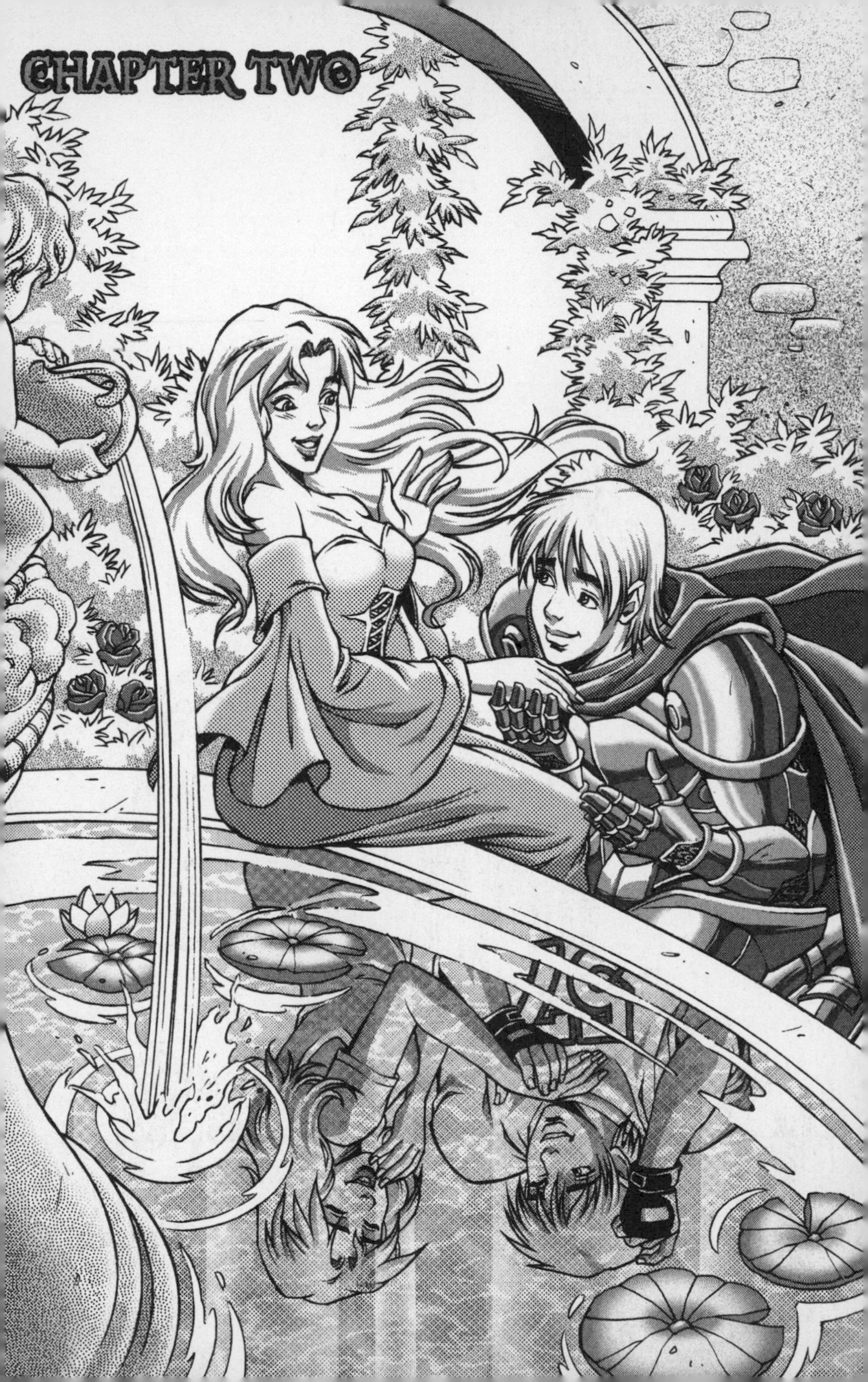

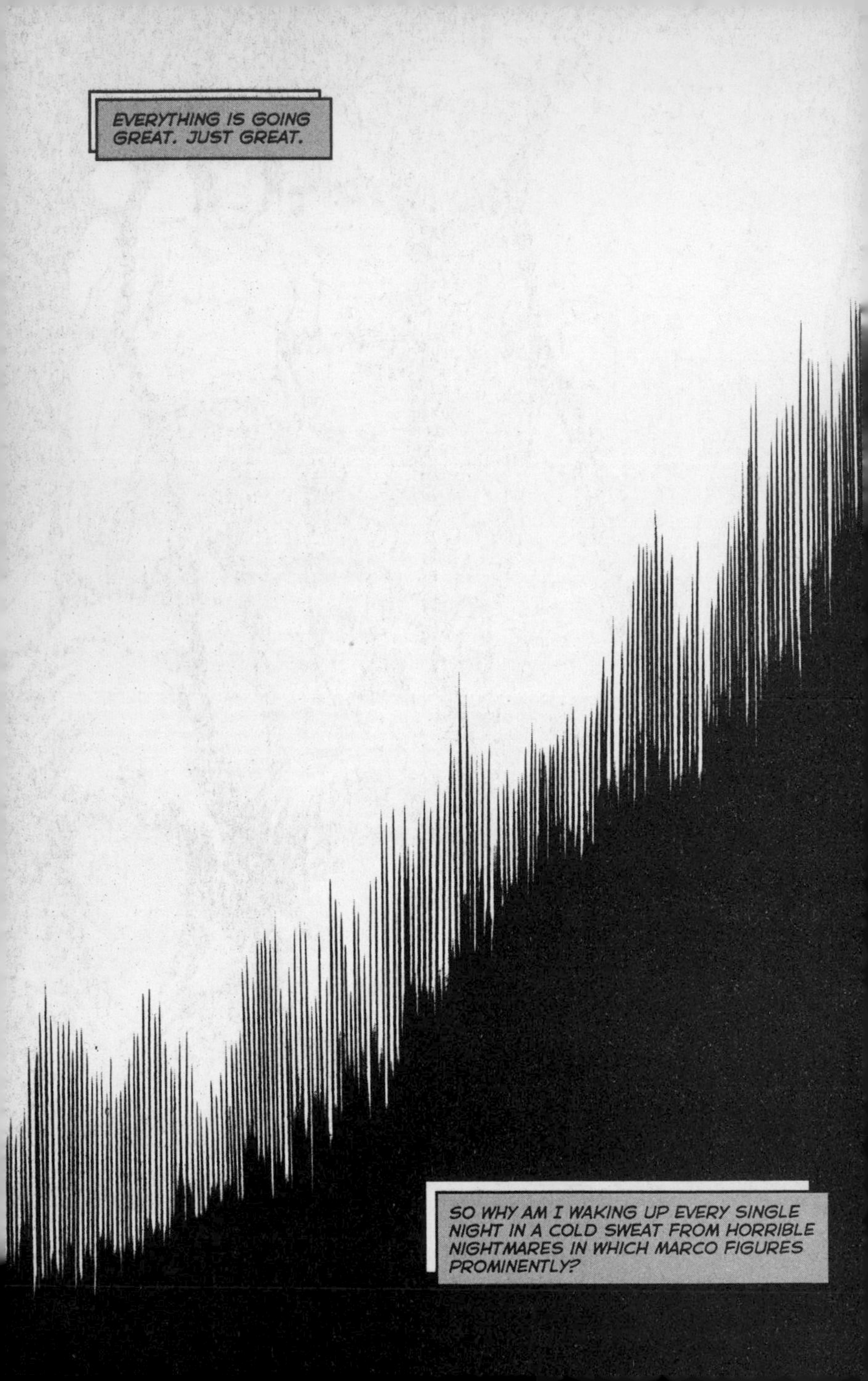
EVERYTHING IS GOING GREAT. JUST GREAT.
SO WHY AM I WAKING UP EVERY SINGLE NIGHT IN A COLD SWEAT FROM HORRIBLE NIGHTMARES IN WHICH MARCO FIGURES PROMINENTLY?

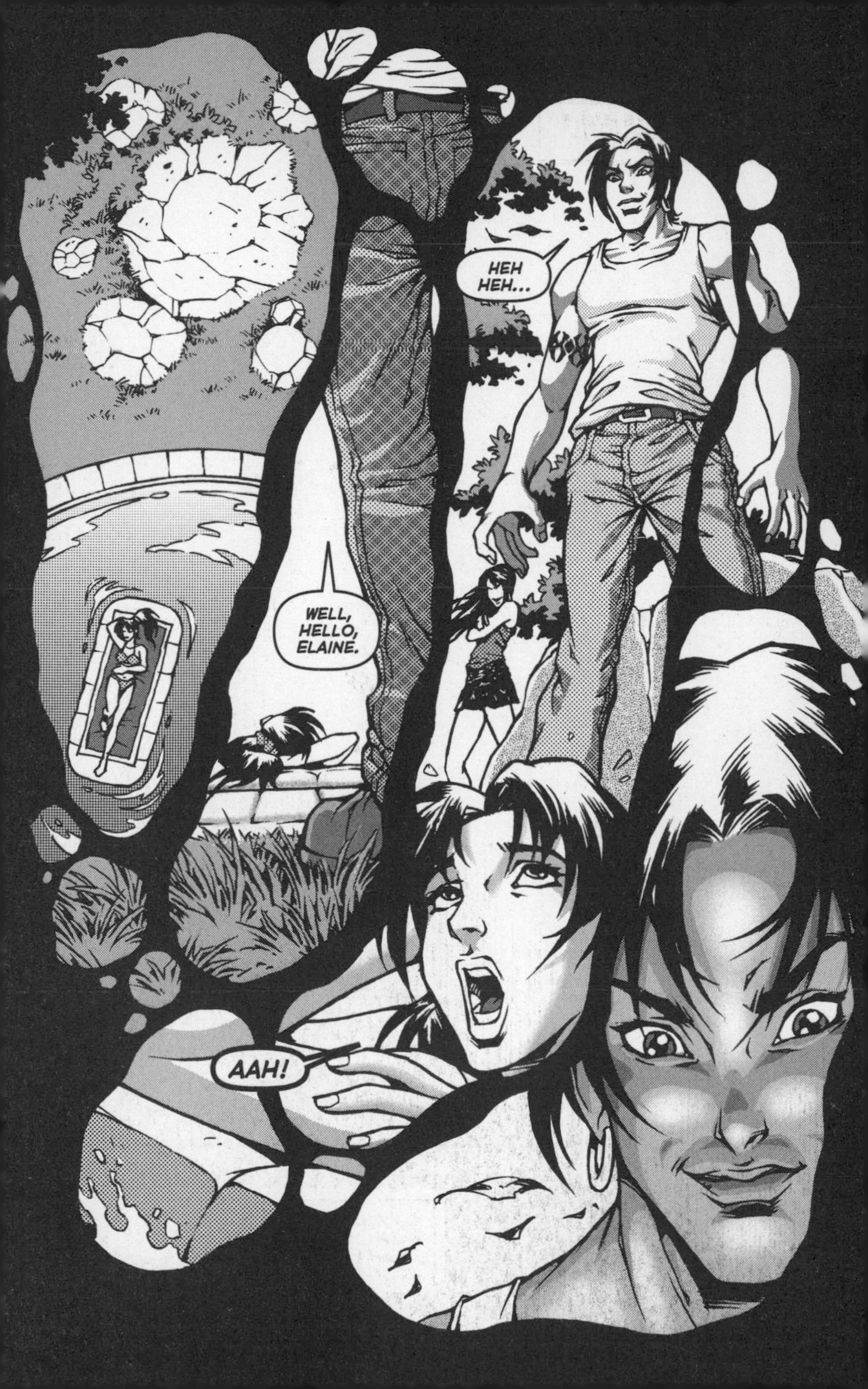
HEH HEH...
WELL, HELLO, ELAINE.
AAH!

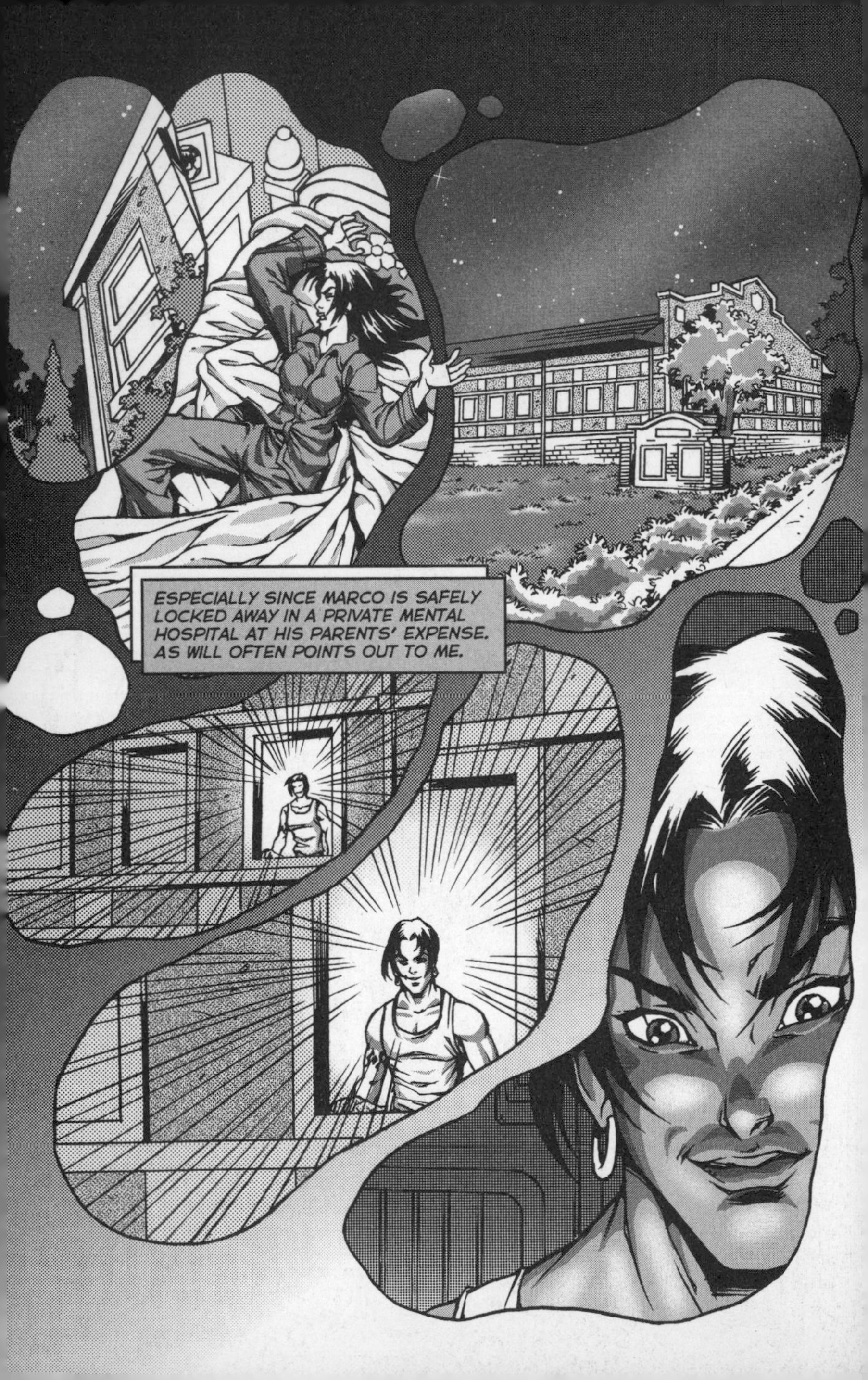
ESPECIALLY SINCE MARCO IS SAFELY LOCKED AWAY IN A PRIVATE MENTAL HOSPITAL AT HIS PARENTS' EXPENSE. AS WILL OFTEN POINTS OUT TO ME.

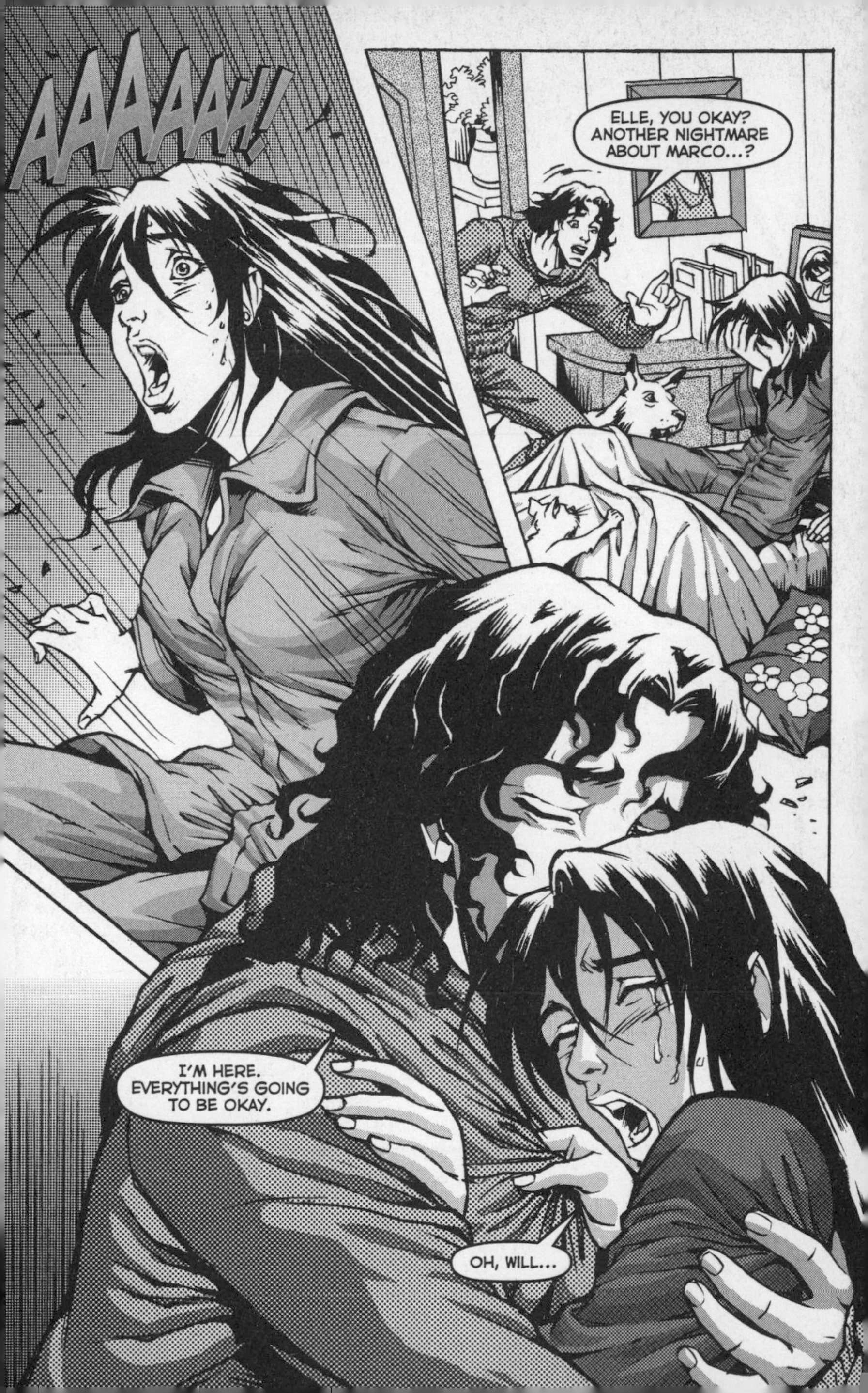
AAAAAH!
ELLE, YOU OKAY? ANOTHER NIGHTMARE ABOUT MARCO...?
I'M HERE. EVERYTHING'S GOING TO BE OKAY.
OH, WILL...

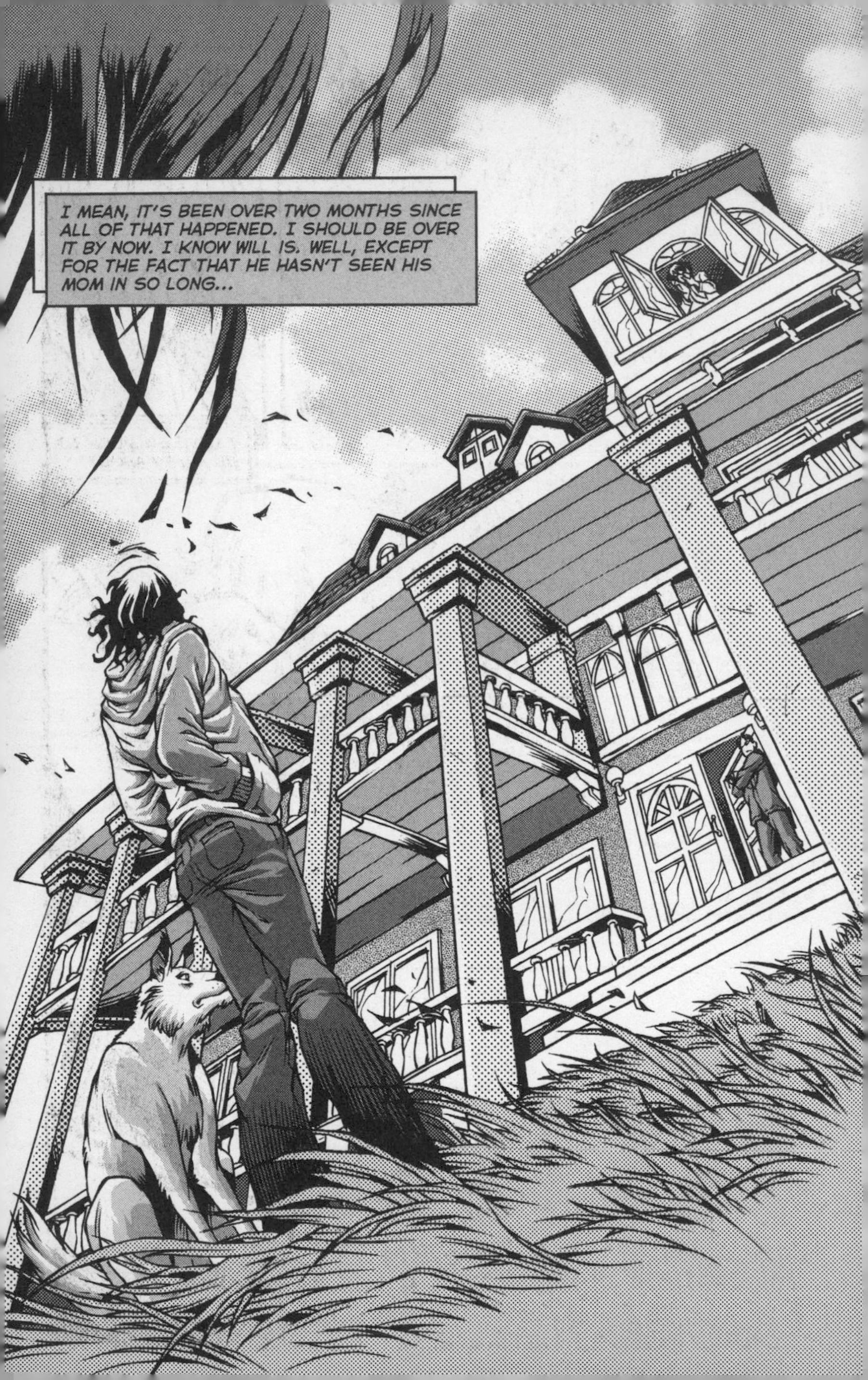
I MEAN, IT'S BEEN OVER TWO MONTHS SINCE ALL OF THAT HAPPENED. I SHOULD BE OVER IT BY NOW. I KNOW WILL IS. WELL, EXCEPT FOR THE FACT THAT HE HASN'T SEEN HIS MOM IN SO LONG...

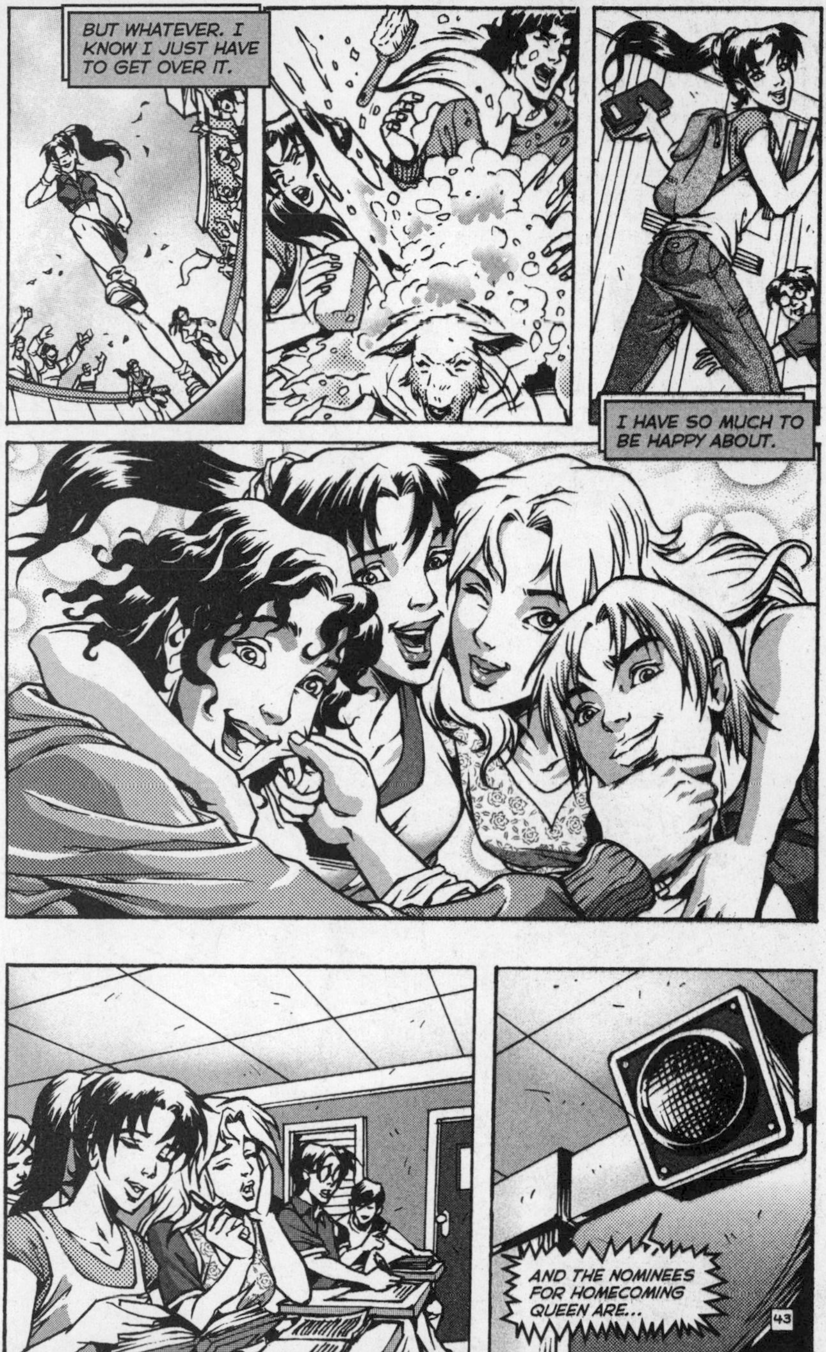
BUT WHATEVER. I KNOW I JUST HAVE TO GET OVER IT.
I HAVE SO MUCH TO BE HAPPY ABOUT.
AND THE NOMINEES FOR HOMECOMING QUEEN ARE...

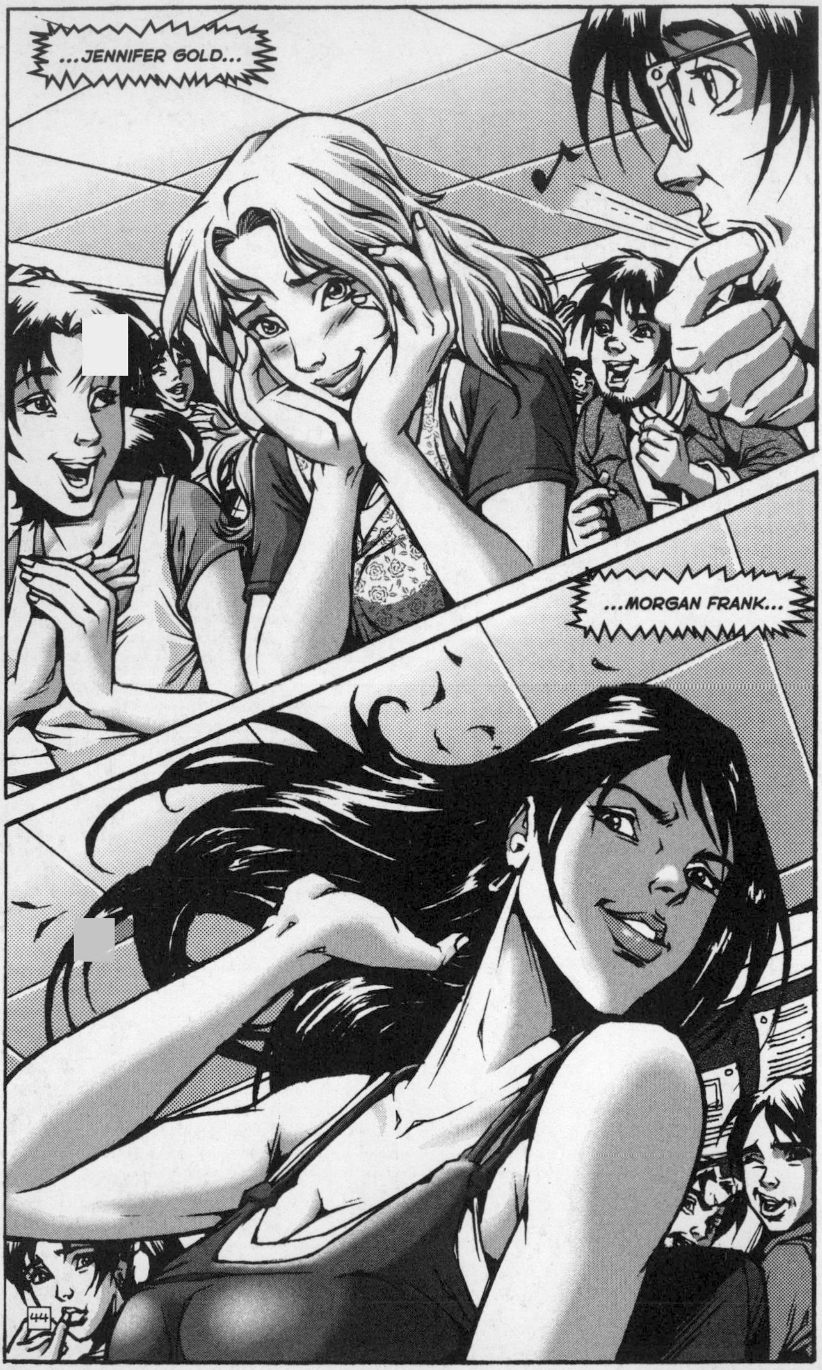
...JENNIFER GOLD...
...MORGAN FRANK...

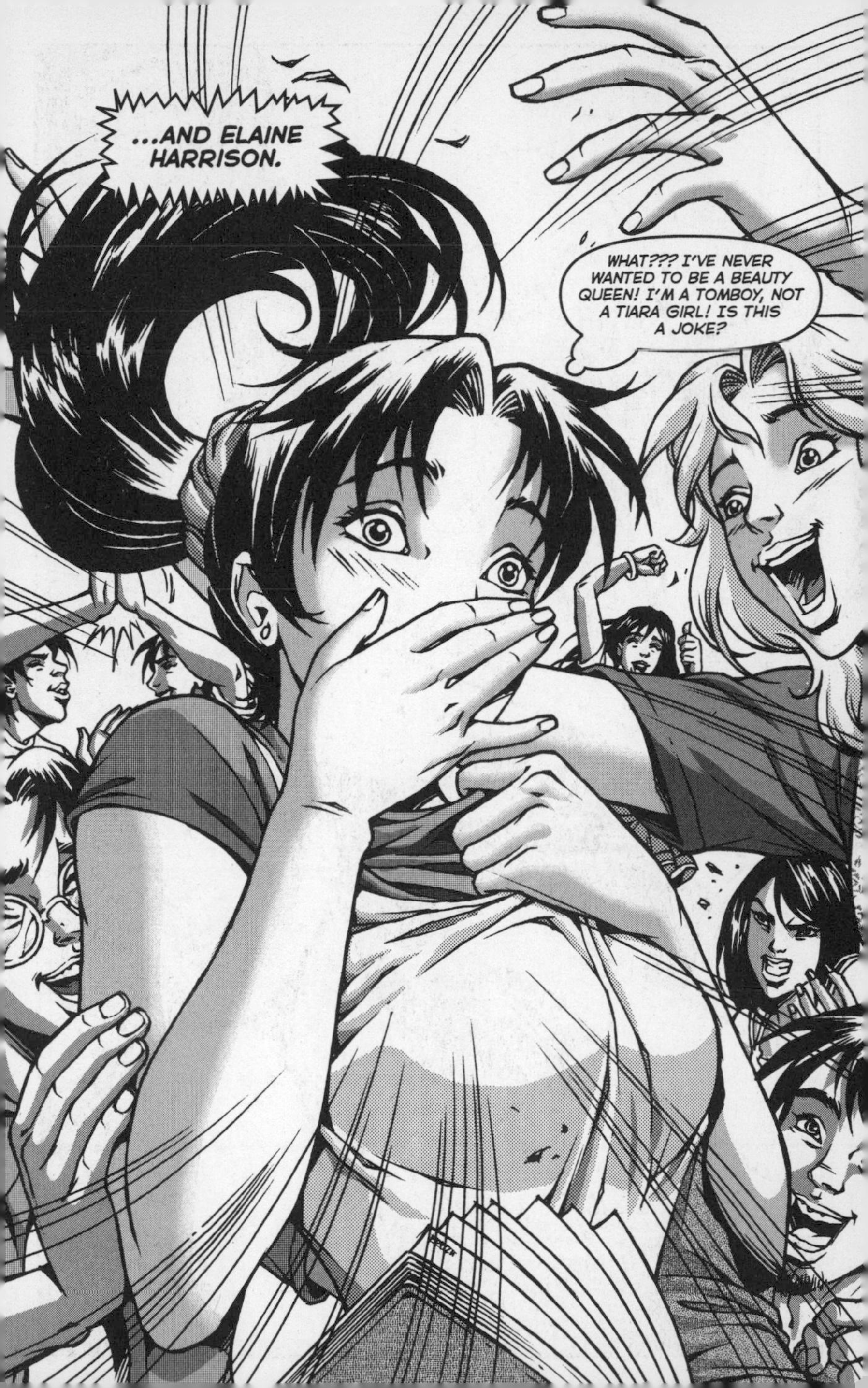
...AND ELAINE HARRISON.
WHAT??? I'VE NEVER WANTED TO BE A BEAUTY QUEEN! I'M A TOMBOY, NOT A TIARA GIRL! IS THIS A JOKE?

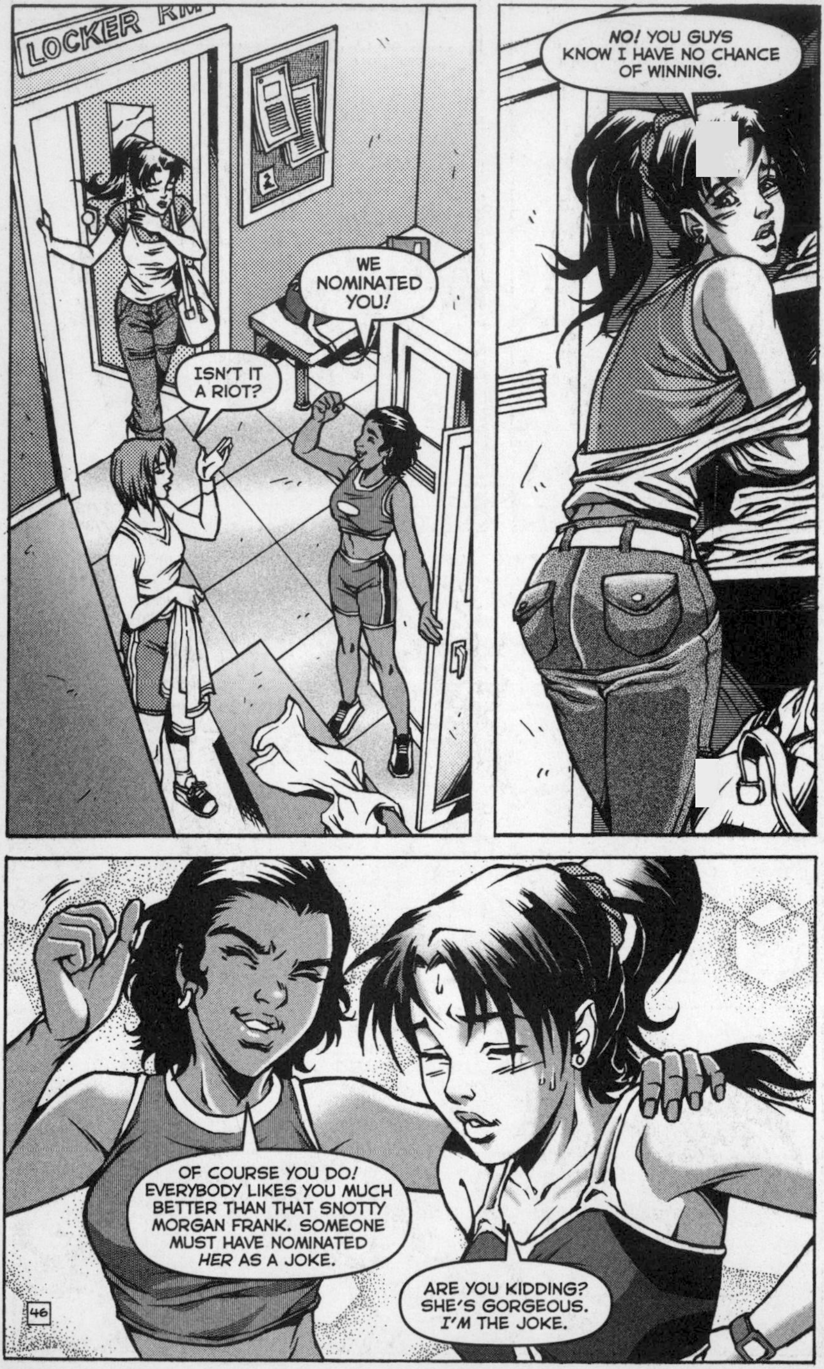
LOCKER RM
WE NOMINATED YOU!
ISN'T IT A RIOT?
NO! YOU GUYS KNOW I HAVE NO CHANCE OF WINNING.
OF COURSE YOU DO! EVERYBODY LIKES YOU MUCH BETTER THAN THAT SNOTTY MORGAN FRANK. SOMEONE MUST HAVE NOMINATED *HER* AS A JOKE.
ARE YOU KIDDING? SHE'S GORGEOUS. *I'M* THE JOKE.

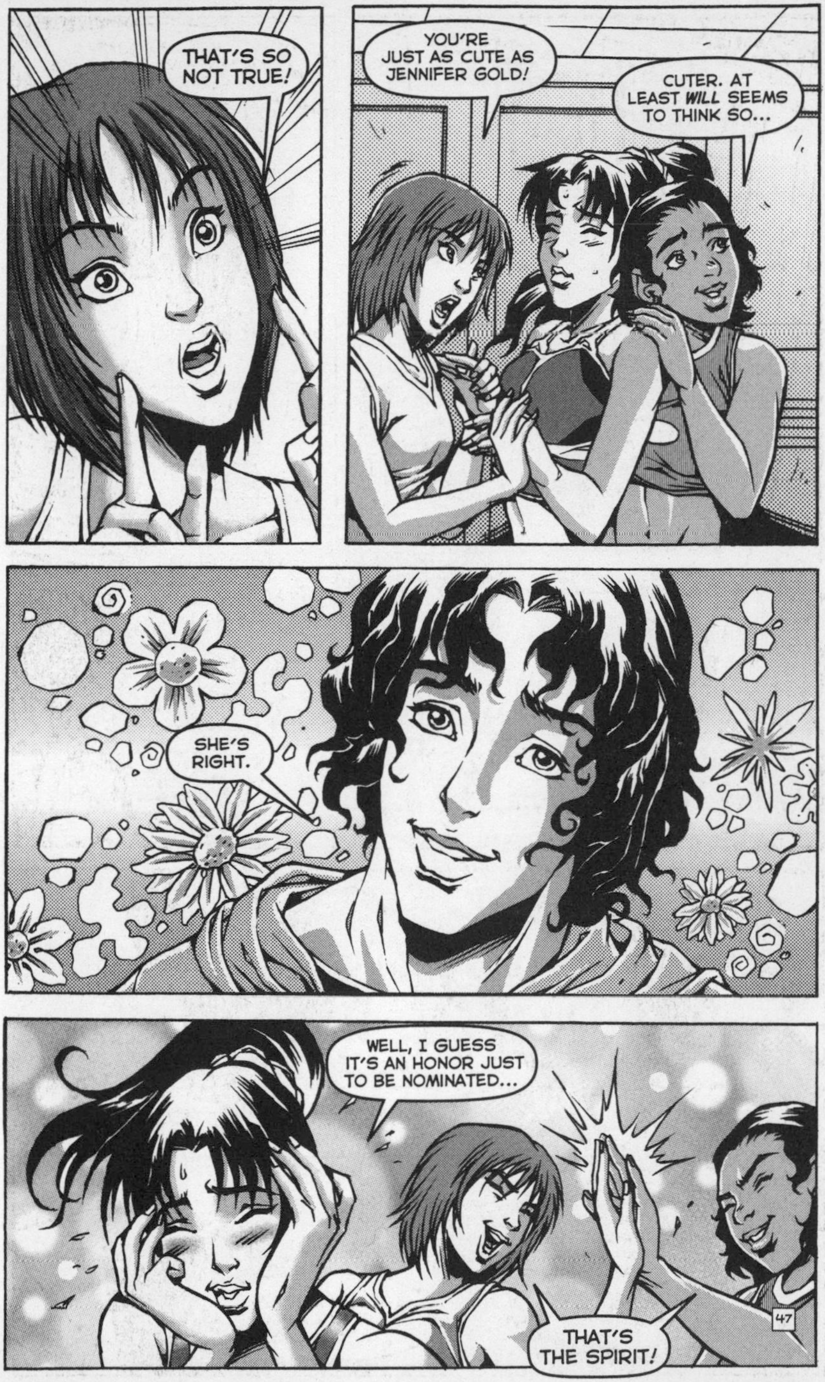
THAT'S SO NOT TRUE!
YOU'RE JUST AS CUTE AS JENNIFER GOLD!
CUTER. AT LEAST *WILL* SEEMS TO THINK SO...
SHE'S RIGHT.
WELL, I GUESS IT'S AN HONOR JUST TO BE NOMINATED...
THAT'S THE SPIRIT!

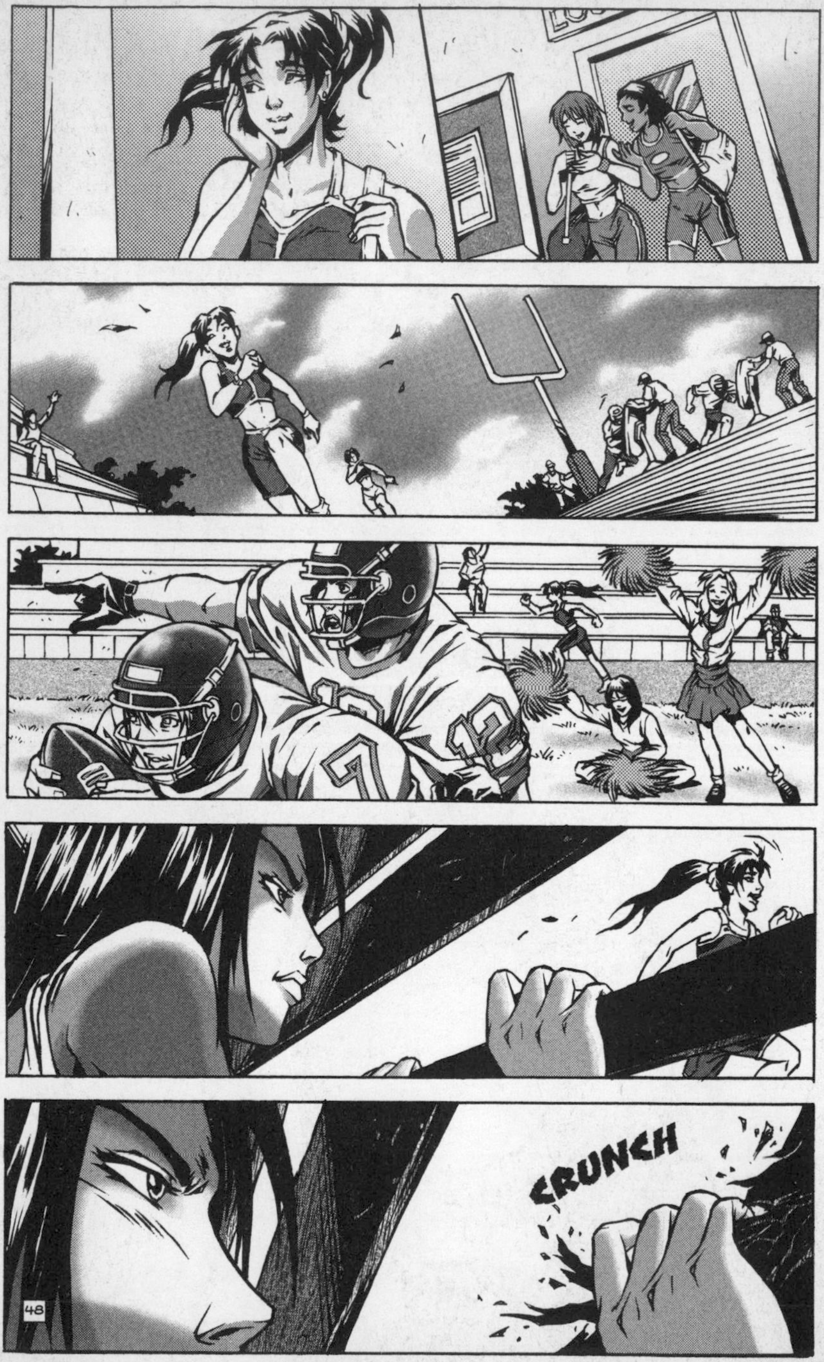
CRUNCH

I DON'T KNOW WHY I LET THEM TALK ME INTO GOING THROUGH IT.
IT'S NOT LIKE I DON'T HAVE OTHER STUFF TO WORRY ABOUT...

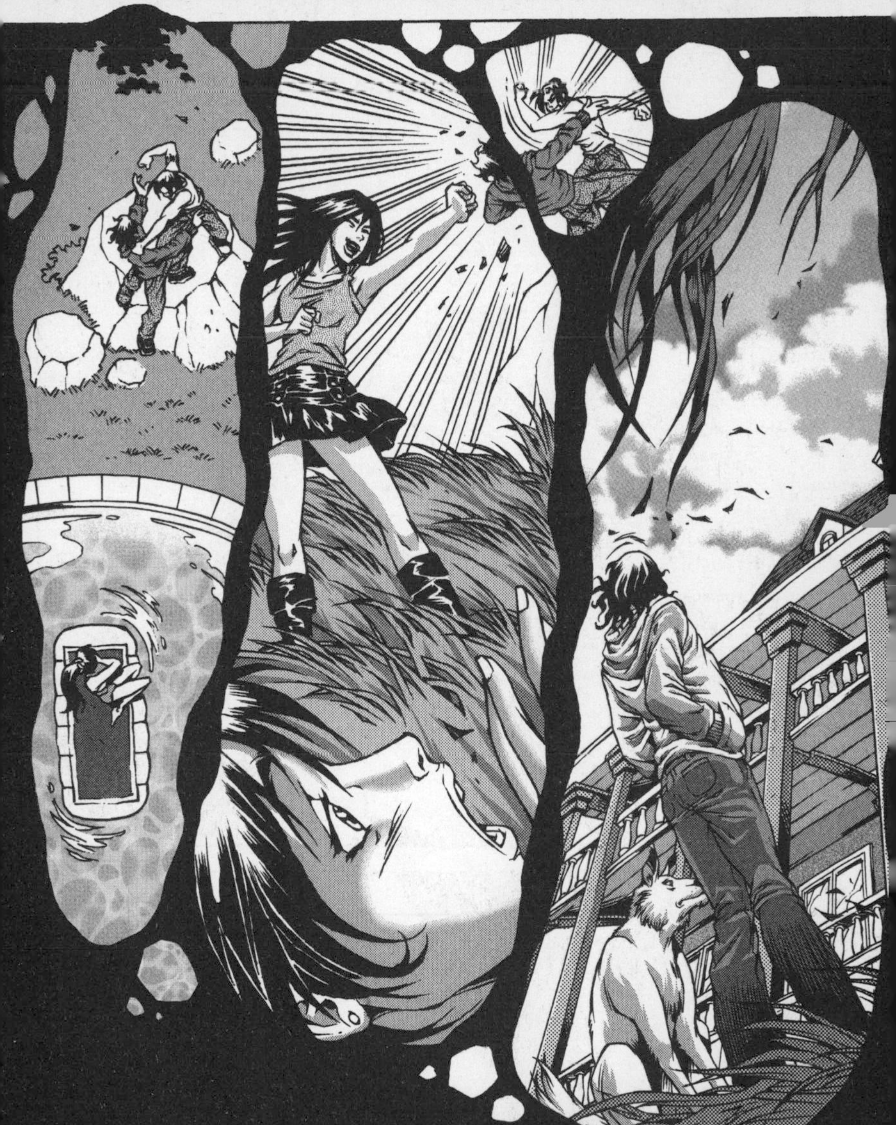

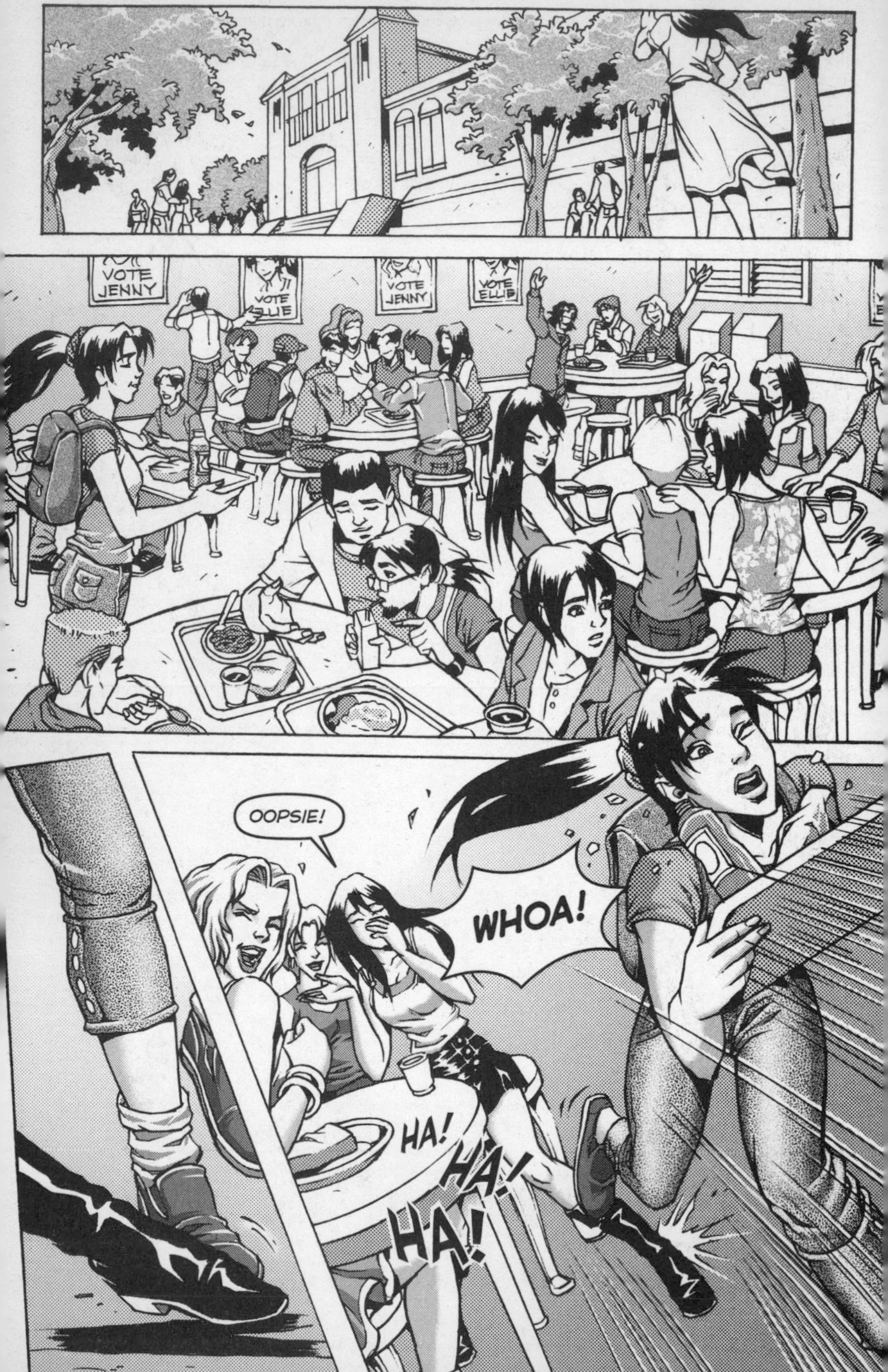
VOTE JENNY
VOTE ELLIE
VOTE JENNY
VOTE ELLIE
OOPSIE!
WHOA!
HA!
HA!
HA!

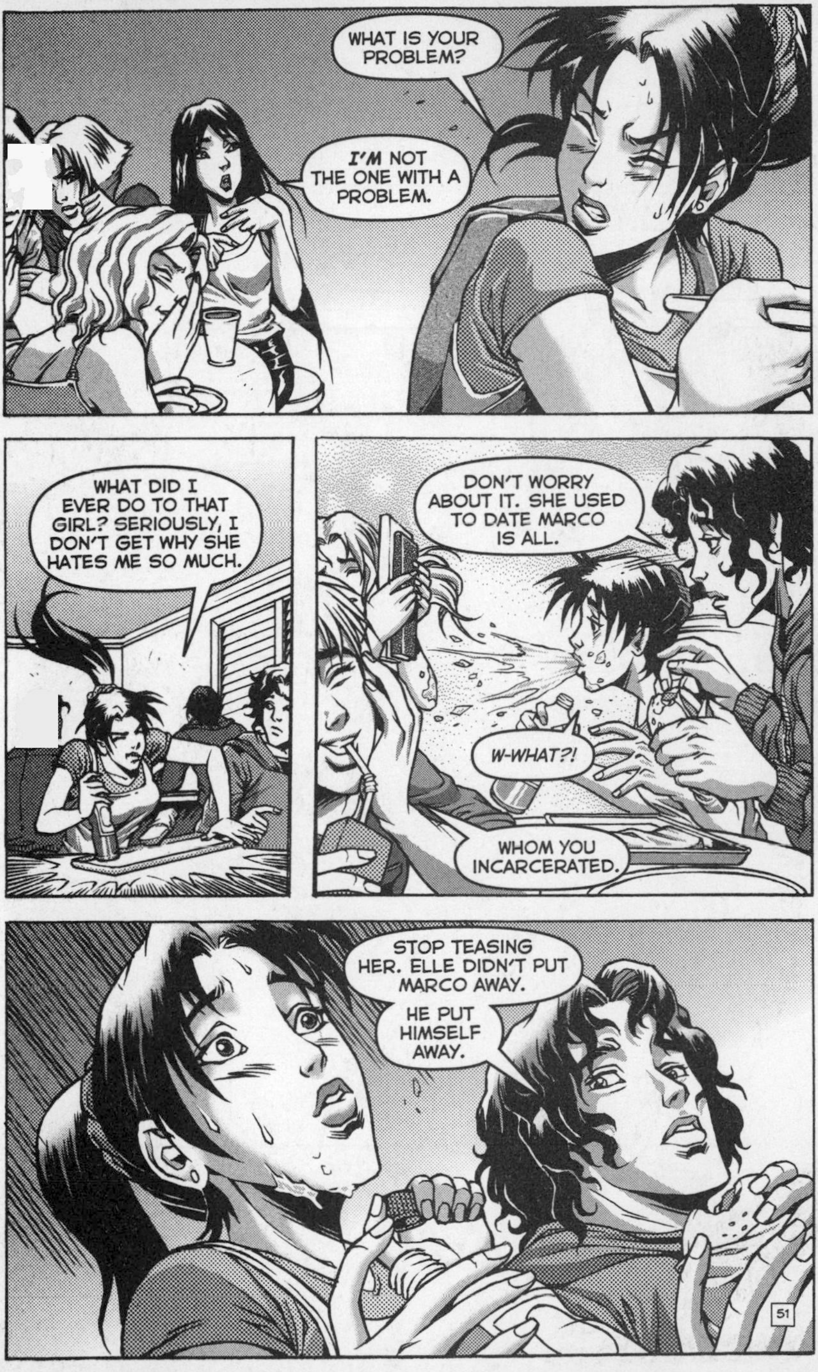
WHAT IS YOUR PROBLEM?
I'M NOT THE ONE WITH A PROBLEM.
WHAT DID I EVER DO TO THAT GIRL? SERIOUSLY, I DON'T GET WHY SHE HATES ME SO MUCH.
DON'T WORRY ABOUT IT. SHE USED TO DATE MARCO IS ALL.
W-WHAT?!
WHOM YOU INCARCERATED.
STOP TEASING HER. ELLE DIDN'T PUT MARCO AWAY.
HE PUT HIMSELF AWAY.

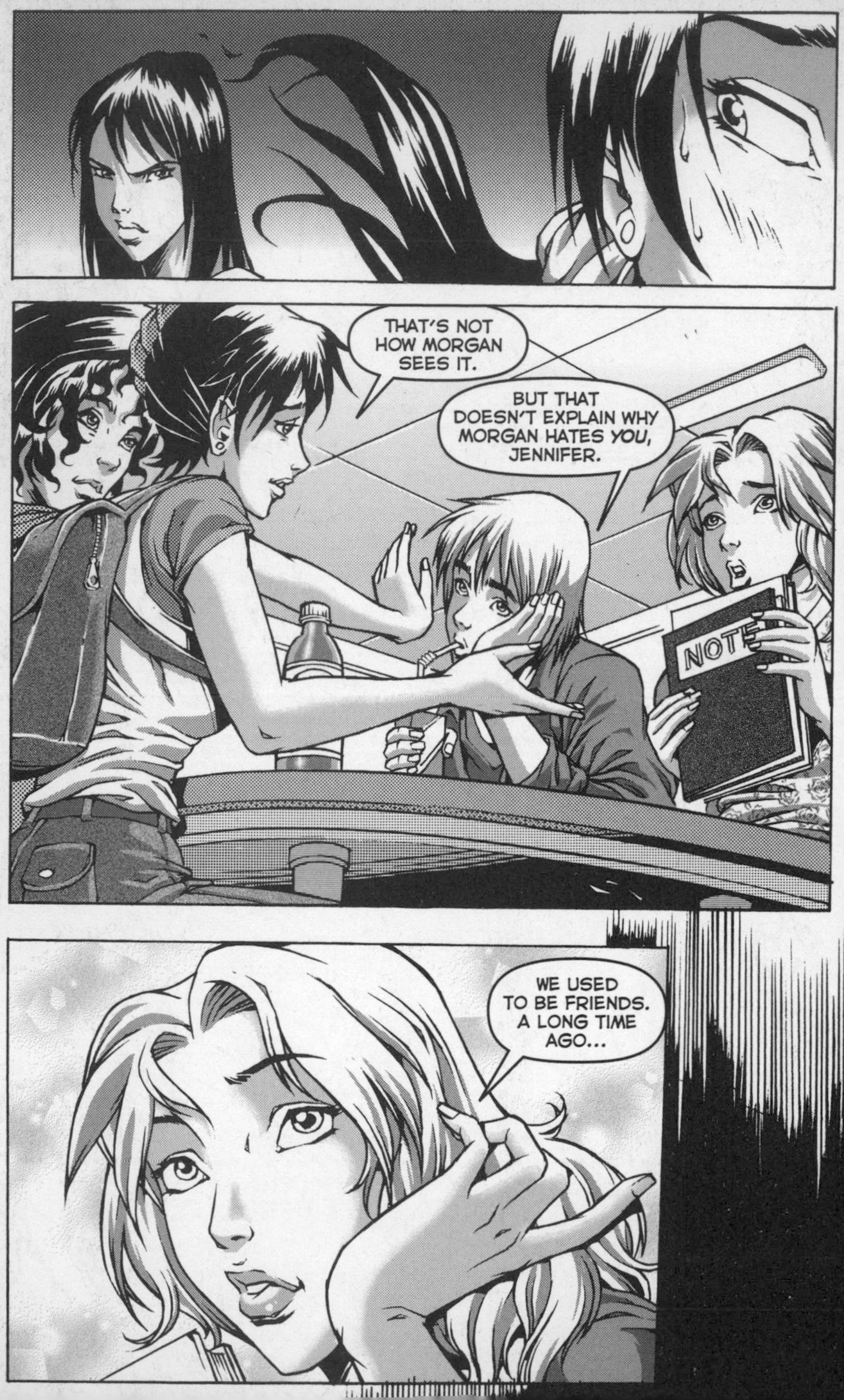
THAT'S NOT HOW MORGAN SEES IT.
BUT THAT DOESN'T EXPLAIN WHY MORGAN HATES *YOU*, JENNIFER.
NOTE
WE USED TO BE FRIENDS. A LONG TIME AGO...

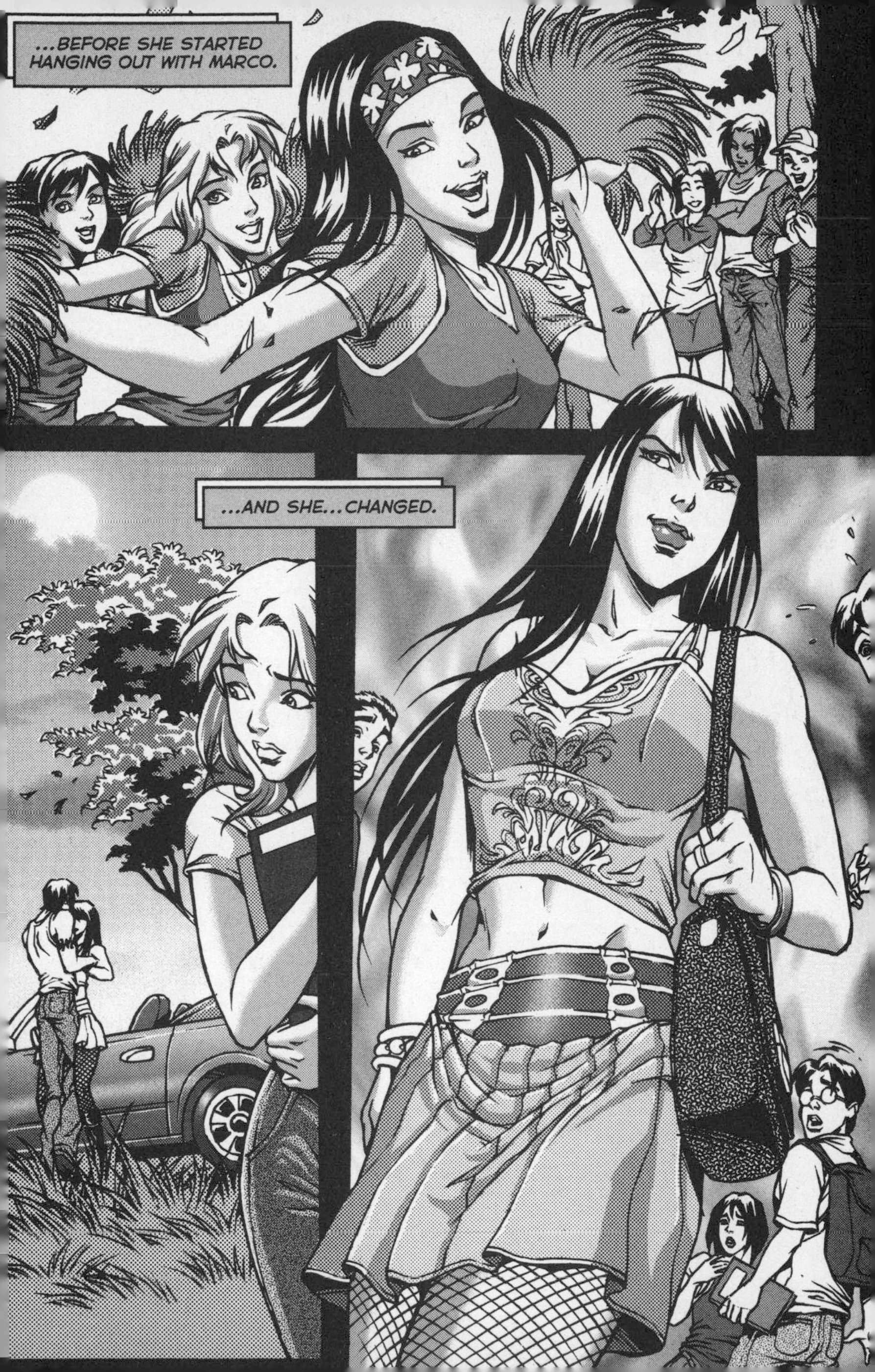
...BEFORE SHE STARTED HANGING OUT WITH MARCO.
...AND SHE...CHANGED.

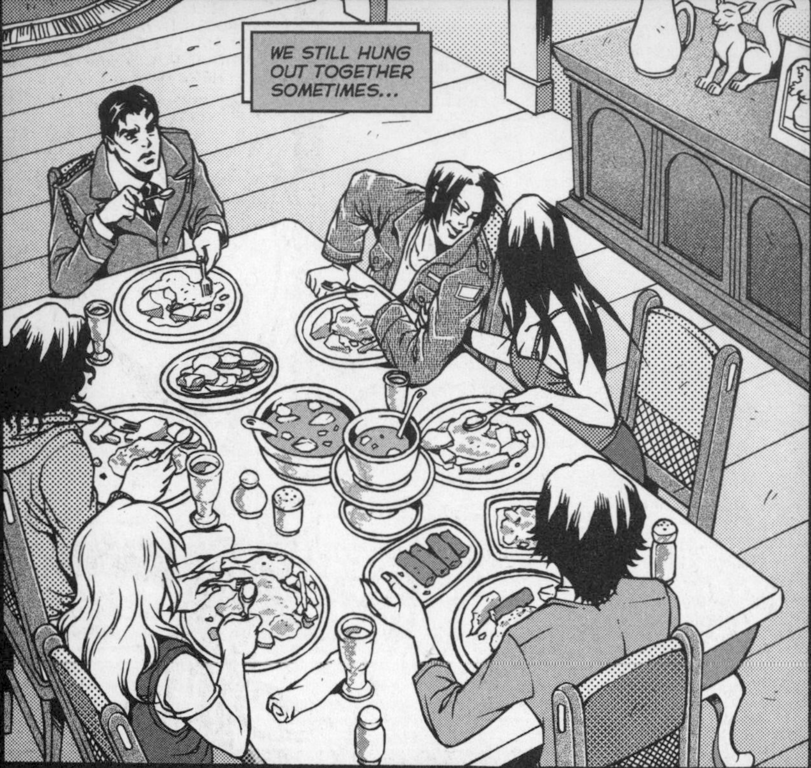
WE STILL HUNG OUT TOGETHER SOMETIMES...
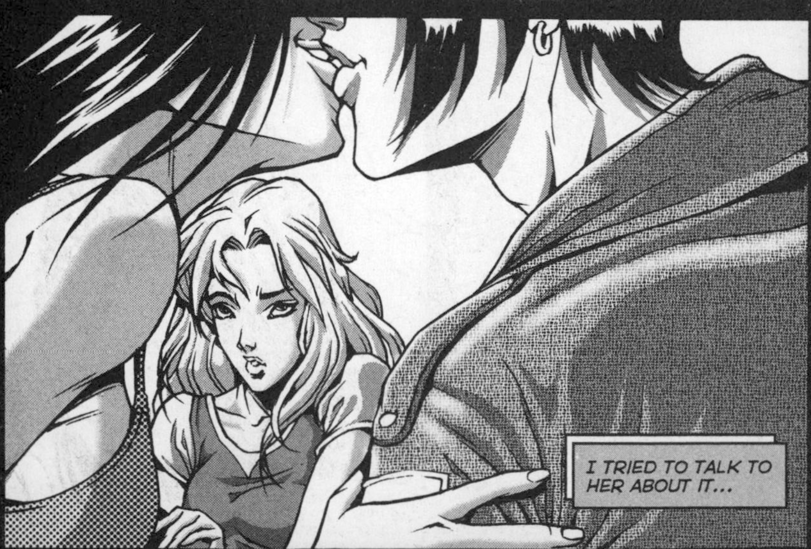
I TRIED TO TALK TO HER ABOUT IT...

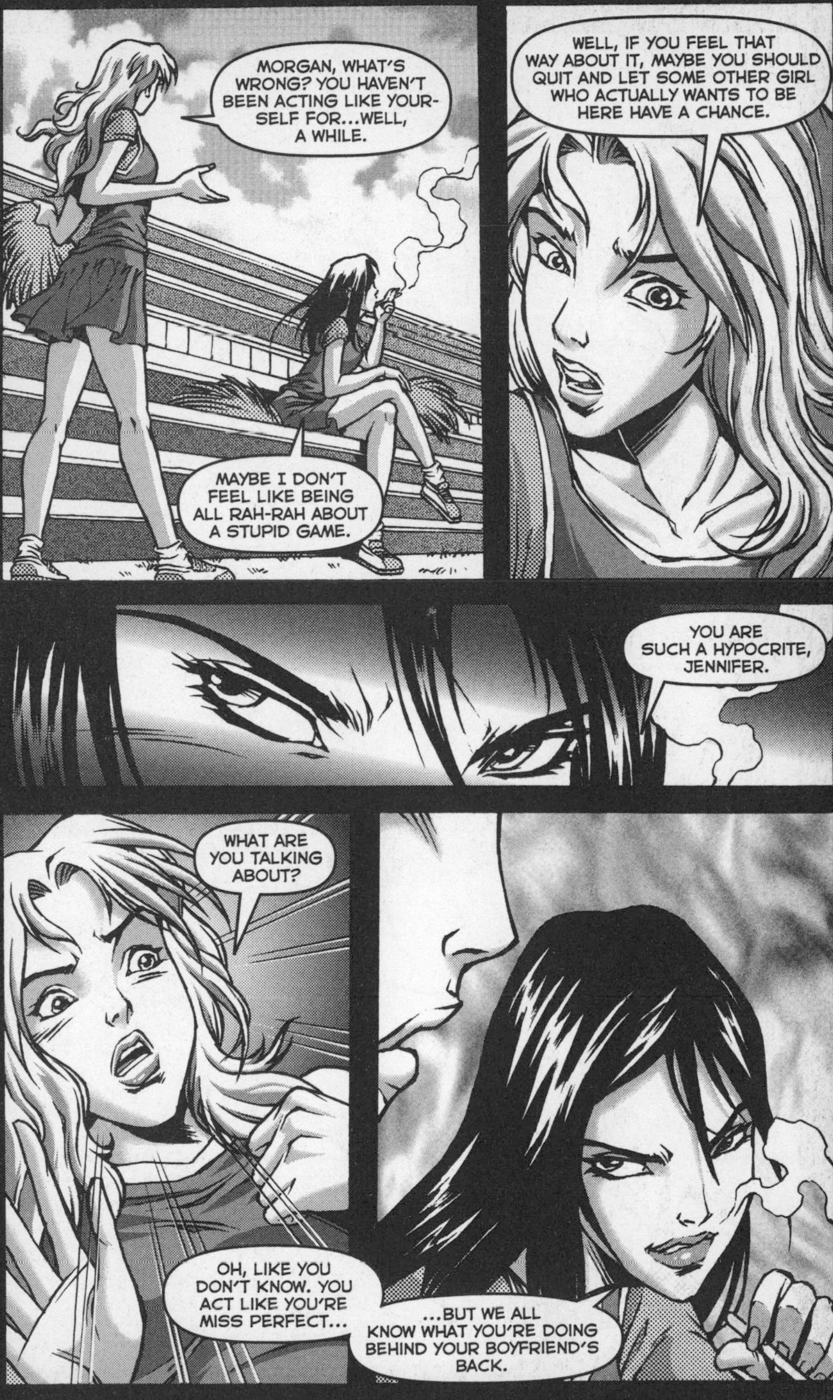
MORGAN, WHAT'S WRONG? YOU HAVEN'T BEEN ACTING LIKE YOUR-SELF FOR...WELL, A WHILE.
MAYBE I DON'T FEEL LIKE BEING ALL RAH-RAH ABOUT A STUPID GAME.
WELL, IF YOU FEEL THAT WAY ABOUT IT, MAYBE YOU SHOULD QUIT AND LET SOME OTHER GIRL WHO ACTUALLY WANTS TO BE HERE HAVE A CHANCE.
YOU ARE SUCH A HYPOCRITE, JENNIFER.
WHAT ARE YOU TALKING ABOUT?
OH, LIKE YOU DON'T KNOW. YOU ACT LIKE YOU'RE MISS PERFECT...
...BUT WE ALL KNOW WHAT YOU'RE DOING BEHIND YOUR BOYFRIEND'S BACK.

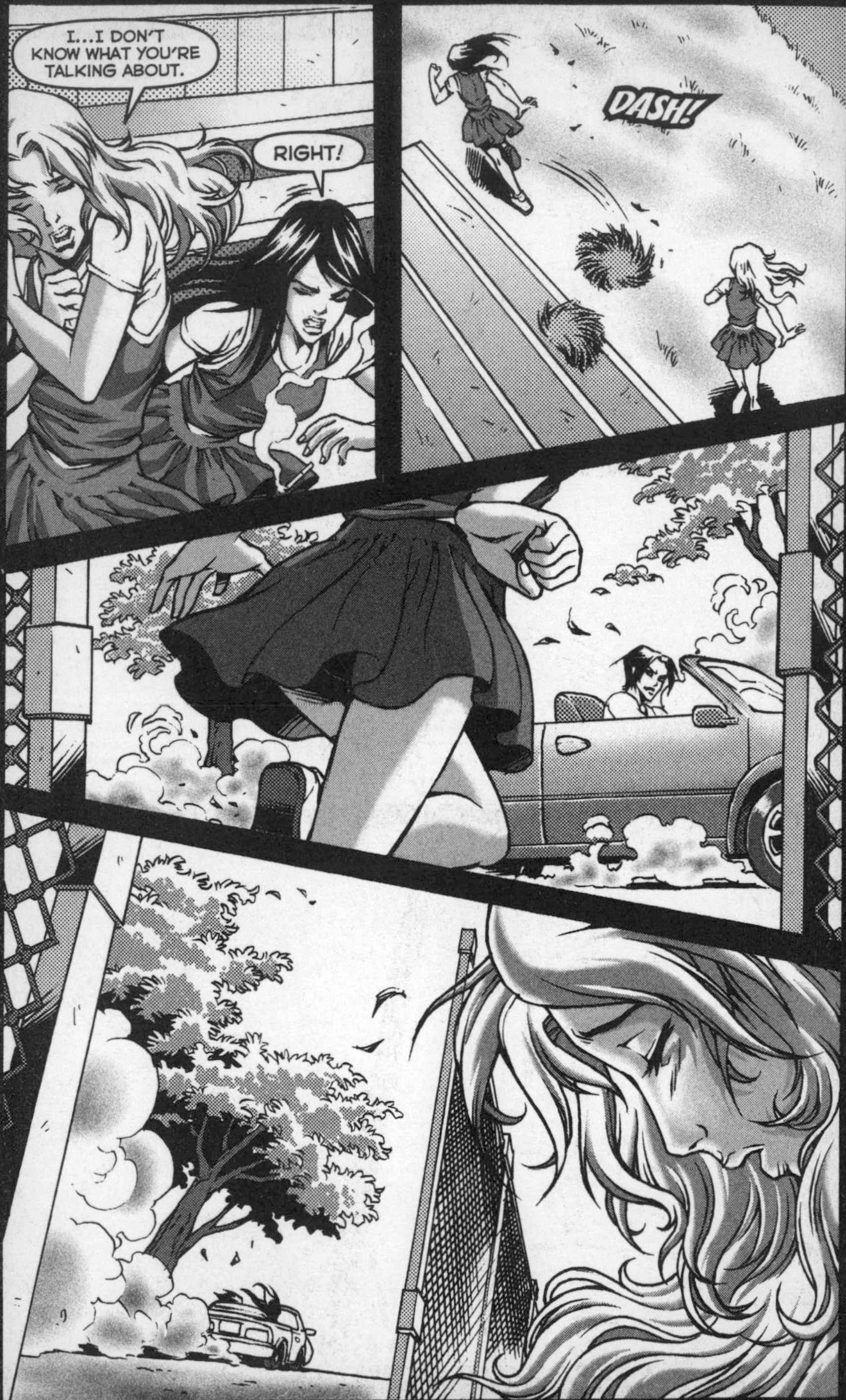
I...I DON'T KNOW WHAT YOU'RE TALKING ABOUT.
RIGHT!
DASH!

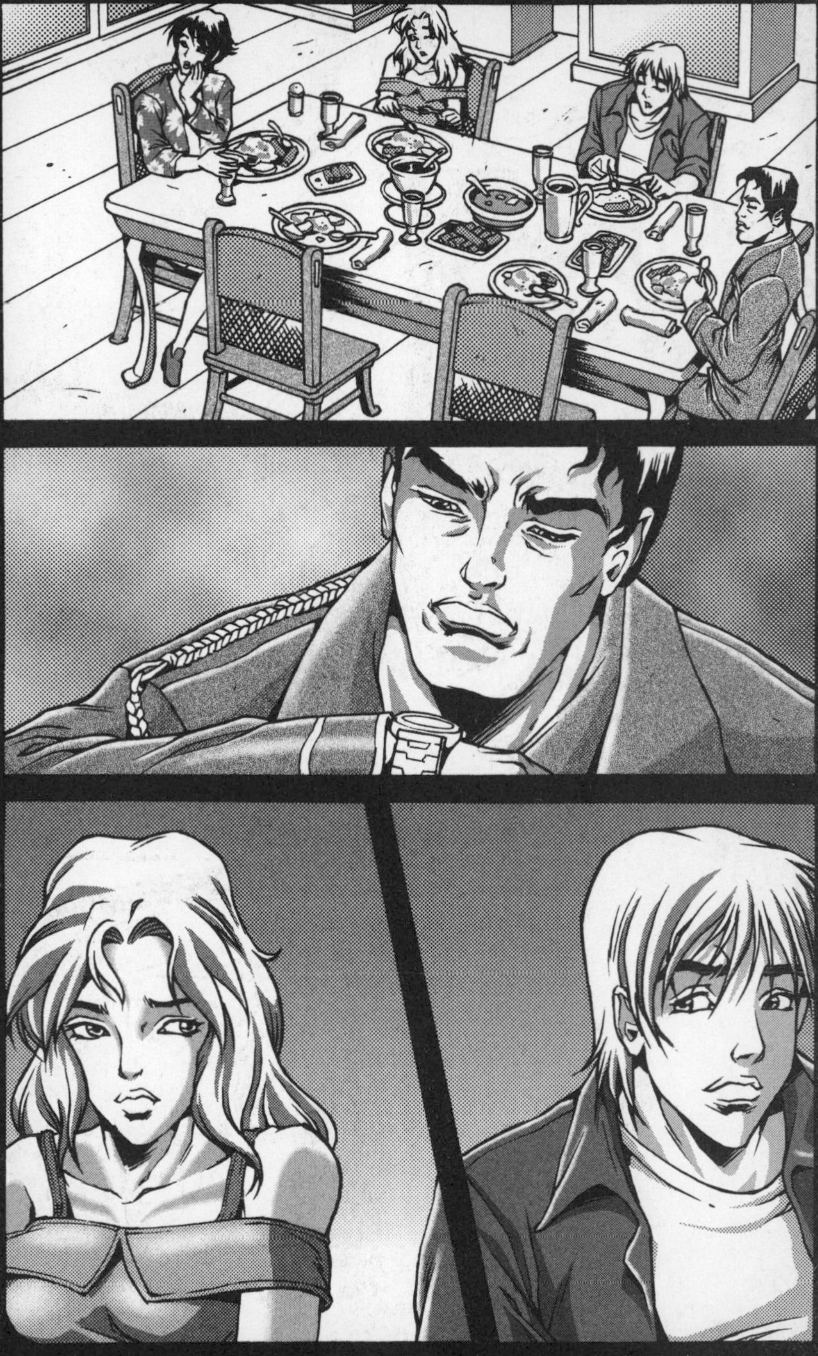

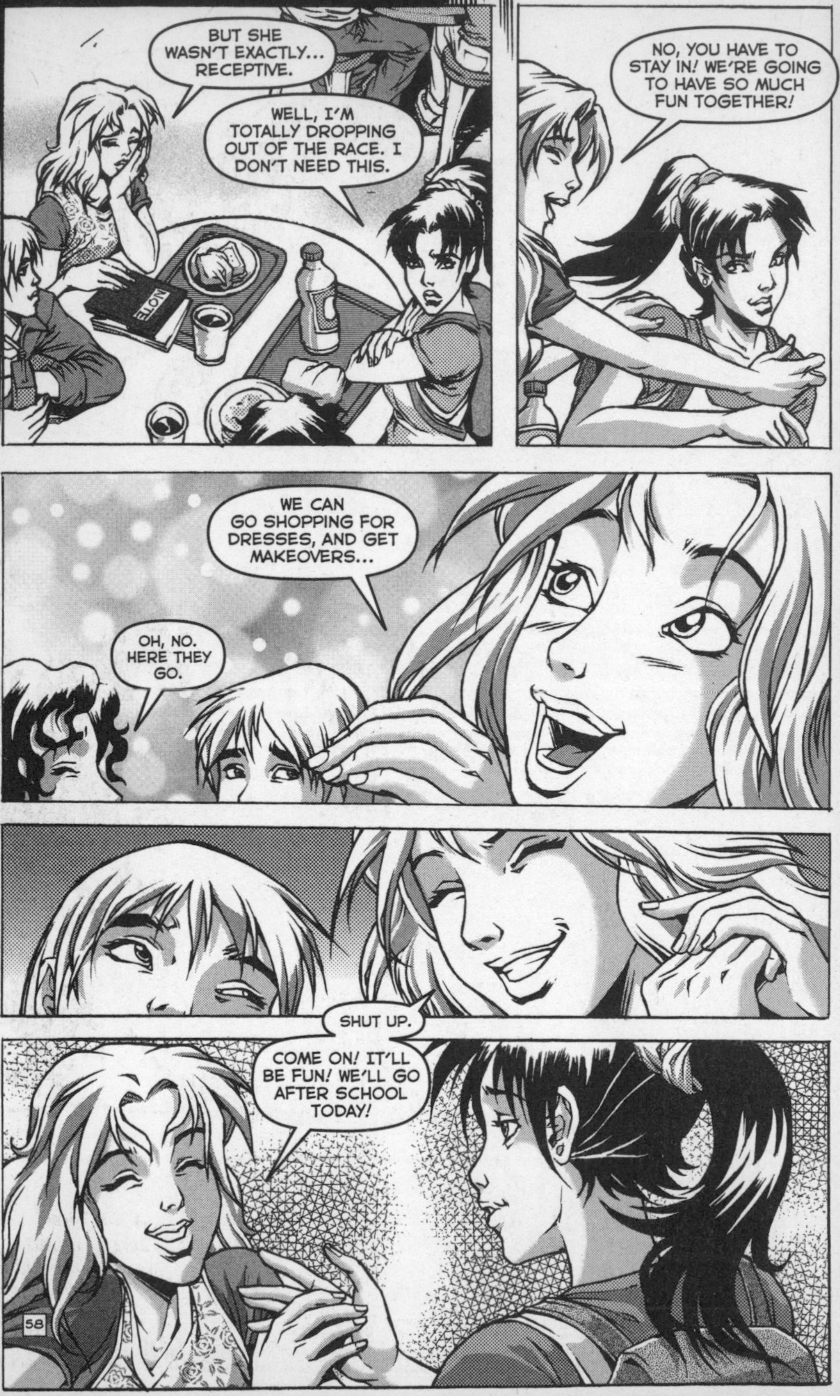
BUT SHE WASN'T EXACTLY... RECEPTIVE.
WELL, I'M TOTALLY DROPPING OUT OF THE RACE. I DON'T NEED THIS.
NOTE
NO, YOU HAVE TO STAY IN! WE'RE GOING TO HAVE SO MUCH FUN TOGETHER!
WE CAN GO SHOPPING FOR DRESSES, AND GET MAKEOVERS...
OH, NO. HERE THEY GO.
SHUT UP.
COME ON! IT'LL BE FUN! WE'LL GO AFTER SCHOOL TODAY!

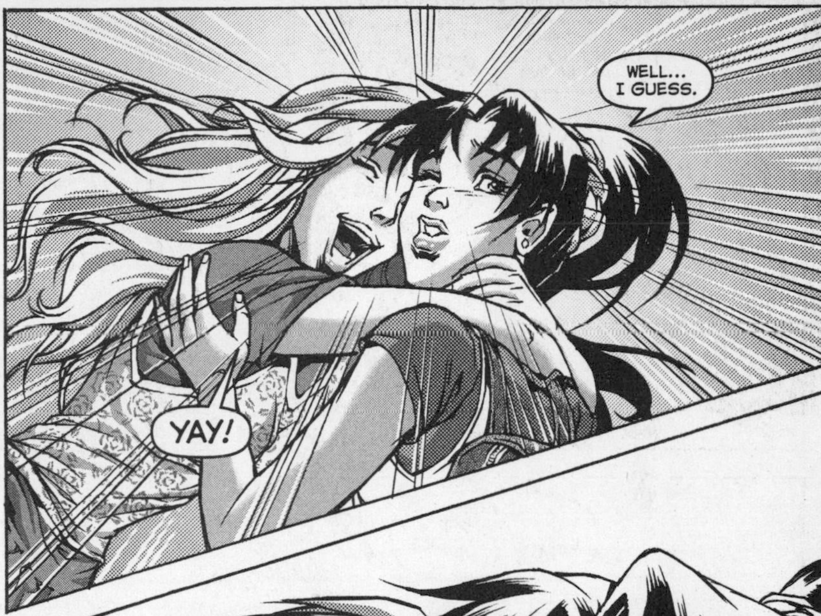
WELL... I GUESS.
YAY!

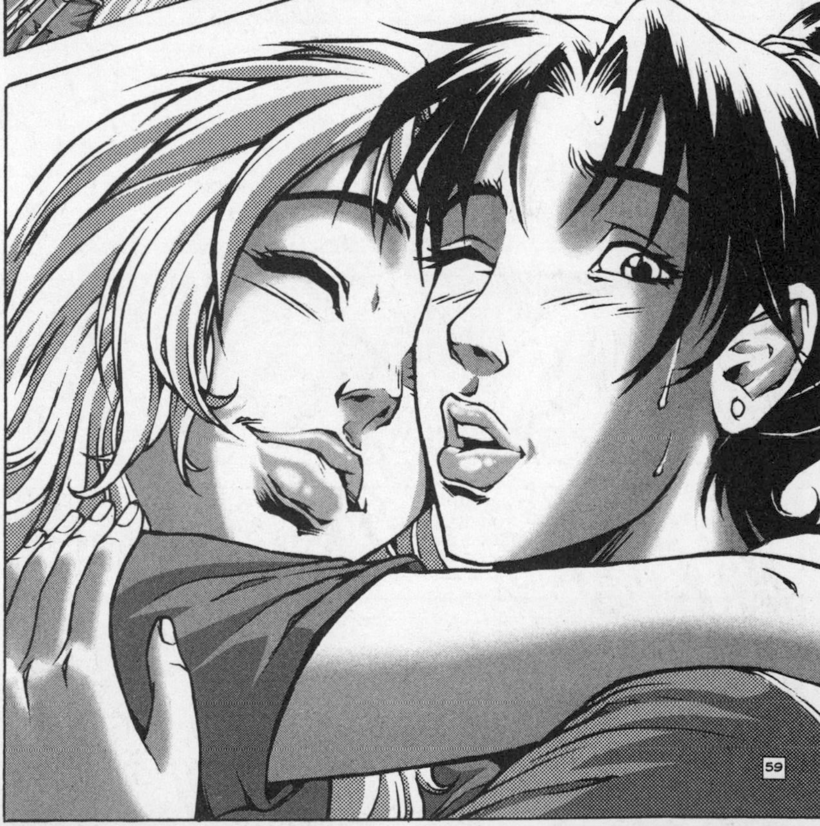

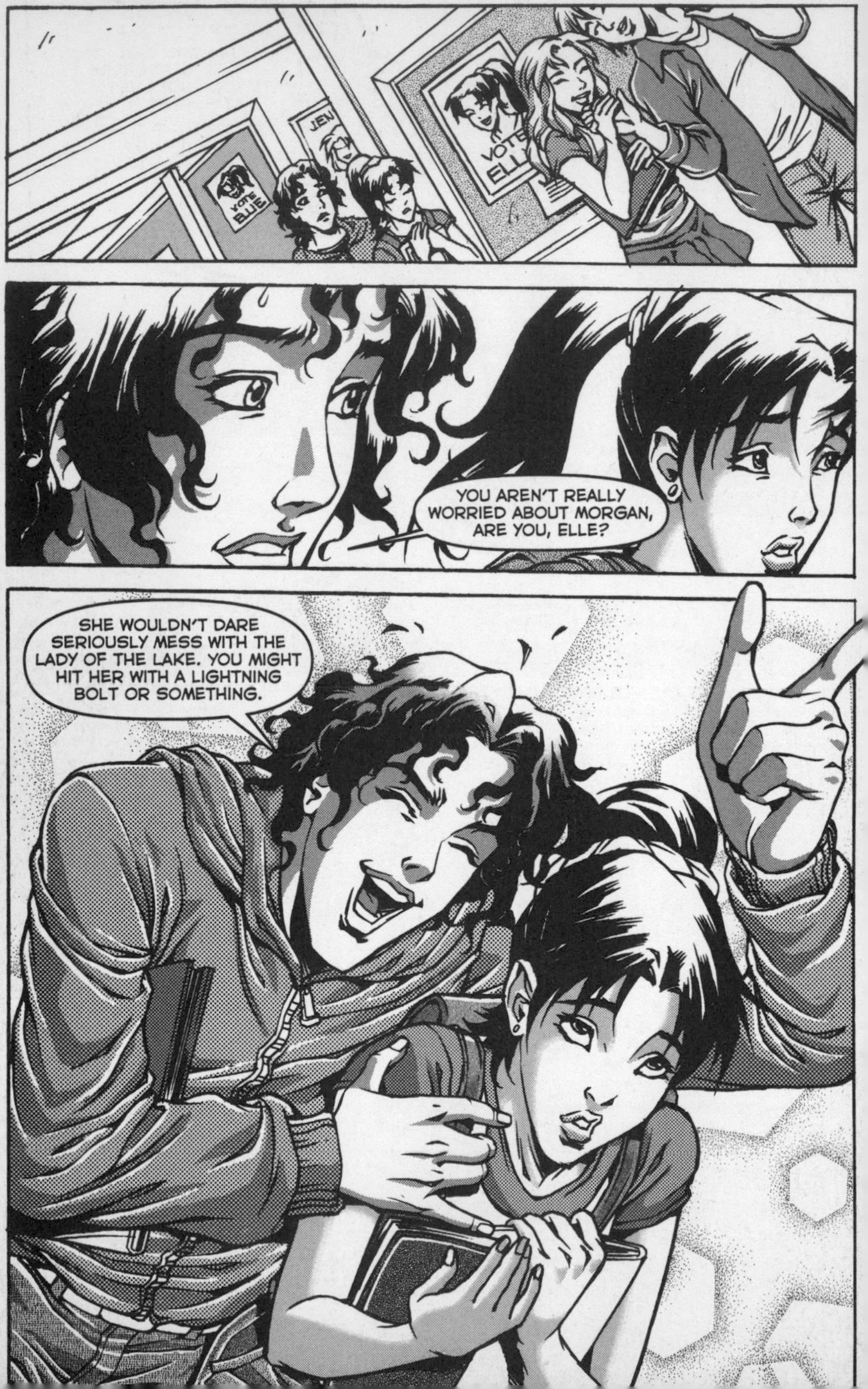
JEN
VOTE BLUE
VOTE ELLE
YOU AREN'T REALLY WORRIED ABOUT MORGAN, ARE YOU, ELLE?
SHE WOULDN'T DARE SERIOUSLY MESS WITH THE LADY OF THE LAKE. YOU MIGHT HIT HER WITH A LIGHTNING BOLT OR SOMETHING.

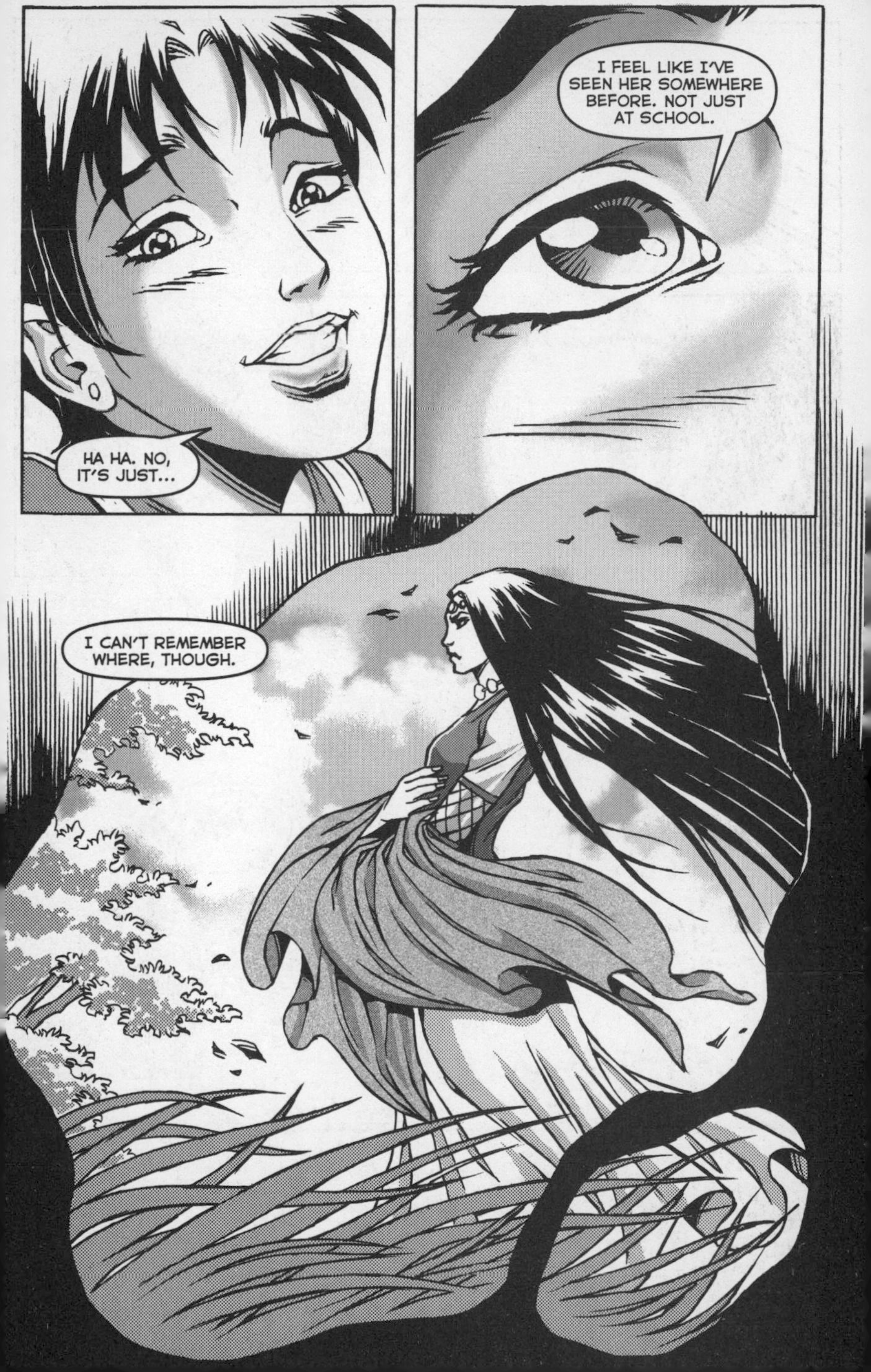
HA HA. NO, IT'S JUST...
I FEEL LIKE I'VE SEEN HER SOMEWHERE BEFORE. NOT JUST AT SCHOOL.
I CAN'T REMEMBER WHERE, THOUGH.

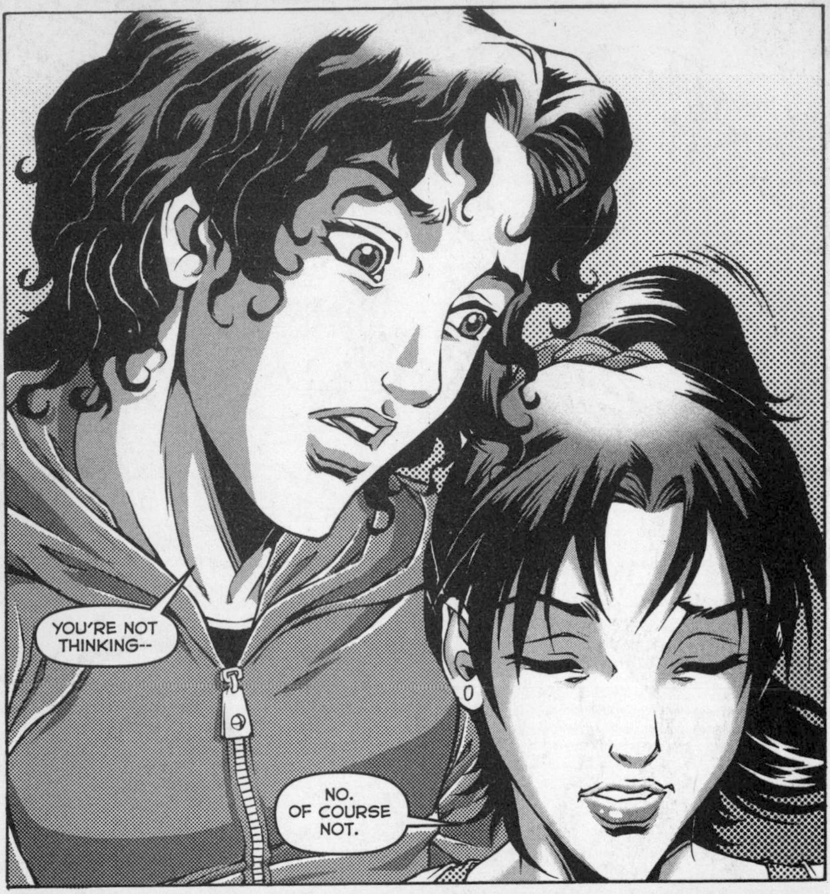
YOU'RE NOT THINKING--
NO. OF COURSE NOT.

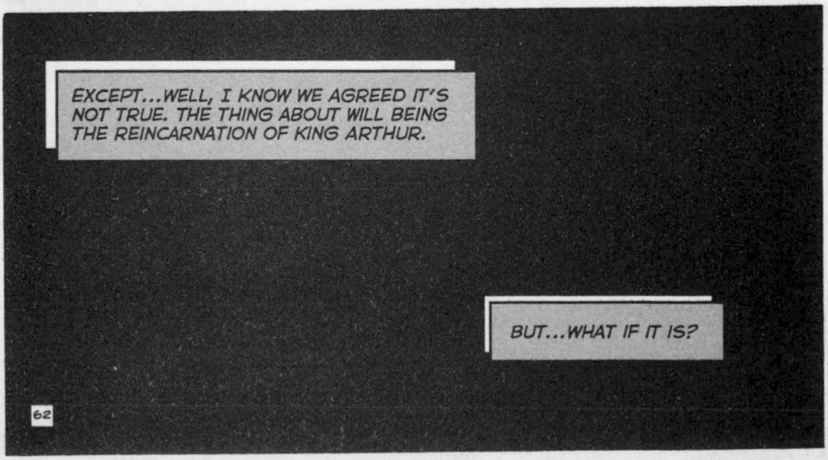
EXCEPT...WELL, I KNOW WE AGREED IT'S NOT TRUE. THE THING ABOUT WILL BEING THE REINCARNATION OF KING ARTHUR.
BUT...WHAT IF IT IS?

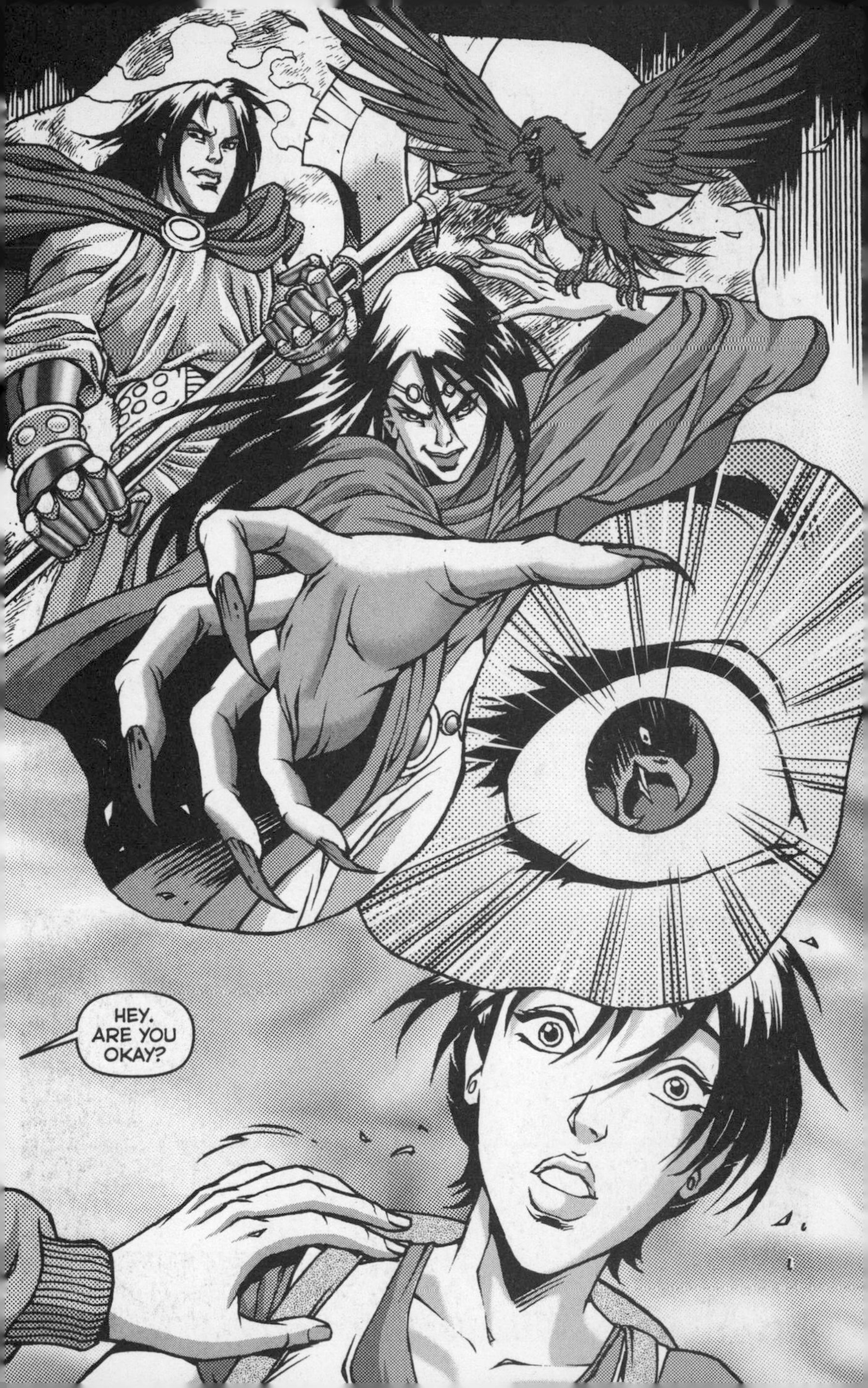
HEY. ARE YOU OKAY?

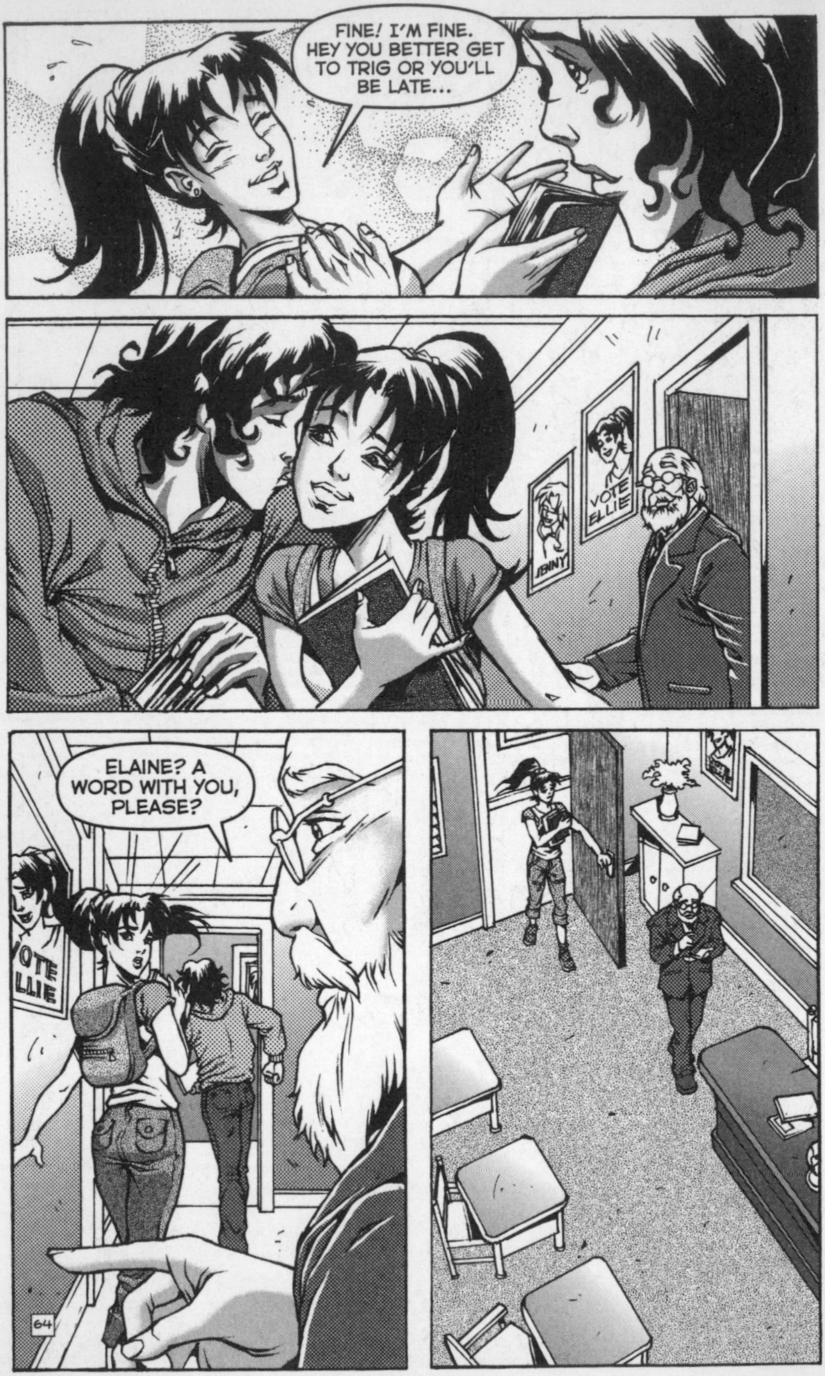
FINE! I'M FINE. HEY YOU BETTER GET TO TRIG OR YOU'LL BE LATE...
JENNY
VOTE ELLIE
ELAINE? A WORD WITH YOU, PLEASE?
VOTE ELLIE

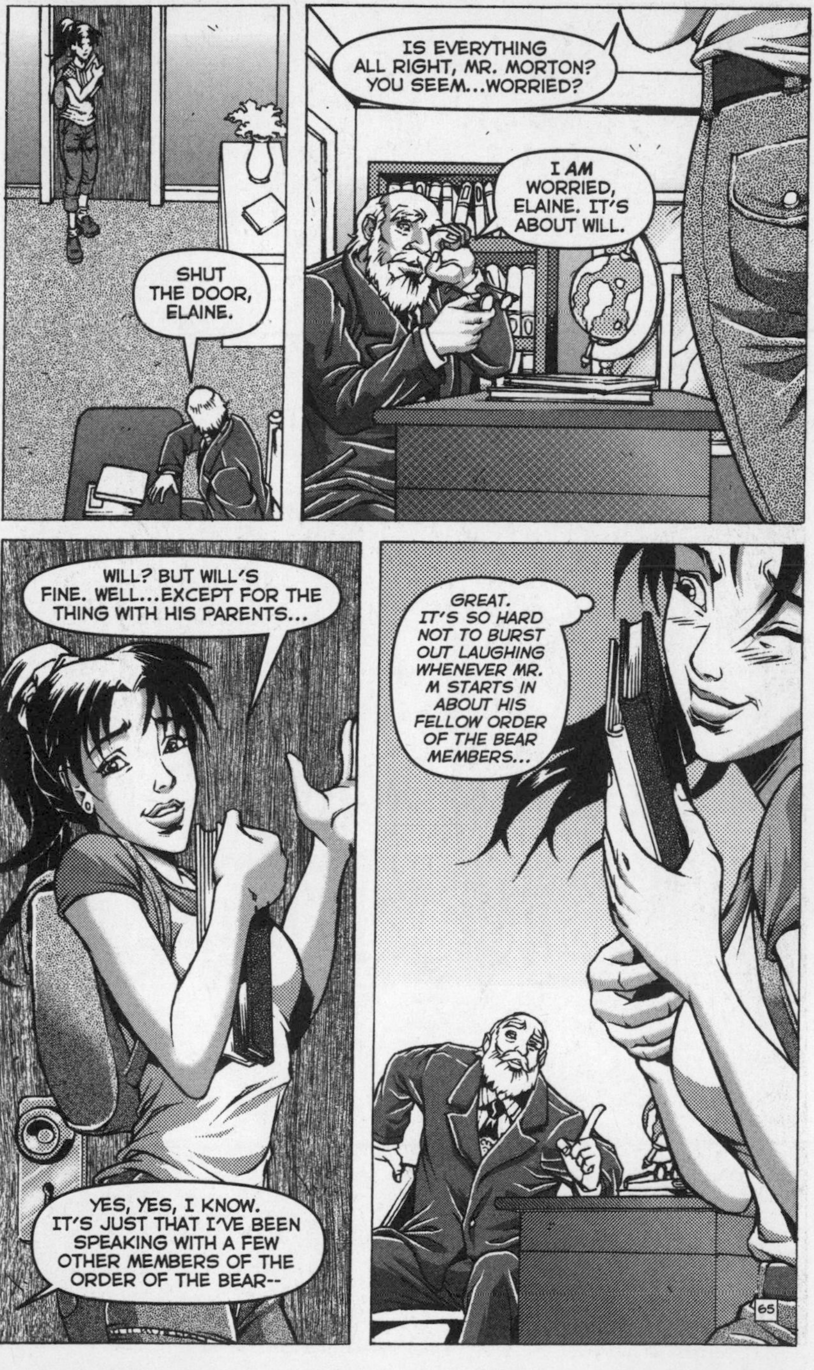
SHUT THE DOOR, ELAINE.
IS EVERYTHING ALL RIGHT, MR. MORTON? YOU SEEM...WORRIED?
I *AM* WORRIED, ELAINE. IT'S ABOUT WILL.
WILL? BUT WILL'S FINE. WELL...EXCEPT FOR THE THING WITH HIS PARENTS...
YES, YES, I KNOW. IT'S JUST THAT I'VE BEEN SPEAKING WITH A FEW OTHER MEMBERS OF THE ORDER OF THE BEAR--
GREAT. IT'S SO HARD NOT TO BURST OUT LAUGHING WHENEVER MR. M STARTS IN ABOUT HIS FELLOW ORDER OF THE BEAR MEMBERS...

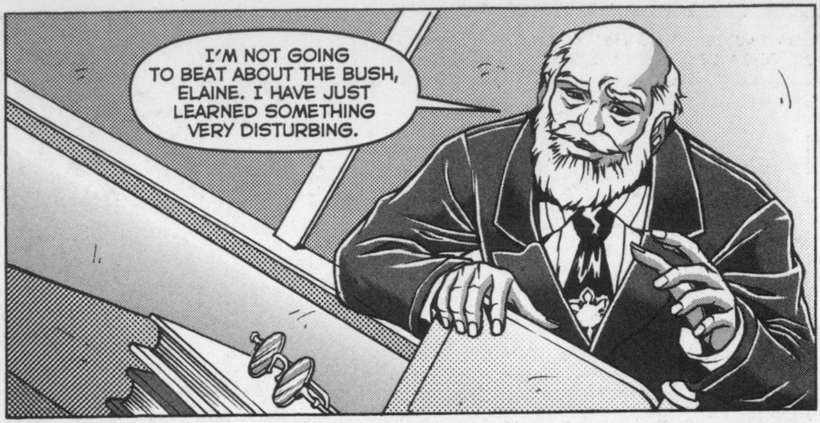
I'M NOT GOING TO BEAT ABOUT THE BUSH, ELAINE. I HAVE JUST LEARNED SOMETHING VERY DISTURBING.

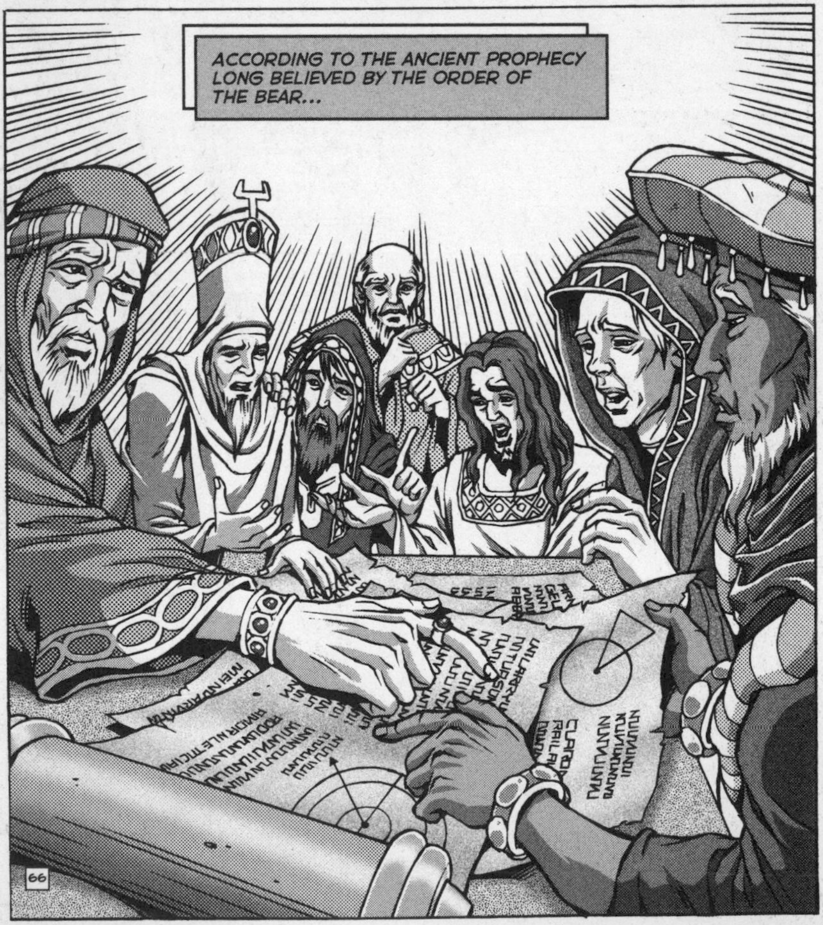
ACCORDING TO THE ANCIENT PROPHECY LONG BELIEVED BY THE ORDER OF THE BEAR...

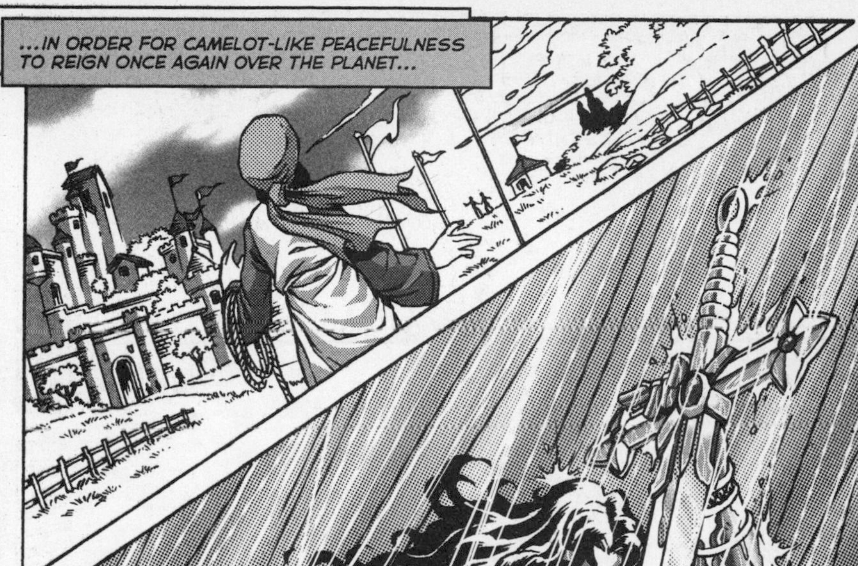
...IN ORDER FOR CAMELOT-LIKE PEACEFULNESS TO REIGN ONCE AGAIN OVER THE PLANET...
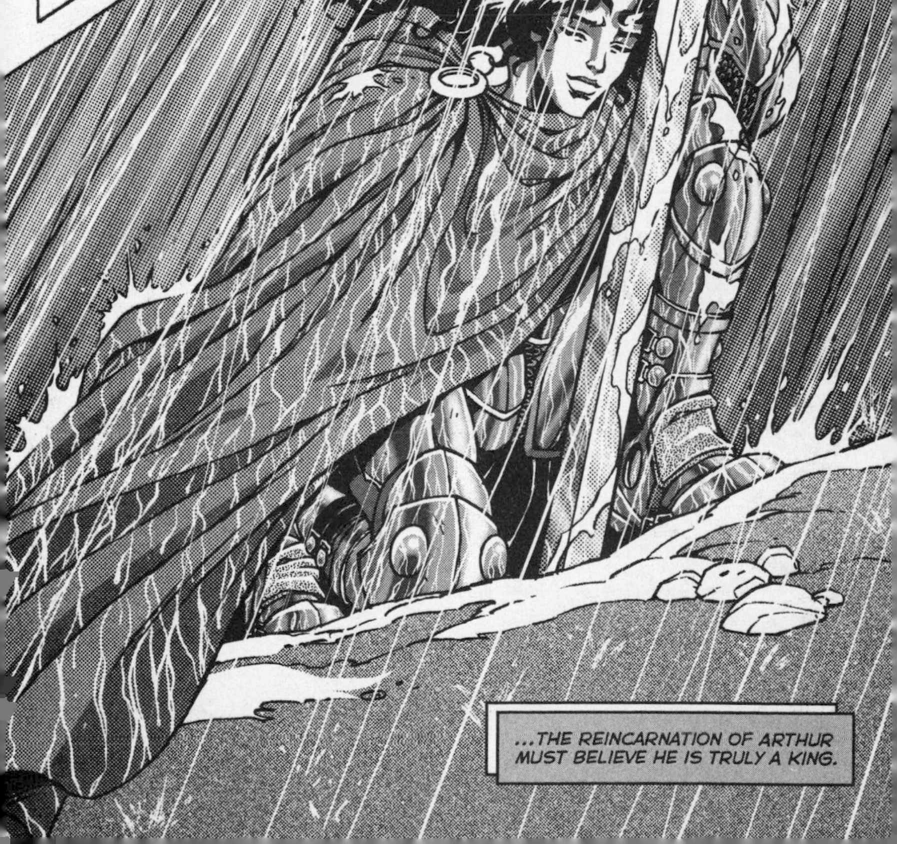
...THE REINCARNATION OF ARTHUR MUST BELIEVE HE IS TRULY A KING.

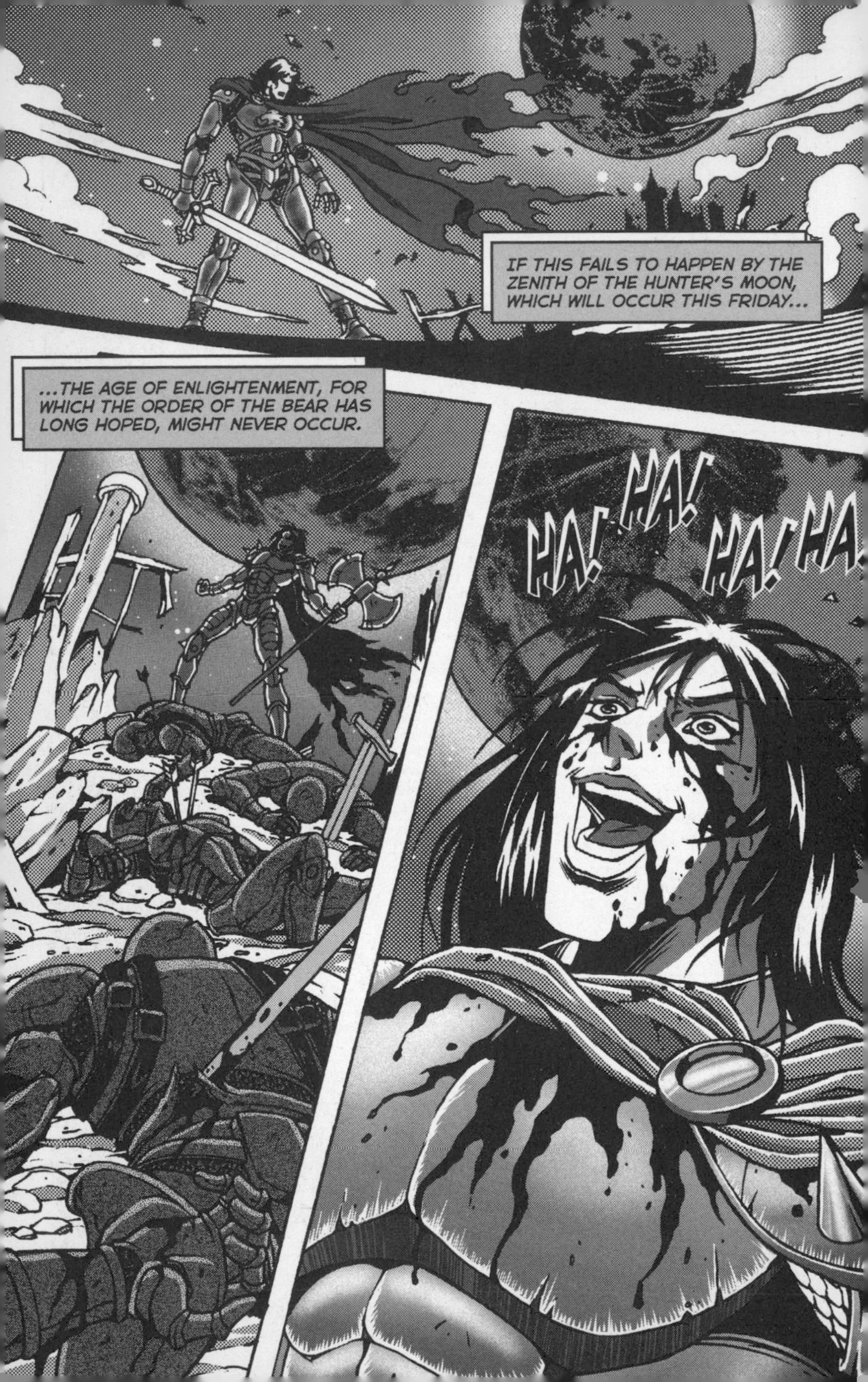
IF THIS FAILS TO HAPPEN BY THE ZENITH OF THE HUNTER'S MOON, WHICH WILL OCCUR THIS FRIDAY...
...THE AGE OF ENLIGHTENMENT, FOR WHICH THE ORDER OF THE BEAR HAS LONG HOPED, MIGHT NEVER OCCUR.
HA! HA! HA! HA

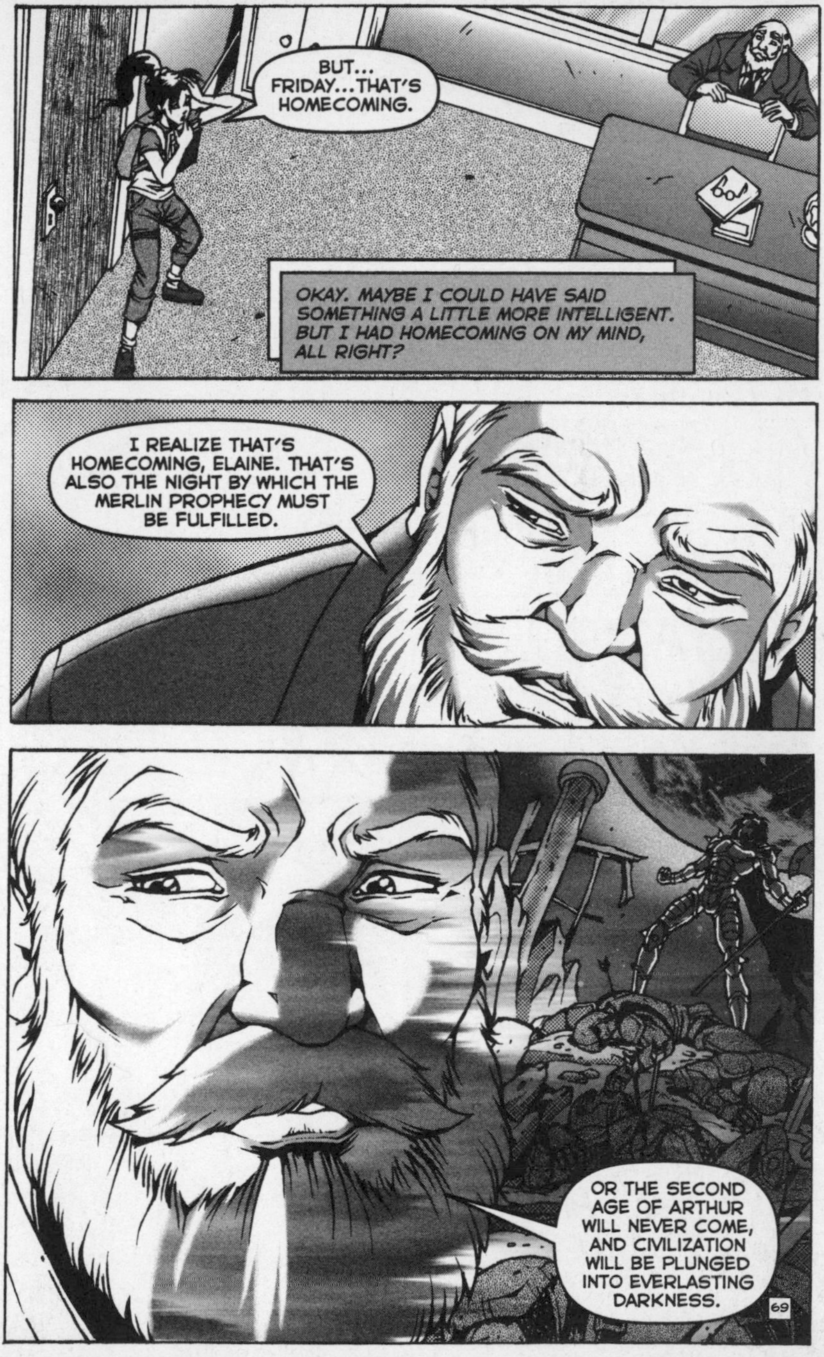
BUT... FRIDAY...THAT'S HOMECOMING.
OKAY. MAYBE I COULD HAVE SAID SOMETHING A LITTLE MORE INTELLIGENT. BUT I HAD HOMECOMING ON MY MIND, ALL RIGHT?
I REALIZE THAT'S HOMECOMING, ELAINE. THAT'S ALSO THE NIGHT BY WHICH THE MERLIN PROPHECY MUST BE FULFILLED.
OR THE SECOND AGE OF ARTHUR WILL NEVER COME, AND CIVILIZATION WILL BE PLUNGED INTO EVERLASTING DARKNESS.

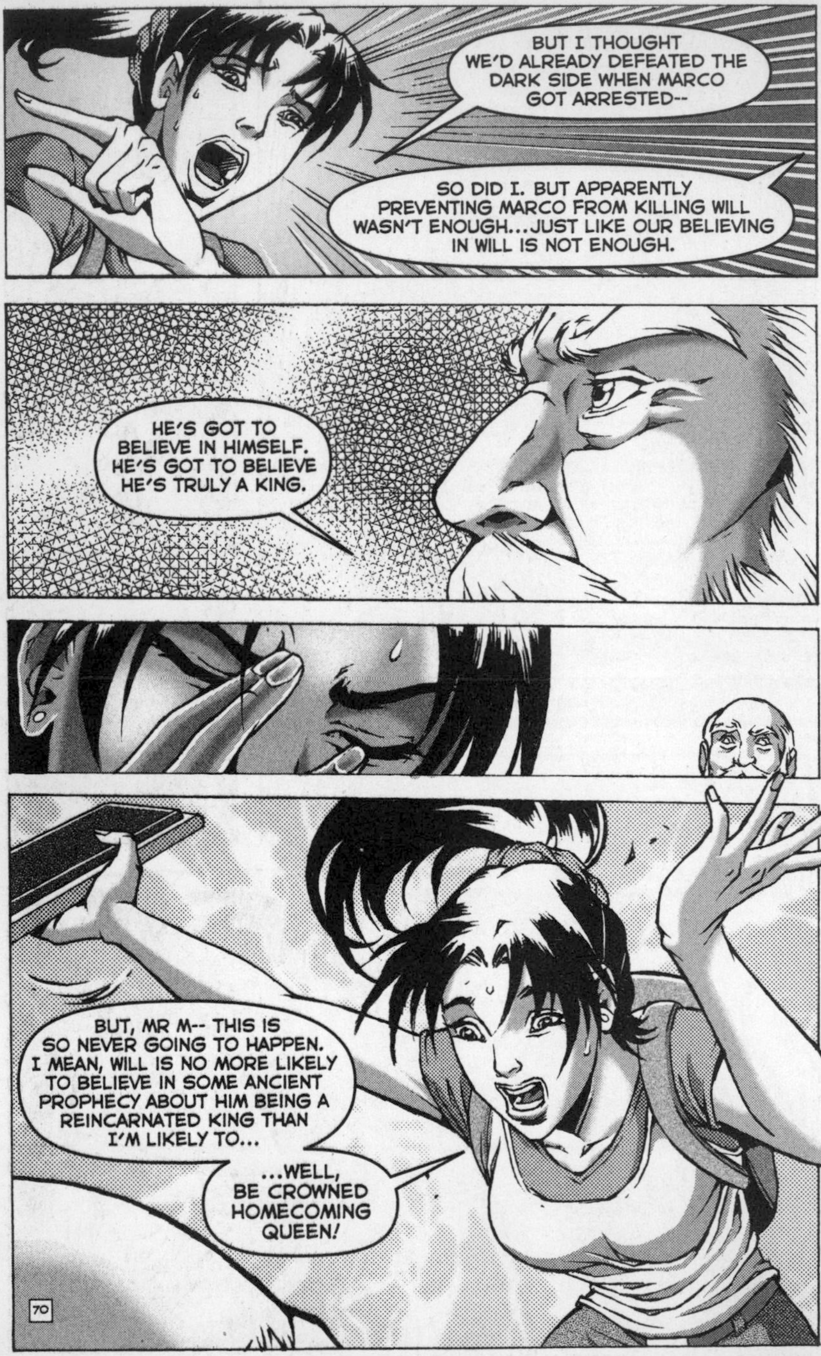
BUT I THOUGHT WE'D ALREADY DEFEATED THE DARK SIDE WHEN MARCO GOT ARRESTED--
SO DID I. BUT APPARENTLY PREVENTING MARCO FROM KILLING WILL WASN'T ENOUGH...JUST LIKE OUR BELIEVING IN WILL IS NOT ENOUGH.
HE'S GOT TO BELIEVE IN HIMSELF. HE'S GOT TO BELIEVE HE'S TRULY A KING.
BUT, MR M-- THIS IS SO NEVER GOING TO HAPPEN. I MEAN, WILL IS NO MORE LIKELY TO BELIEVE IN SOME ANCIENT PROPHECY ABOUT HIM BEING A REINCARNATED KING THAN I'M LIKELY TO...
...WELL, BE CROWNED HOMECOMING QUEEN!

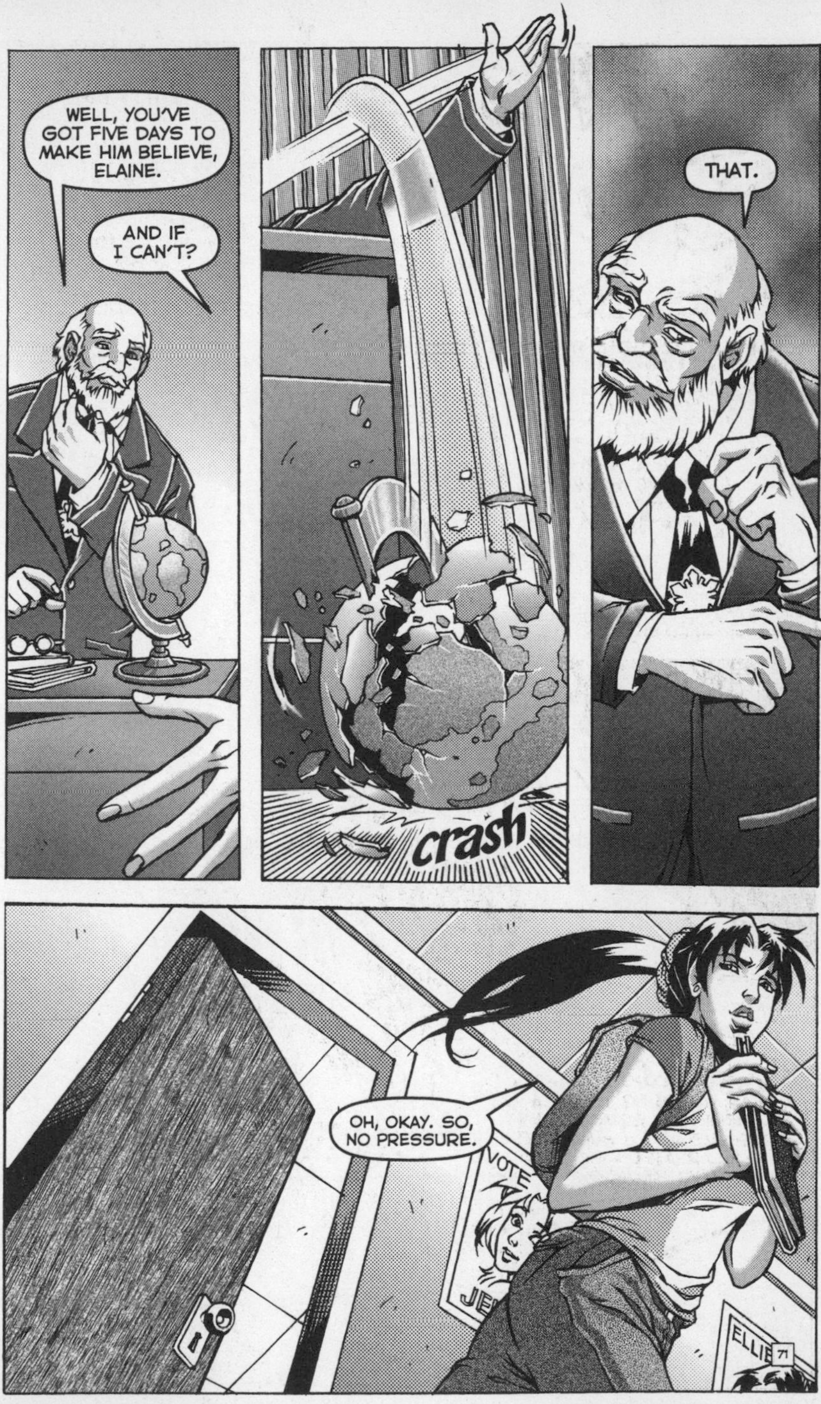
WELL, YOU'VE GOT FIVE DAYS TO MAKE HIM BELIEVE, ELAINE.
AND IF I CAN'T?
crash
THAT.
OH, OKAY. SO, NO PRESSURE.
VOTE
ELLIE

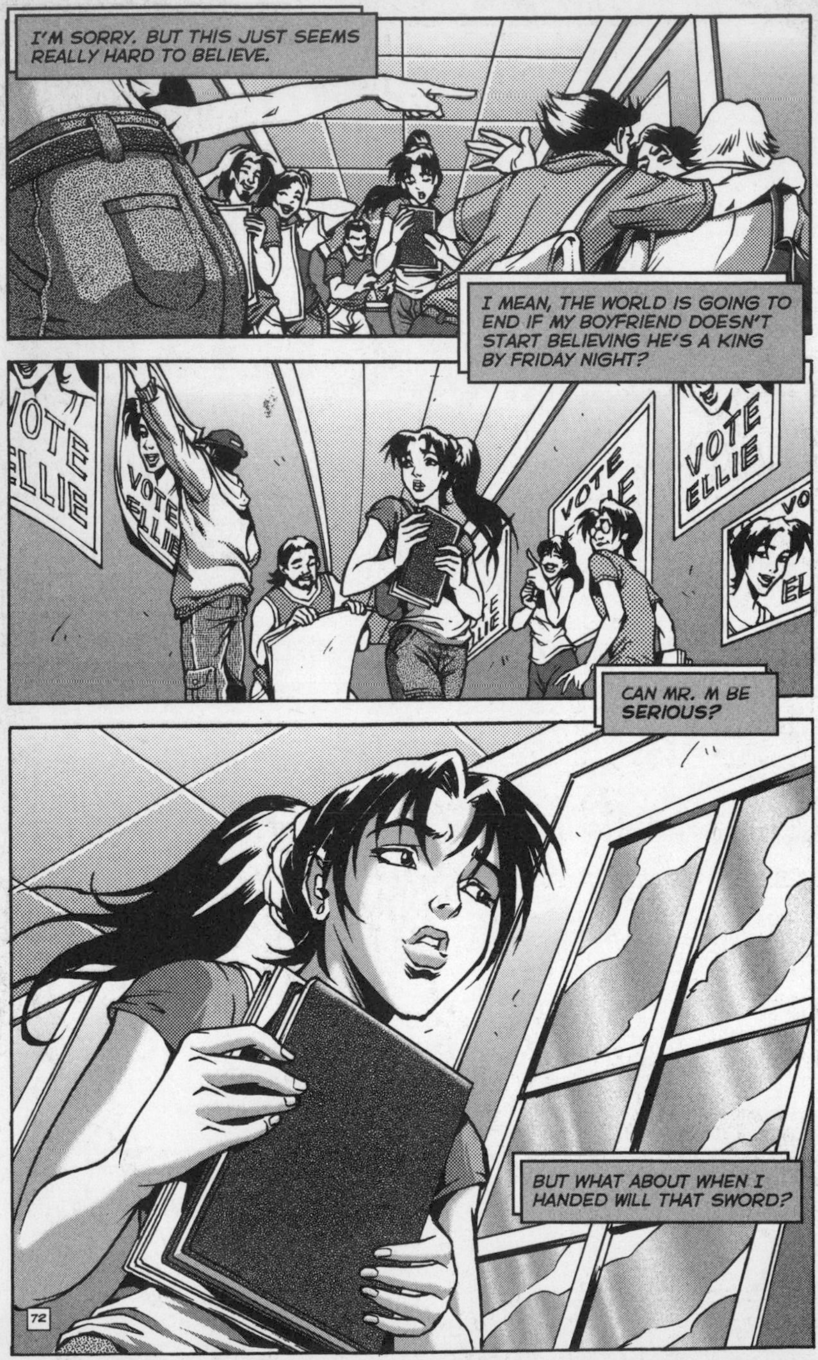
I'M SORRY. BUT THIS JUST SEEMS REALLY HARD TO BELIEVE.
I MEAN, THE WORLD IS GOING TO END IF MY BOYFRIEND DOESN'T START BELIEVING HE'S A KING BY FRIDAY NIGHT?
VOTE ELLIE
VOTE ELLIE
VOTE ELLIE
VOTE ELLIE
CAN MR. M BE SERIOUS?
BUT WHAT ABOUT WHEN I HANDED WILL THAT SWORD?

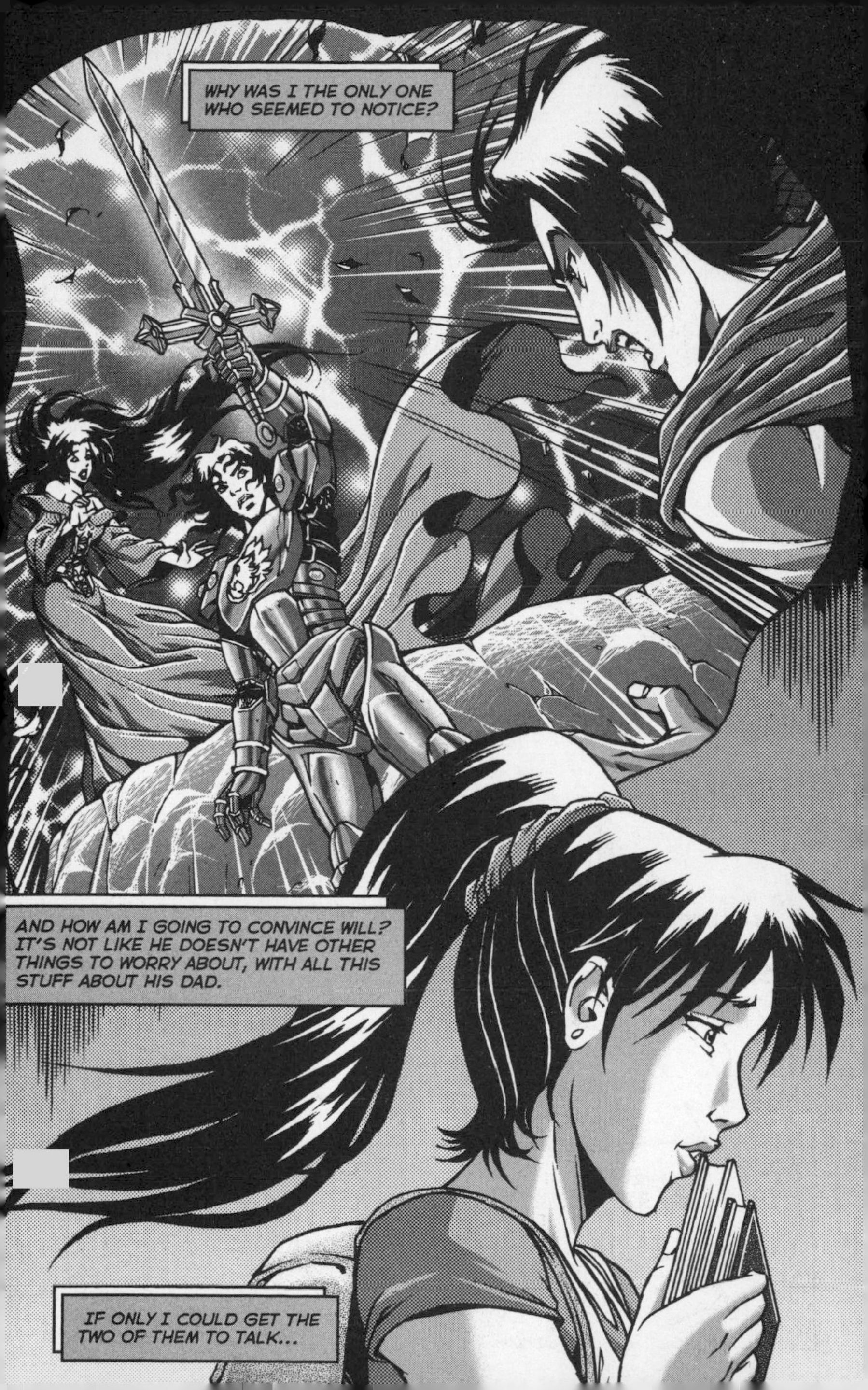
WHY WAS I THE ONLY ONE WHO SEEMED TO NOTICE?
AND HOW AM I GOING TO CONVINCE WILL? IT'S NOT LIKE HE DOESN'T HAVE OTHER THINGS TO WORRY ABOUT, WITH ALL THIS STUFF ABOUT HIS DAD.
IF ONLY I COULD GET THE TWO OF THEM TO TALK...

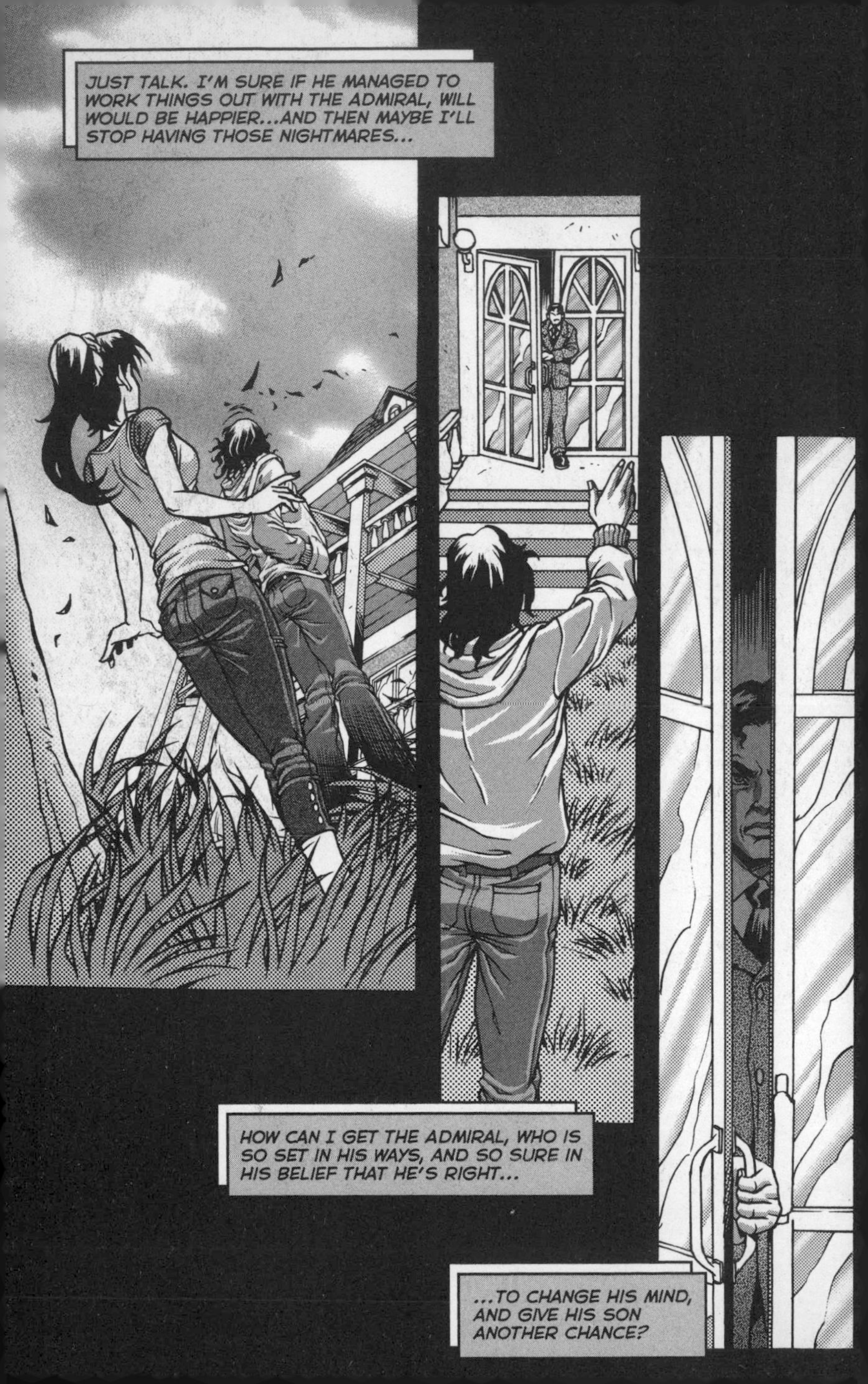
JUST TALK. I'M SURE IF HE MANAGED TO WORK THINGS OUT WITH THE ADMIRAL, WILL WOULD BE HAPPIER...AND THEN MAYBE I'LL STOP HAVING THOSE NIGHTMARES...
HOW CAN I GET THE ADMIRAL, WHO IS SO SET IN HIS WAYS, AND SO SURE IN HIS BELIEF THAT HE'S RIGHT...
...TO CHANGE HIS MIND, AND GIVE HIS SON ANOTHER CHANCE?

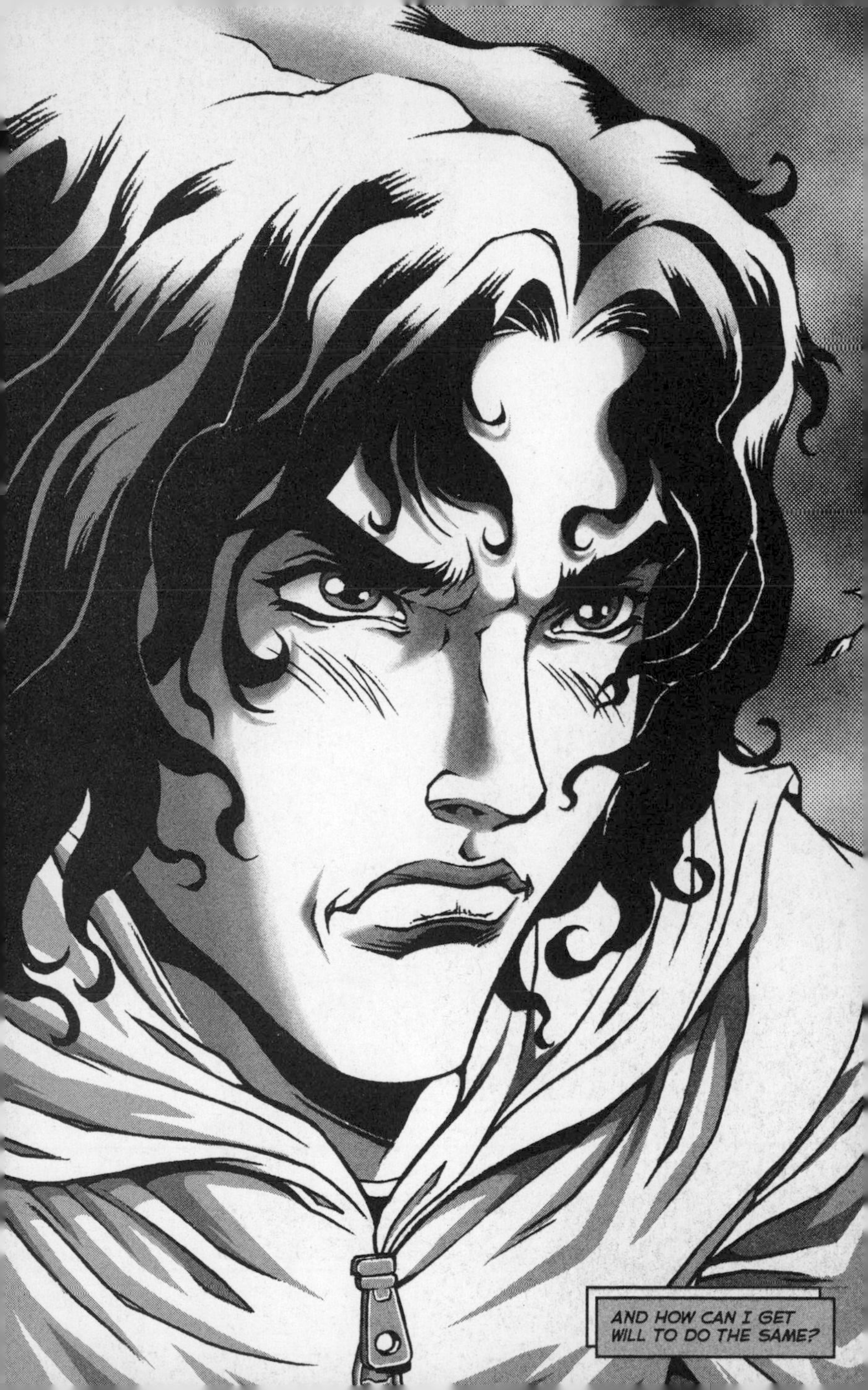
AND HOW CAN I GET
WILL TO DO THE SAME?

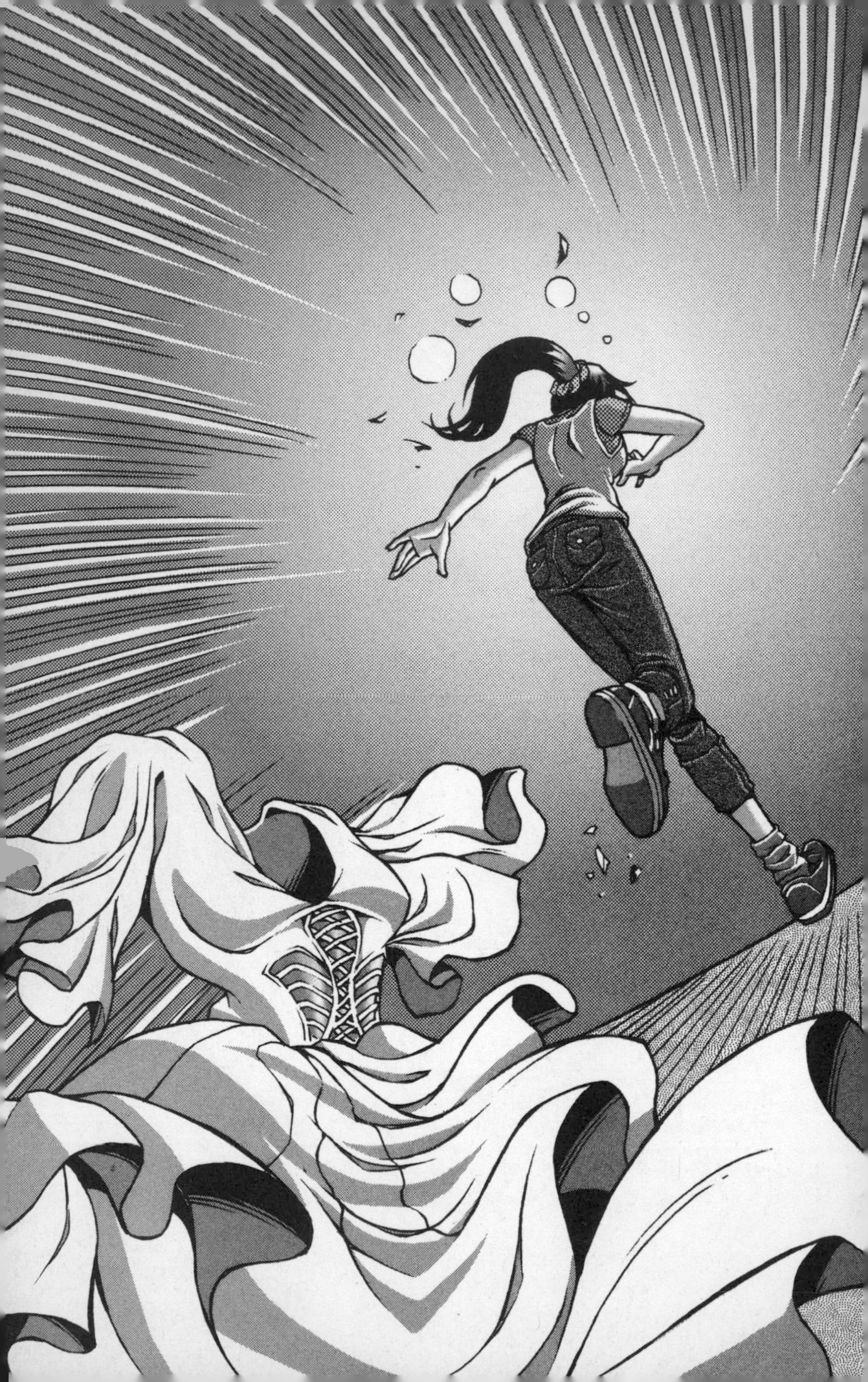

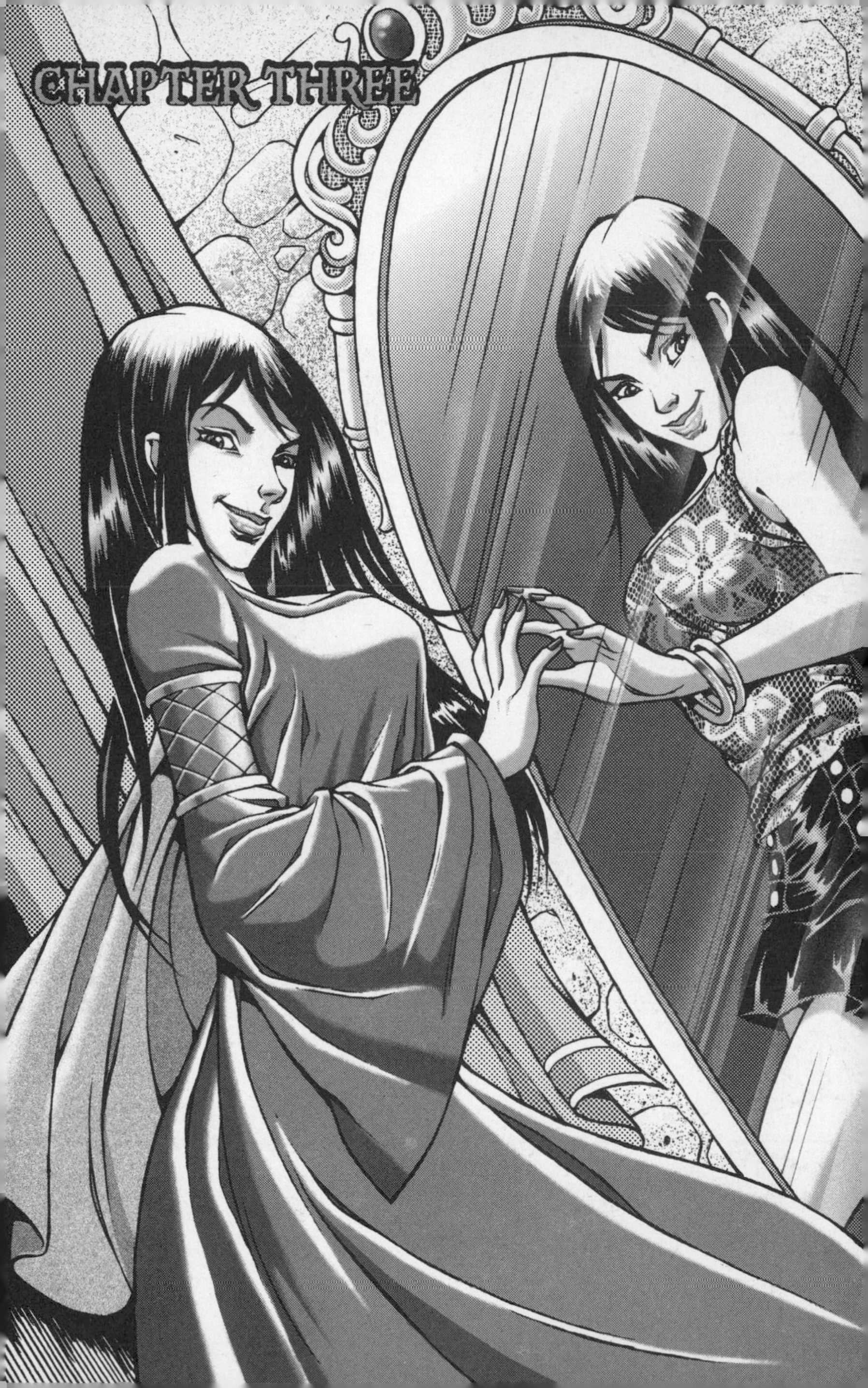
CHAPTER THREE

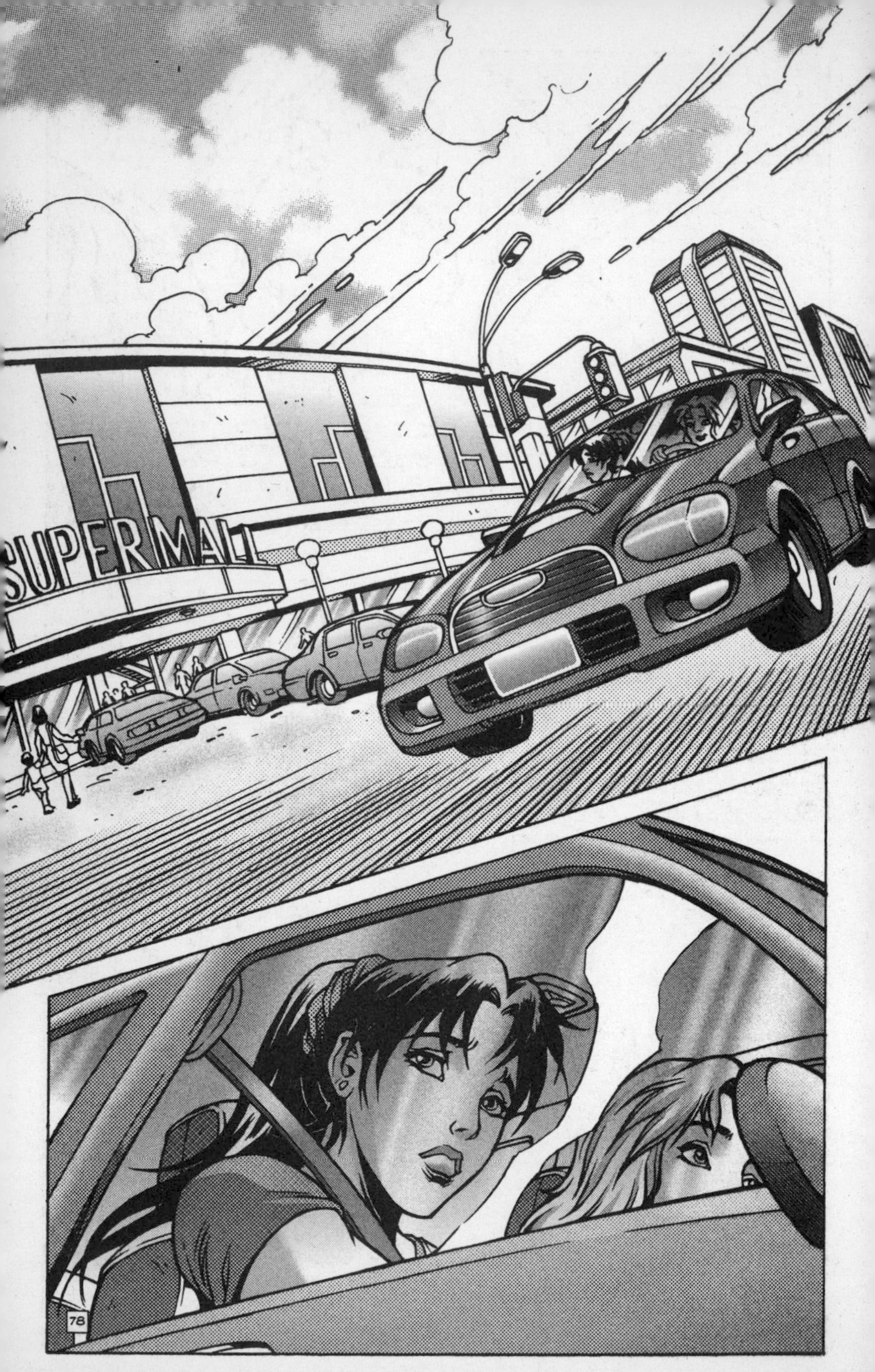
SUPERMALL

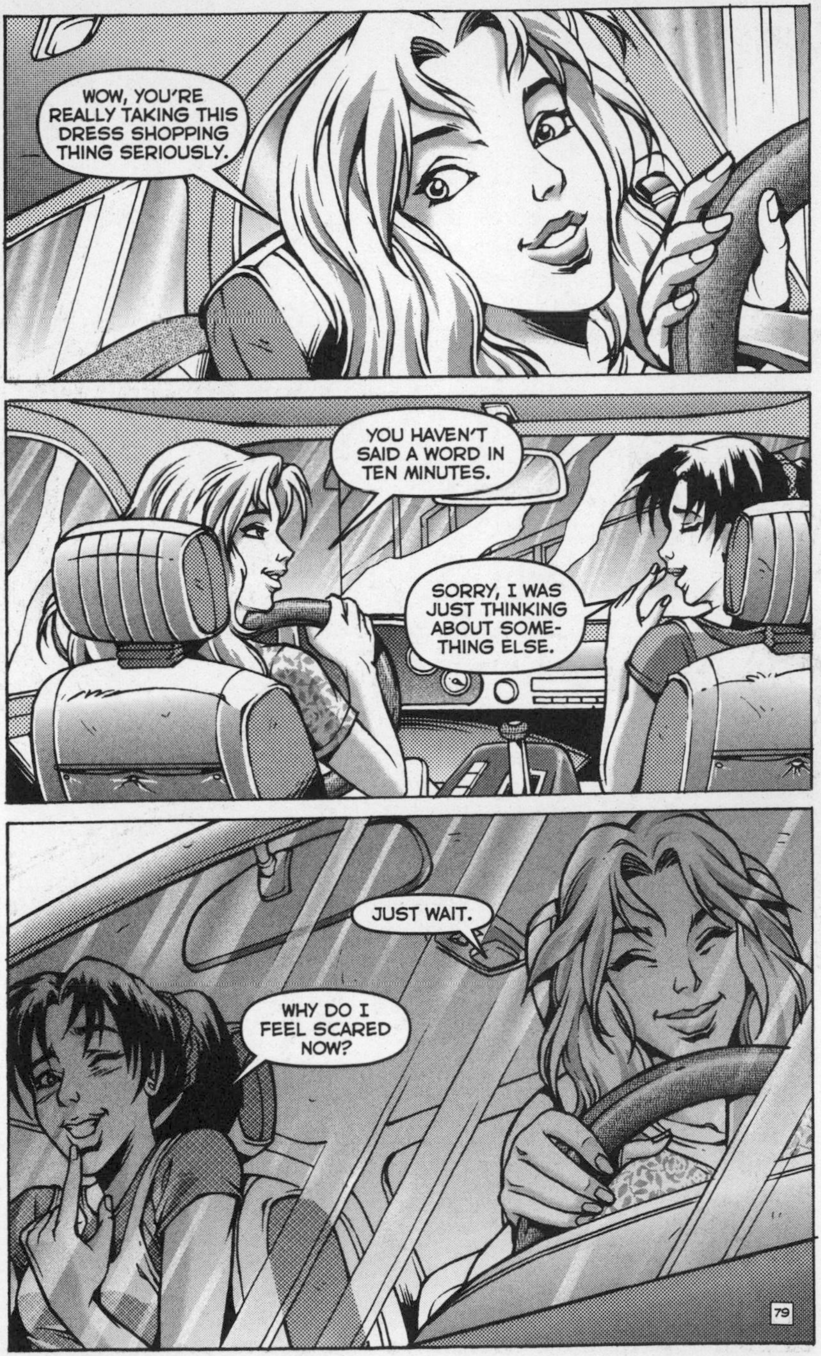
WOW, YOU'RE REALLY TAKING THIS DRESS SHOPPING THING SERIOUSLY.
YOU HAVEN'T SAID A WORD IN TEN MINUTES.
SORRY, I WAS JUST THINKING ABOUT SOME-THING ELSE.
JUST WAIT.
WHY DO I FEEL SCARED NOW?

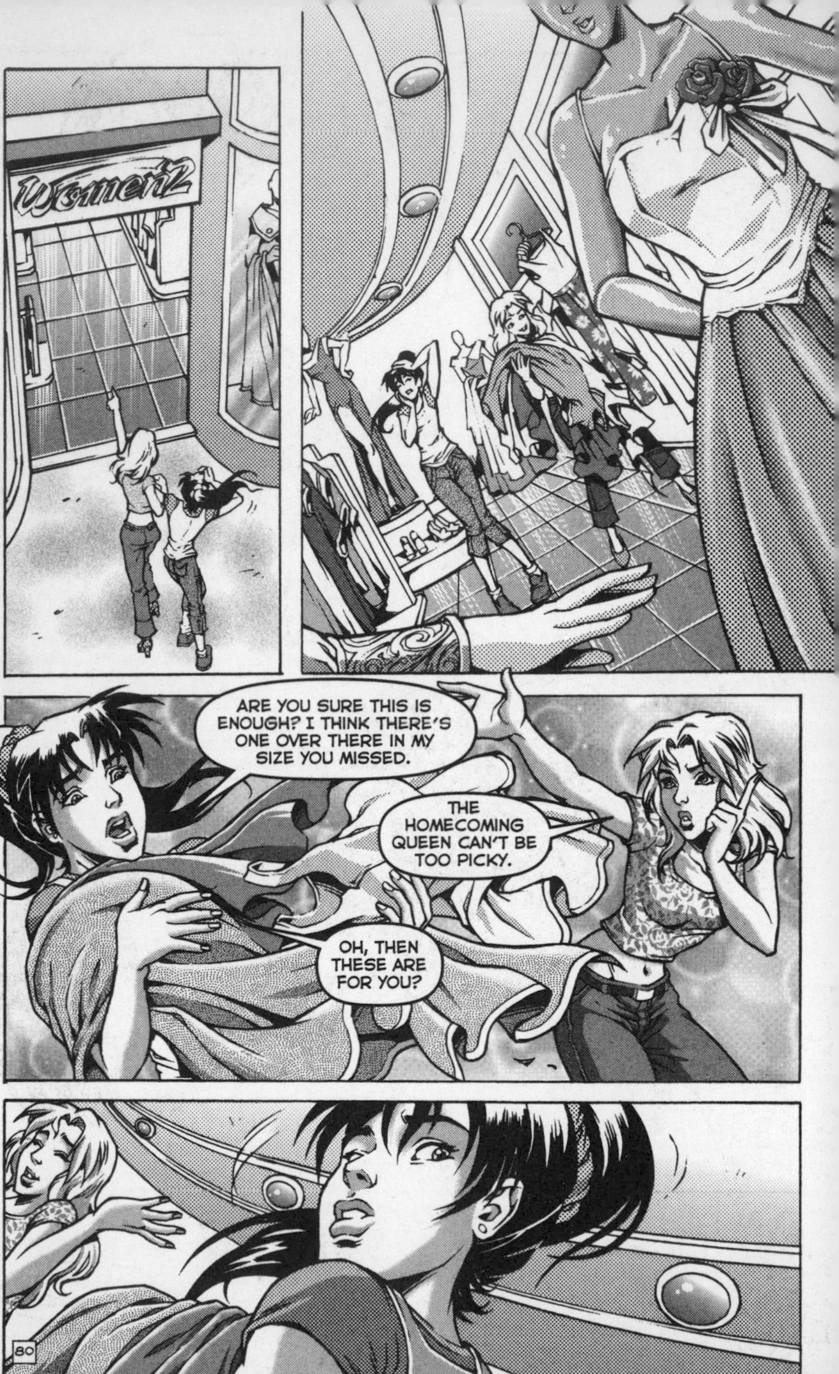
Women2
ARE YOU SURE THIS IS ENOUGH? I THINK THERE'S ONE OVER THERE IN MY SIZE YOU MISSED.
THE HOMECOMING QUEEN CAN'T BE TOO PICKY.
OH, THEN THESE ARE FOR YOU?

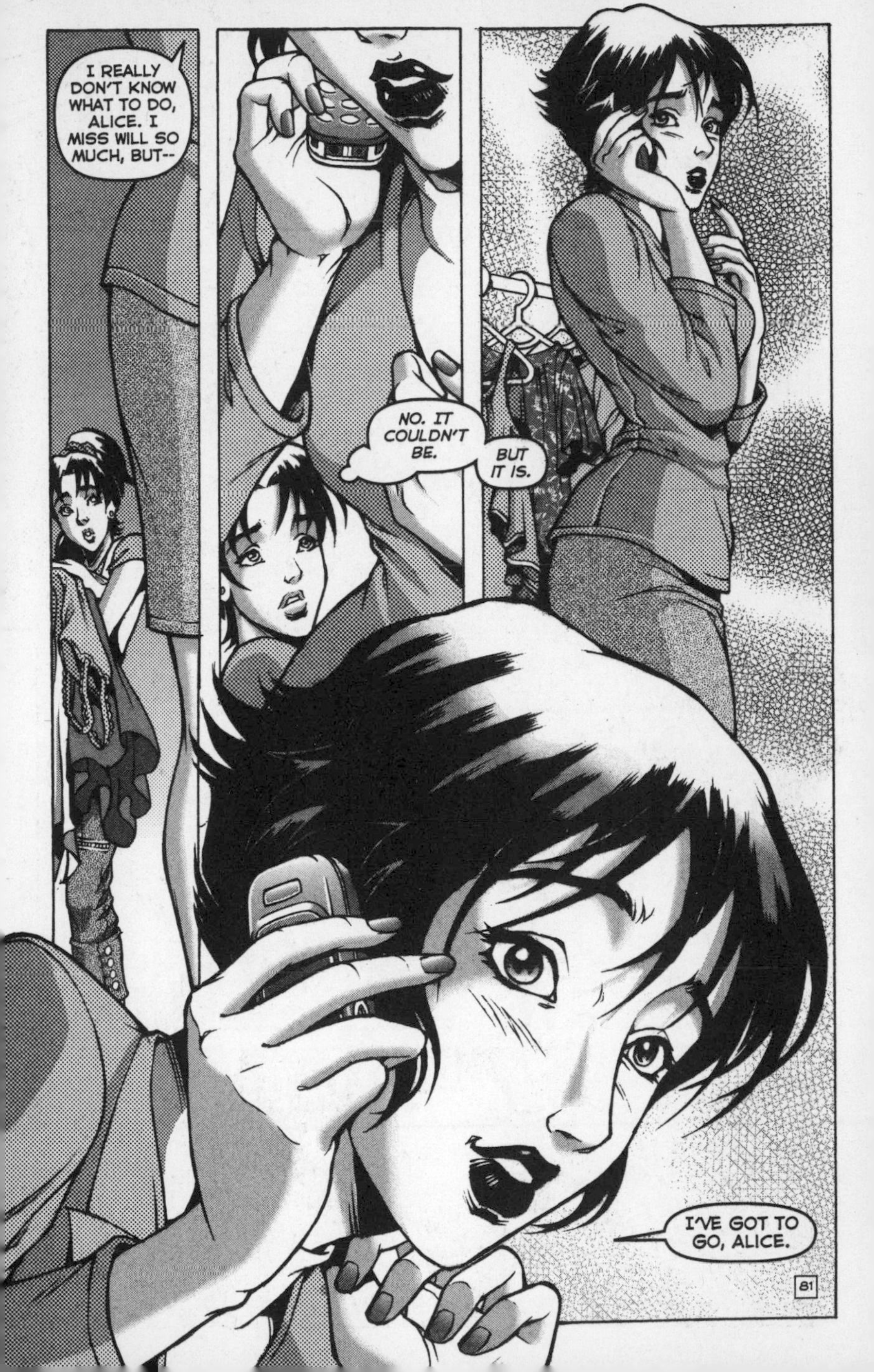
I REALLY DON'T KNOW WHAT TO DO, ALICE. I MISS WILL SO MUCH, BUT--
NO. IT COULDN'T BE.
BUT IT IS.
I'VE GOT TO GO, ALICE.

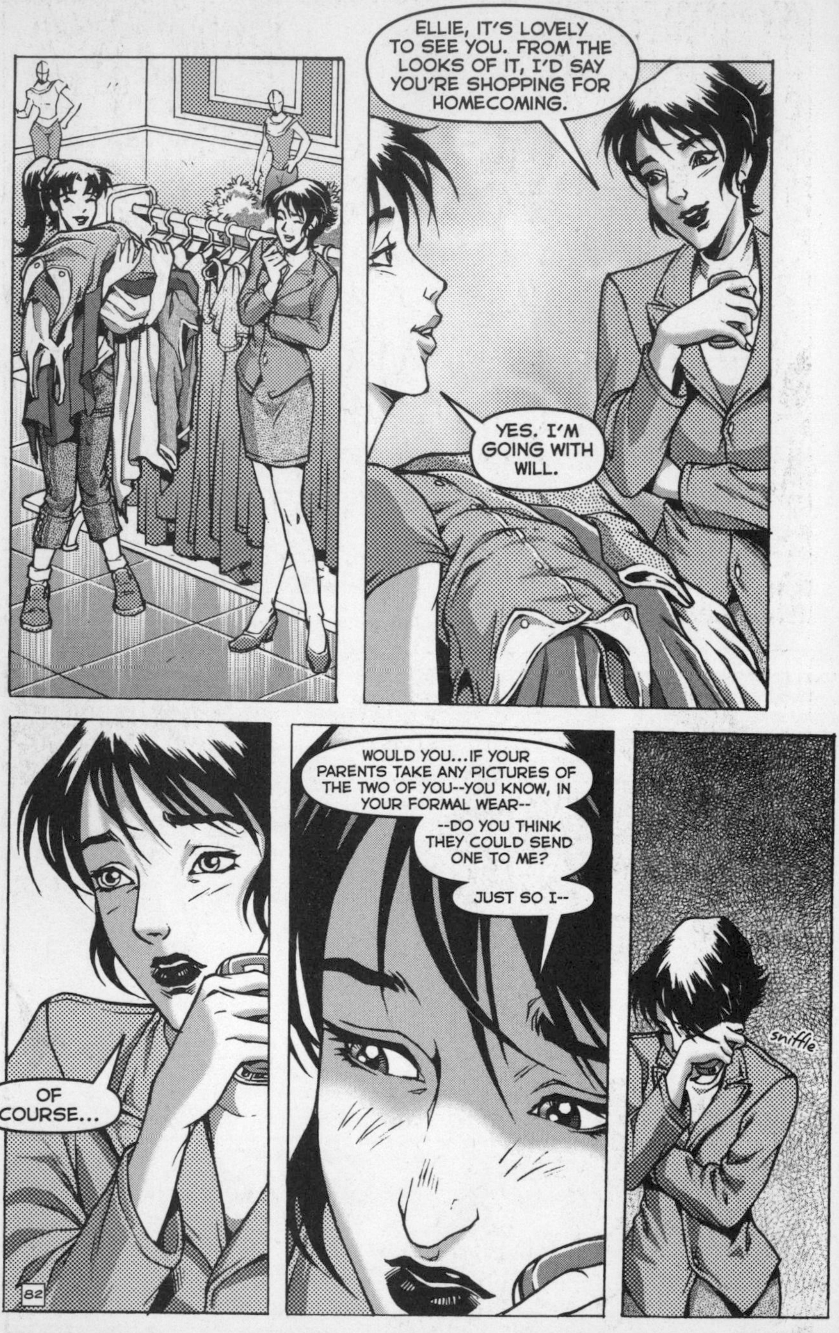
ELLIE, IT'S LOVELY TO SEE YOU. FROM THE LOOKS OF IT, I'D SAY YOU'RE SHOPPING FOR HOMECOMING.
YES. I'M GOING WITH WILL.
OF COURSE...
WOULD YOU...IF YOUR PARENTS TAKE ANY PICTURES OF THE TWO OF YOU--YOU KNOW, IN YOUR FORMAL WEAR--
--DO YOU THINK THEY COULD SEND ONE TO ME?
JUST SO I--
sniffle

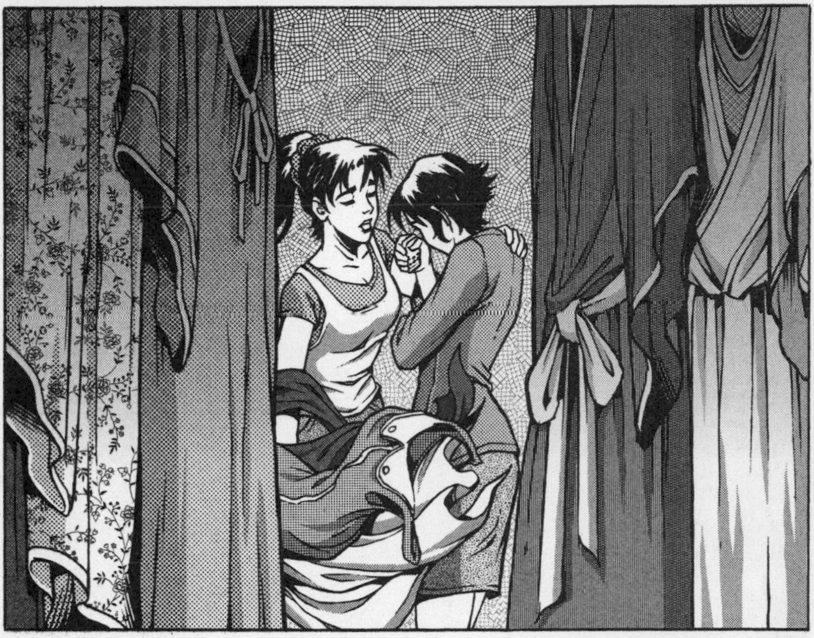

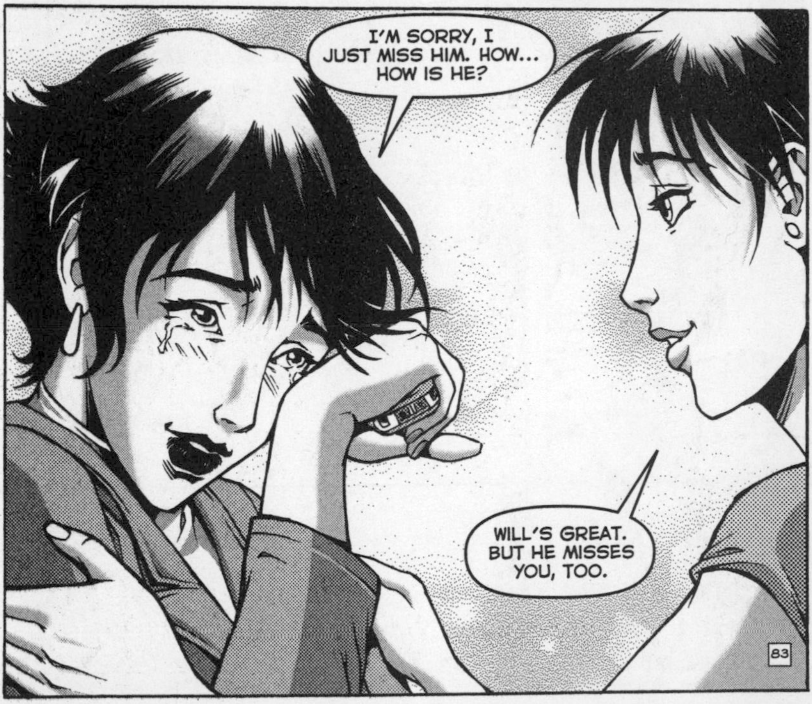
I'M SORRY, I JUST MISS HIM. HOW... HOW IS HE?
WILL'S GREAT. BUT HE MISSES YOU, TOO.

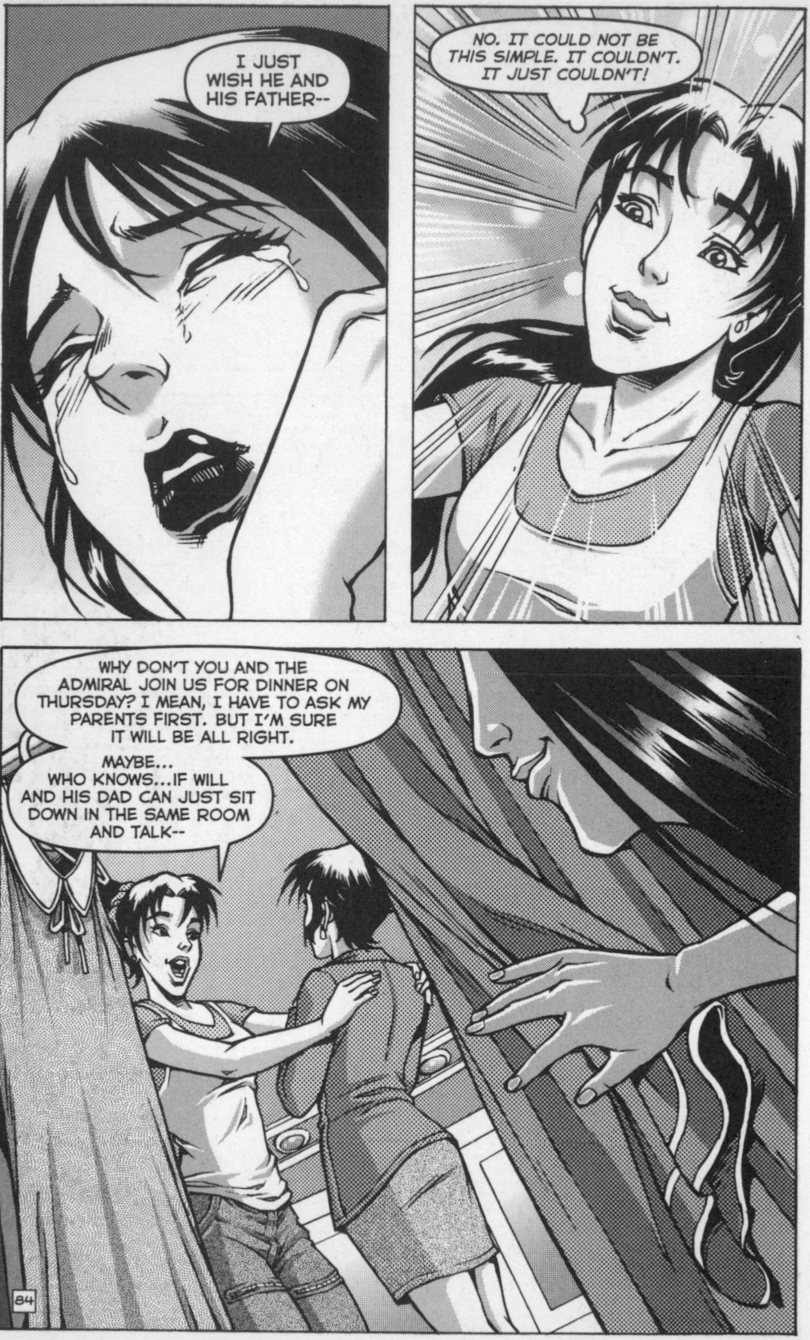
I JUST WISH HE AND HIS FATHER--
NO. IT COULD NOT BE THIS SIMPLE. IT COULDN'T. IT JUST COULDN'T!
WHY DON'T YOU AND THE ADMIRAL JOIN US FOR DINNER ON THURSDAY? I MEAN, I HAVE TO ASK MY PARENTS FIRST. BUT I'M SURE IT WILL BE ALL RIGHT.
MAYBE... WHO KNOWS...IF WILL AND HIS DAD CAN JUST SIT DOWN IN THE SAME ROOM AND TALK--

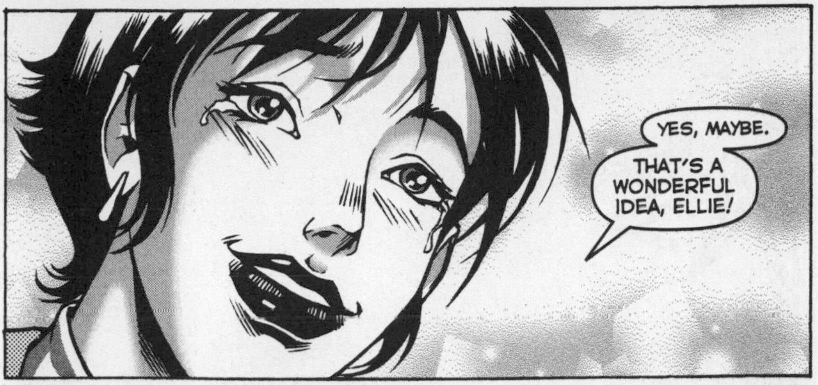
YES, MAYBE.
THAT'S A WONDERFUL IDEA, ELLIE!

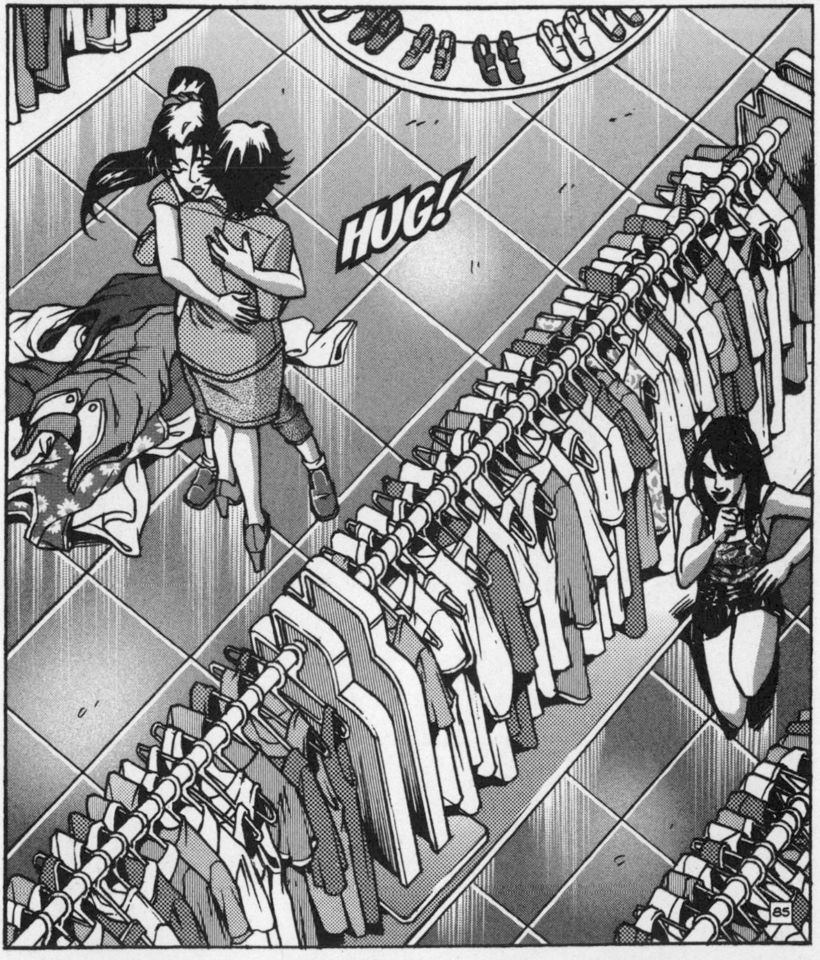
HUG!

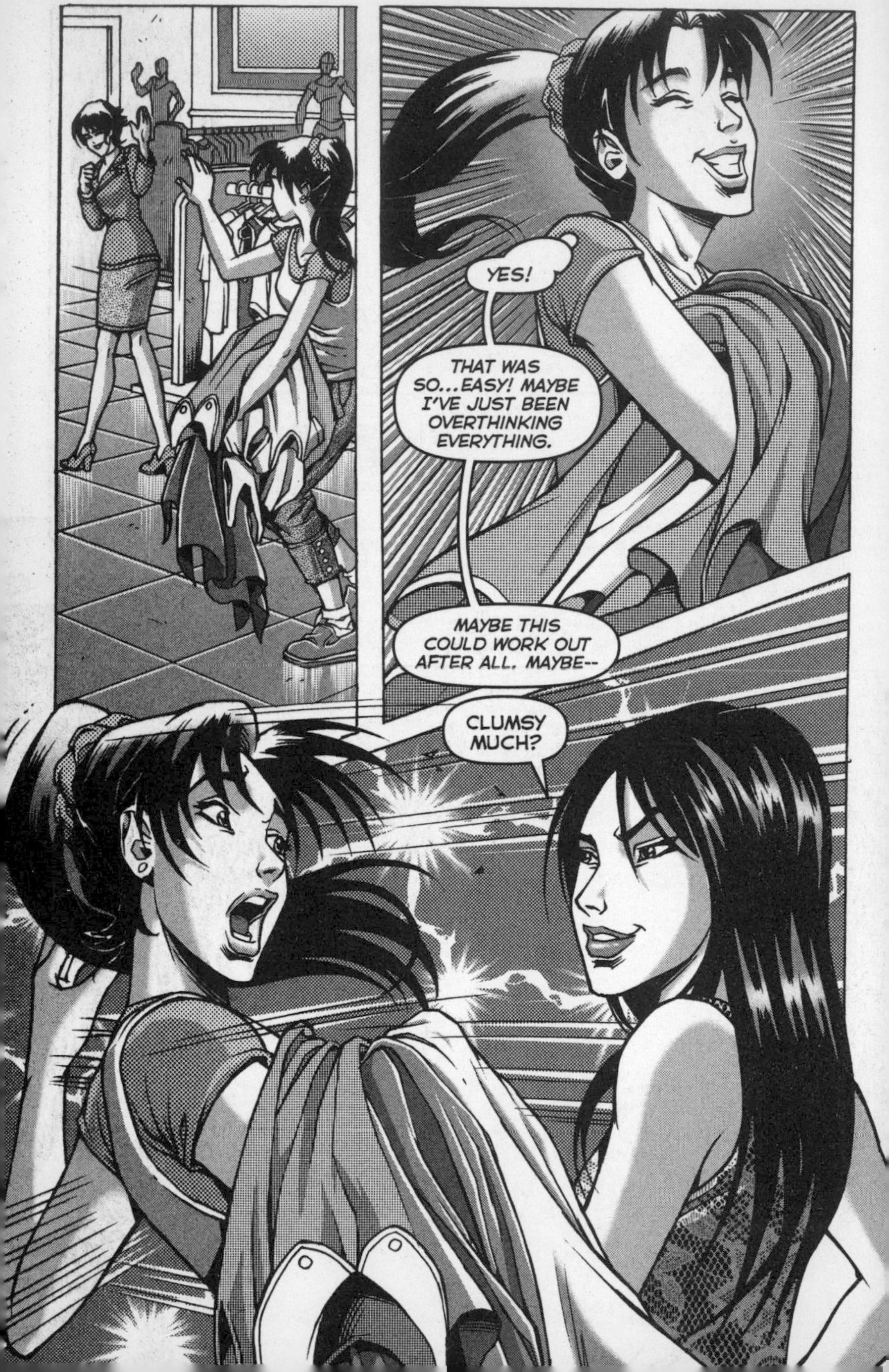
YES!
THAT WAS SO...EASY! MAYBE I'VE JUST BEEN OVERTHINKING EVERYTHING.
MAYBE THIS COULD WORK OUT AFTER ALL. MAYBE--
CLUMSY MUCH?

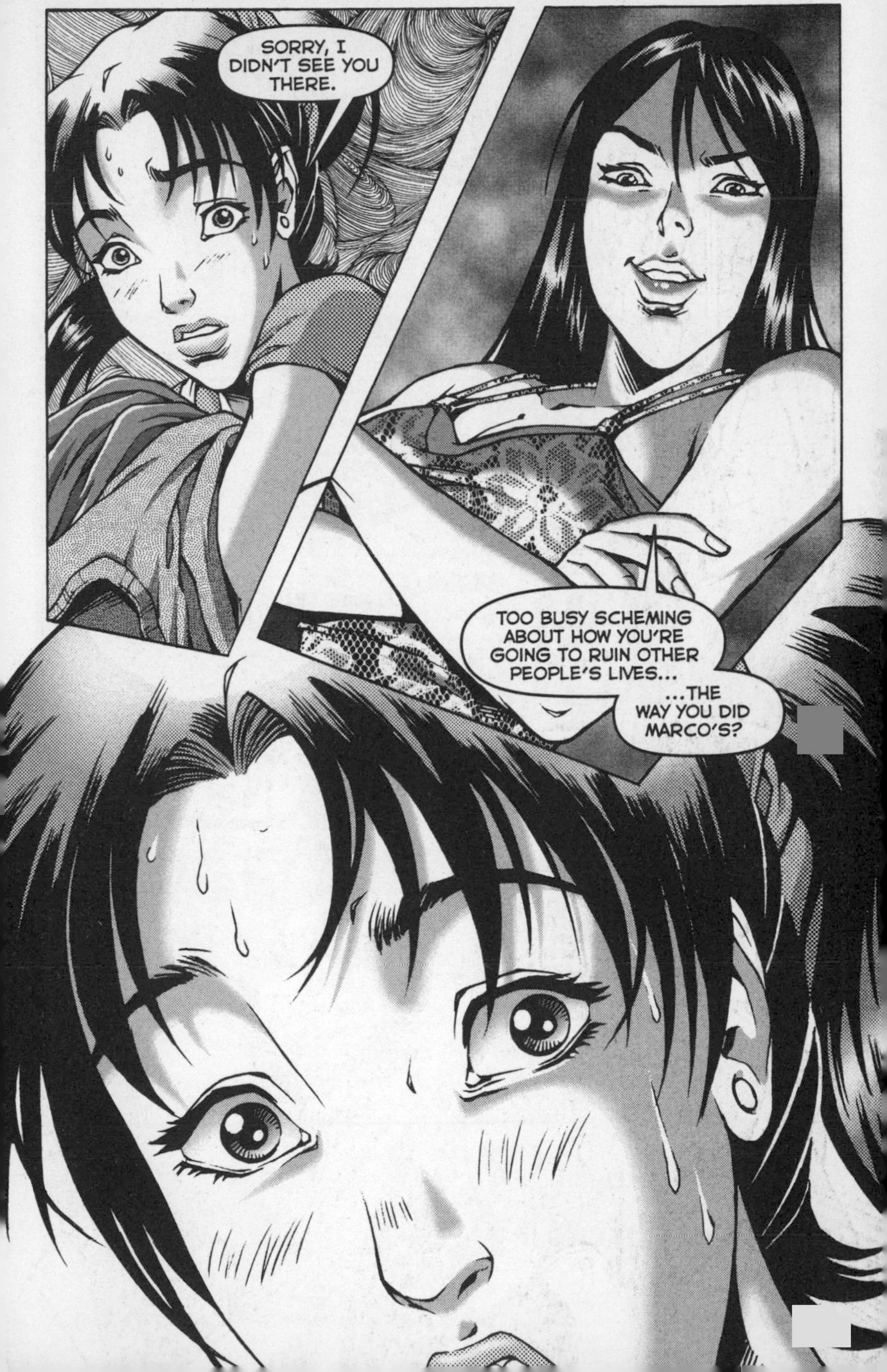
SORRY, I DIDN'T SEE YOU THERE.
TOO BUSY SCHEMING ABOUT HOW YOU'RE GOING TO RUIN OTHER PEOPLE'S LIVES...
...THE WAY YOU DID MARCO'S?

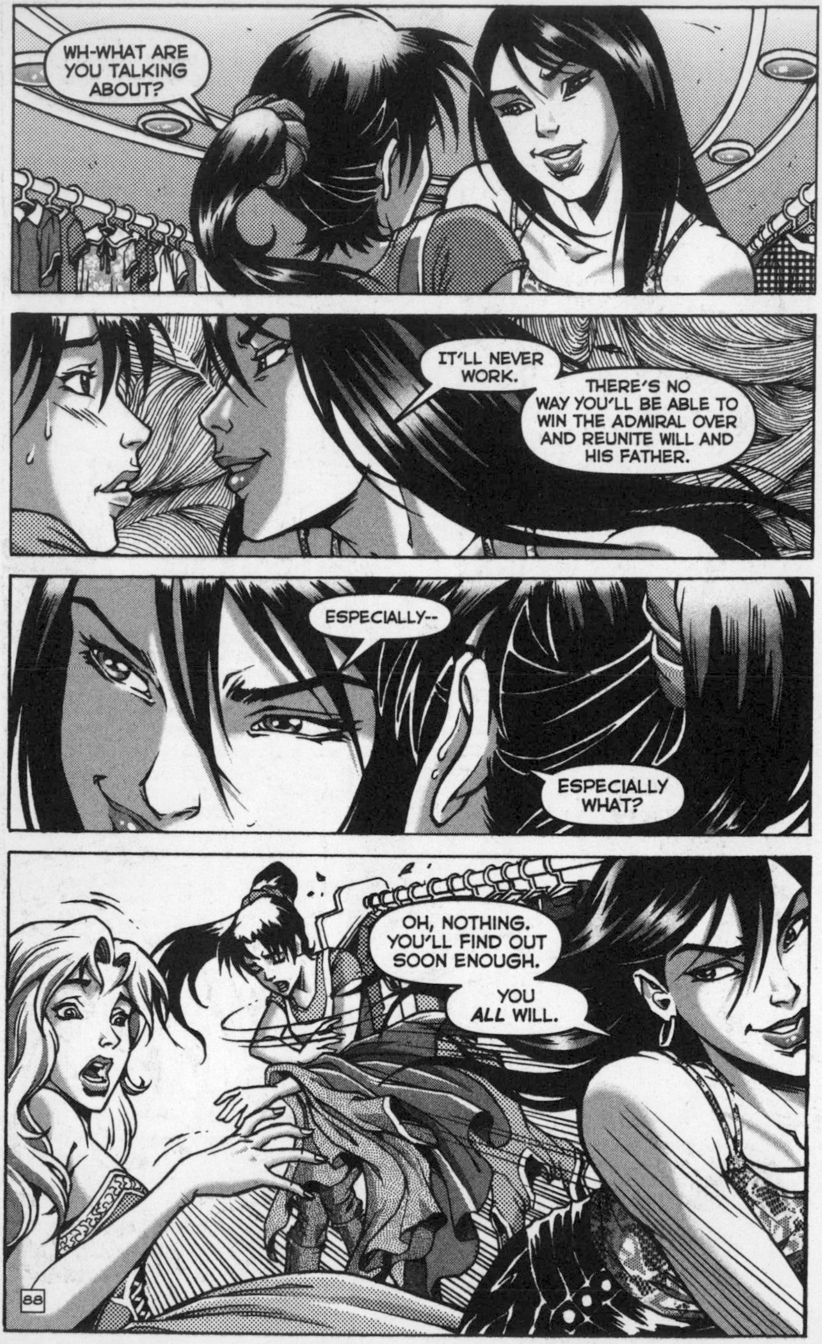
WH-WHAT ARE YOU TALKING ABOUT?
IT'LL NEVER WORK.
THERE'S NO WAY YOU'LL BE ABLE TO WIN THE ADMIRAL OVER AND REUNITE WILL AND HIS FATHER.
ESPECIALLY--
ESPECIALLY WHAT?
OH, NOTHING. YOU'LL FIND OUT SOON ENOUGH.
YOU *ALL* WILL.

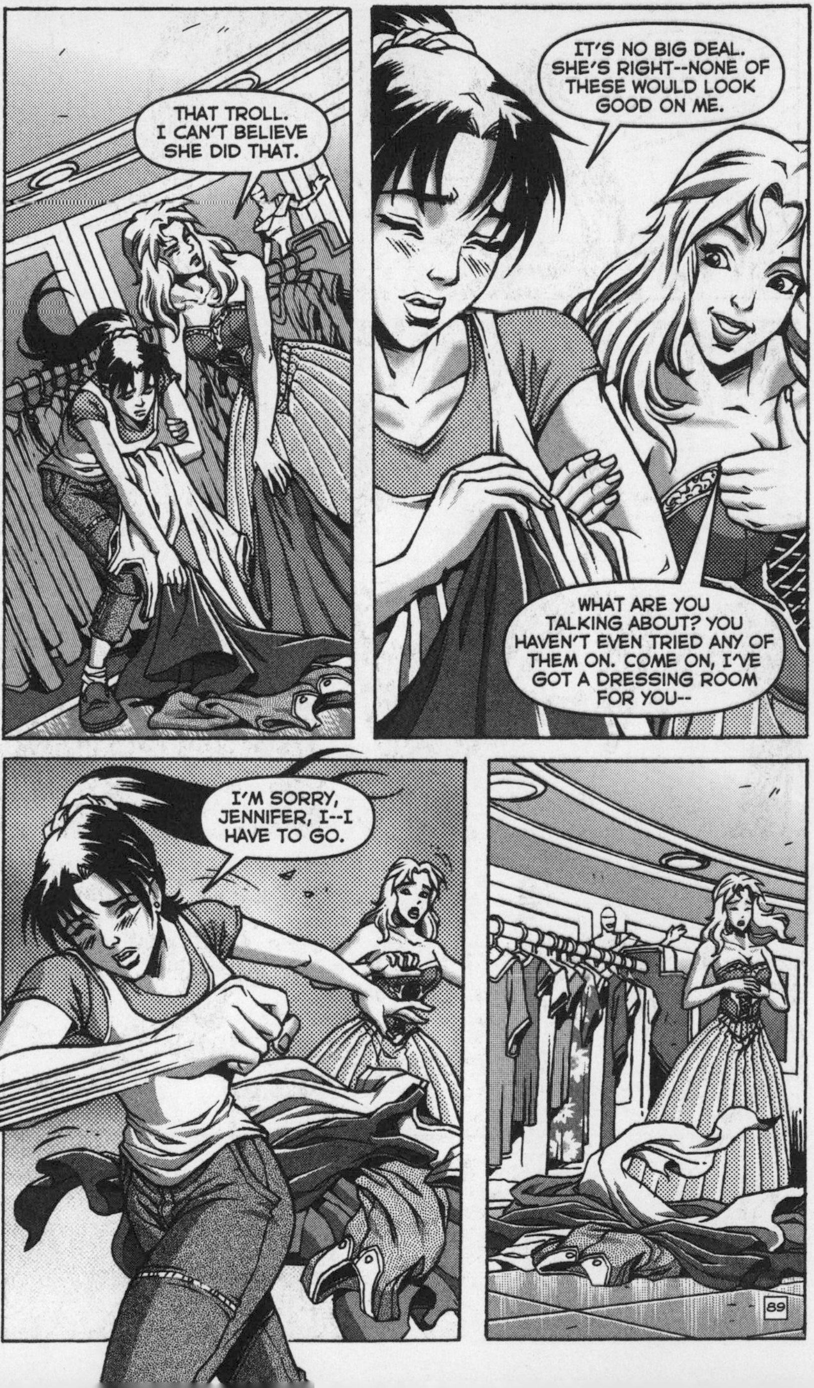
THAT TROLL. I CAN'T BELIEVE SHE DID THAT.
IT'S NO BIG DEAL. SHE'S RIGHT--NONE OF THESE WOULD LOOK GOOD ON ME.
WHAT ARE YOU TALKING ABOUT? YOU HAVEN'T EVEN TRIED ANY OF THEM ON. COME ON, I'VE GOT A DRESSING ROOM FOR YOU--
I'M SORRY, JENNIFER, I--I HAVE TO GO.

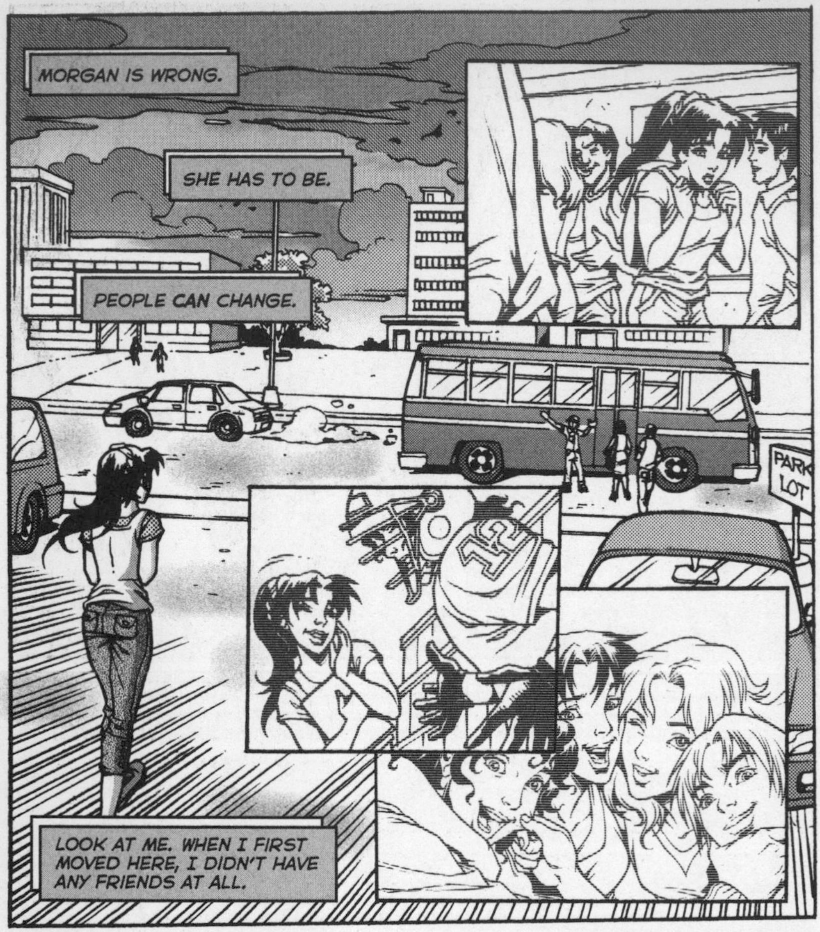
MORGAN IS WRONG.
SHE HAS TO BE.
PEOPLE CAN CHANGE.
PARK LOT
LOOK AT ME. WHEN I FIRST MOVED HERE, I DIDN'T HAVE ANY FRIENDS AT ALL.

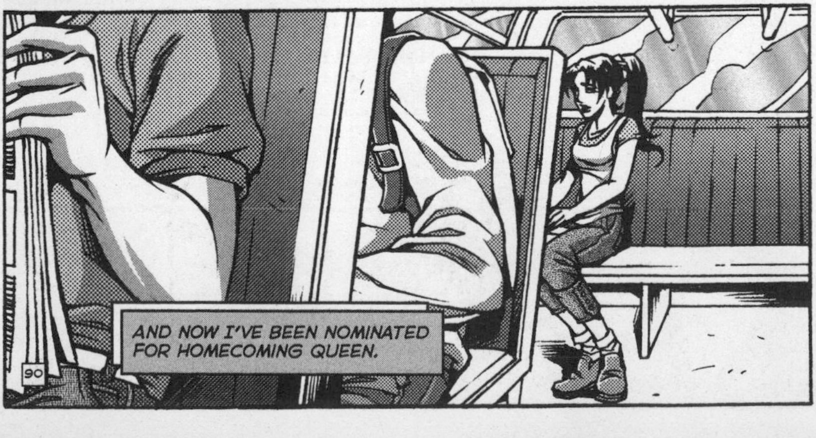
AND NOW I'VE BEEN NOMINATED FOR HOMECOMING QUEEN.

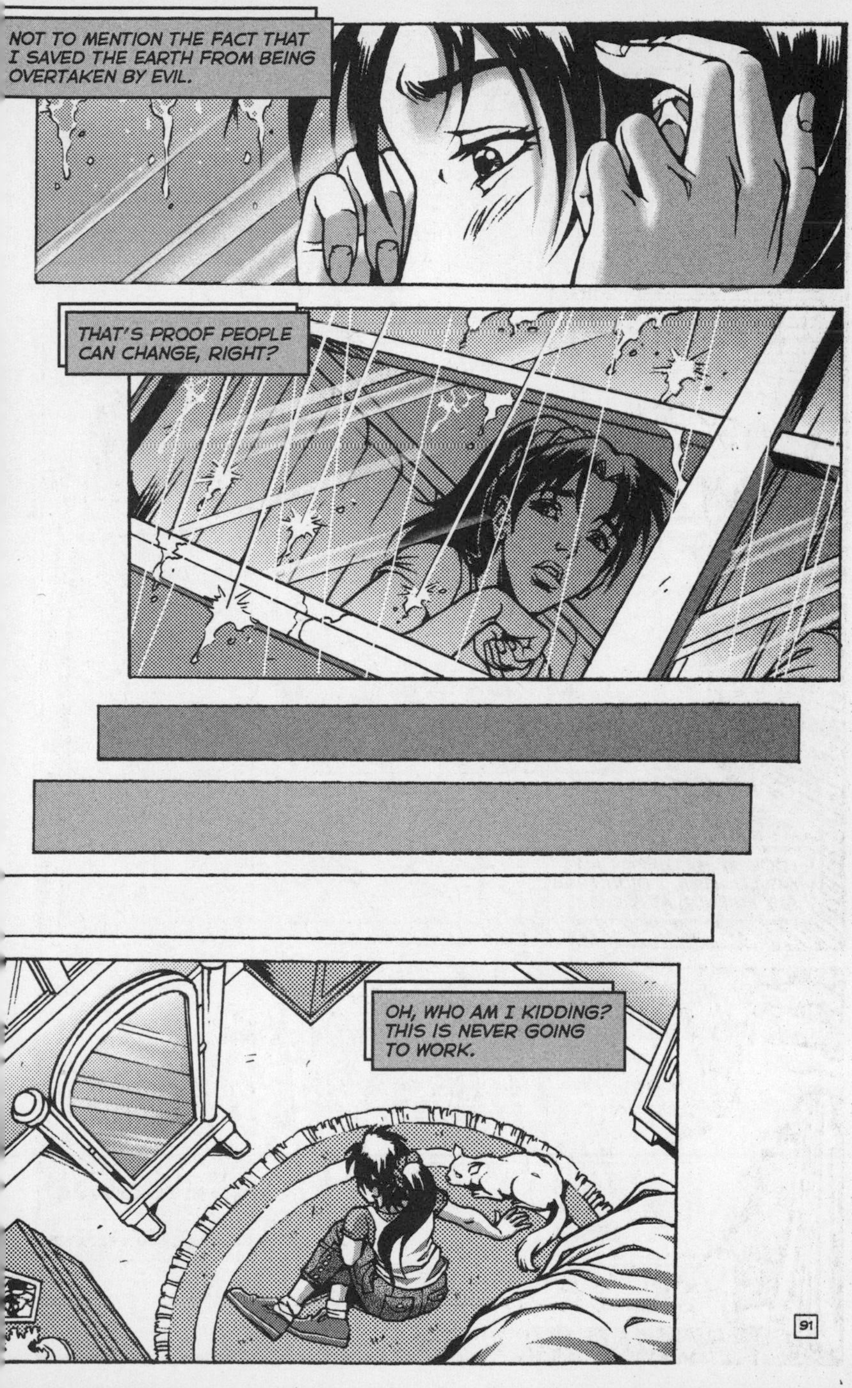
NOT TO MENTION THE FACT THAT I SAVED THE EARTH FROM BEING OVERTAKEN BY EVIL.
THAT'S PROOF PEOPLE CAN CHANGE, RIGHT?
OH, WHO AM I KIDDING? THIS IS NEVER GOING TO WORK.

OKAY, SO DO I TELL HIM ABOUT DINNER FIRST, OR ABOUT THE WHOLE "IF YOU DON'T BELIEVE YOU'RE A KING, THE WORLD WILL END" FIRST?

KNOCK! KNOCK!

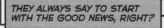

THEY ALWAYS SAY TO START WITH THE GOOD NEWS, RIGHT?

OR IS IT START WITH THE BAD NEWS?

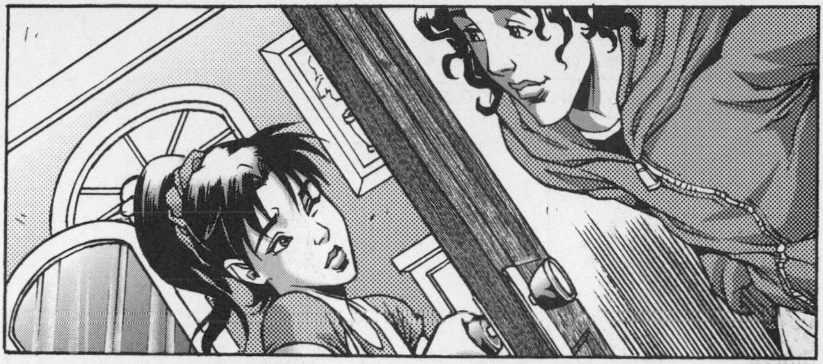

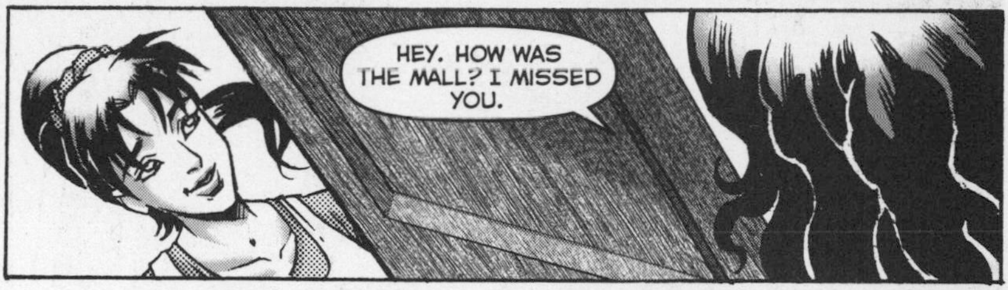
HEY. HOW WAS THE MALL? I MISSED YOU.

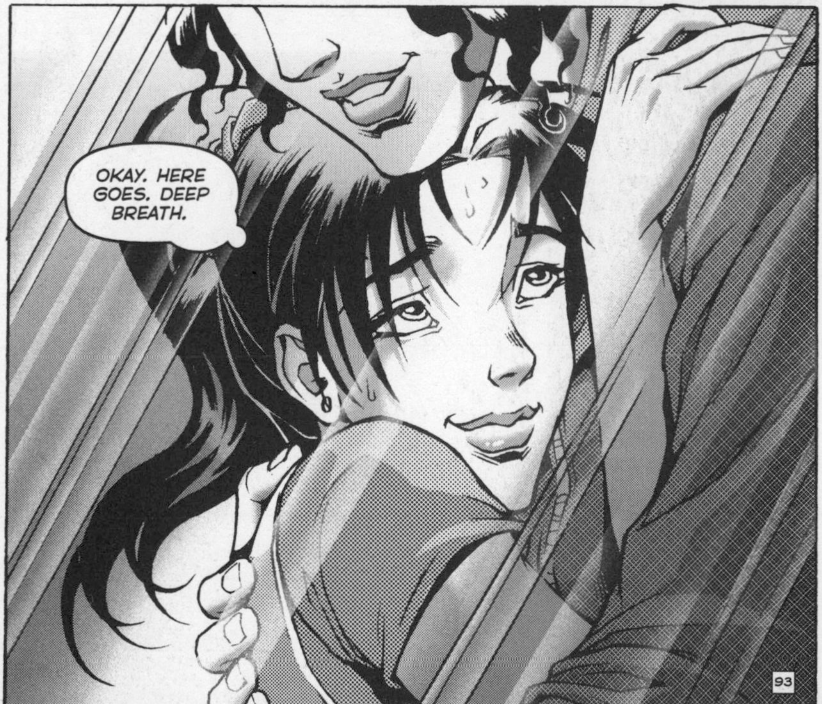
OKAY. HERE GOES. DEEP BREATH.

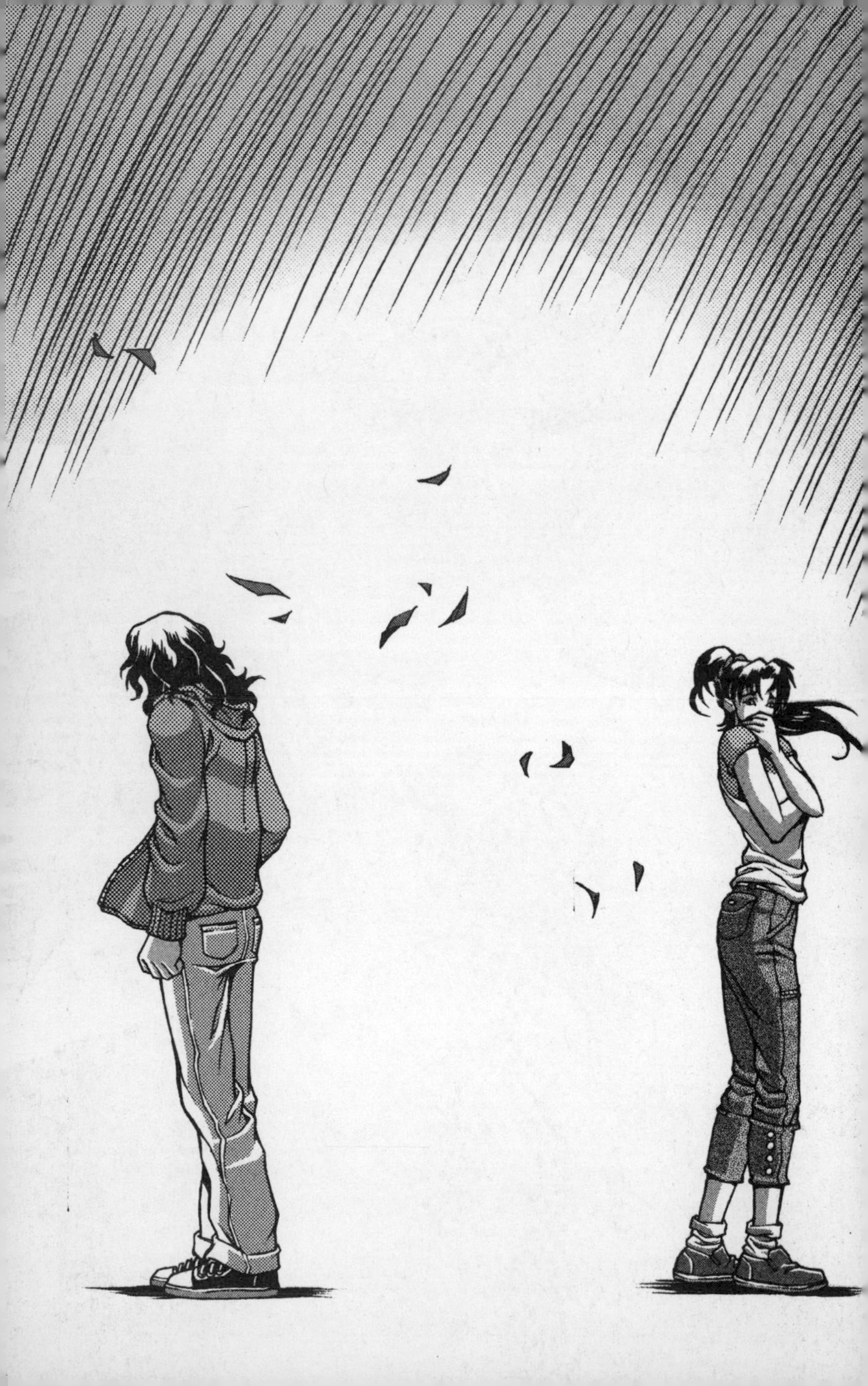

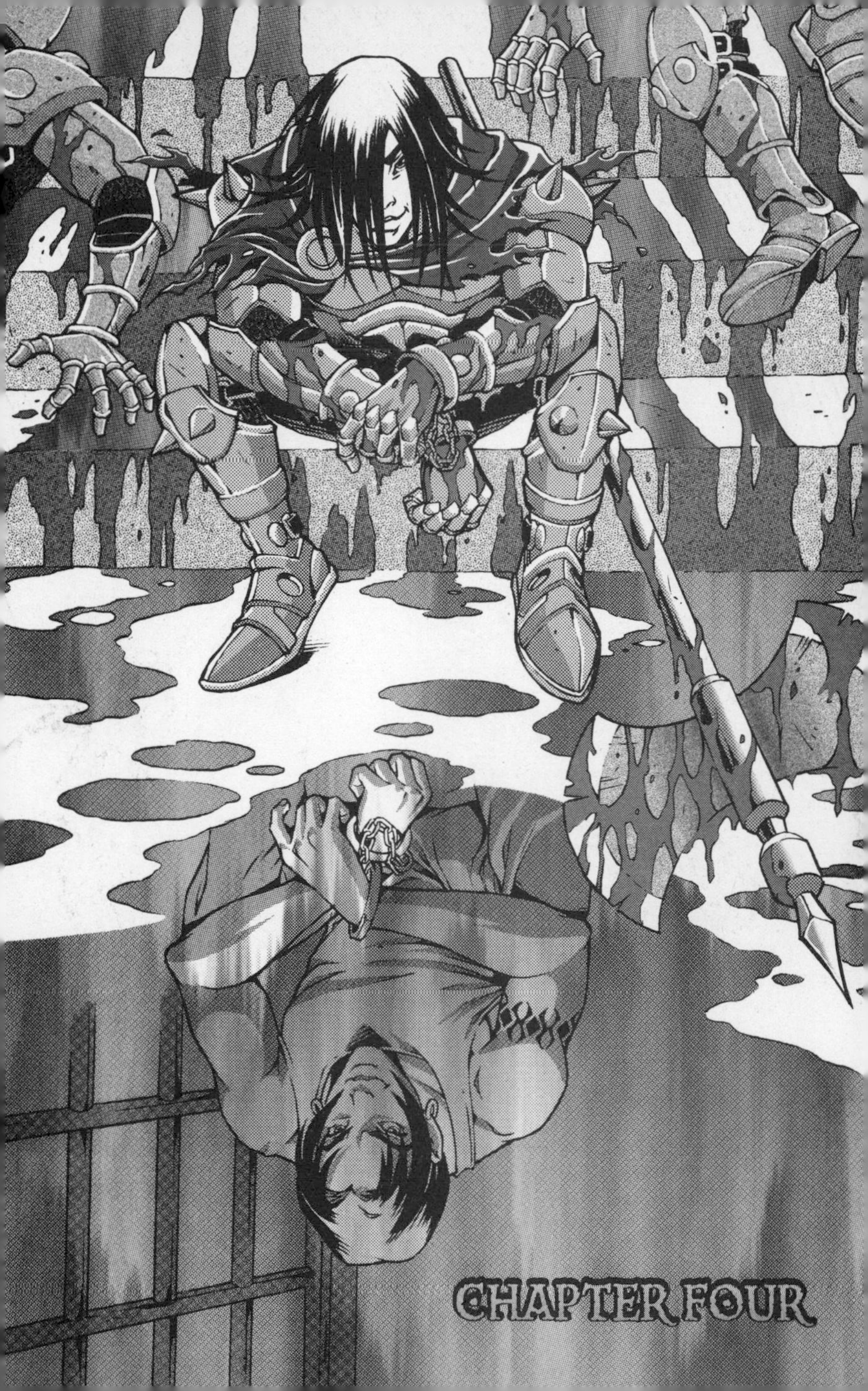
CHAPTER FOUR

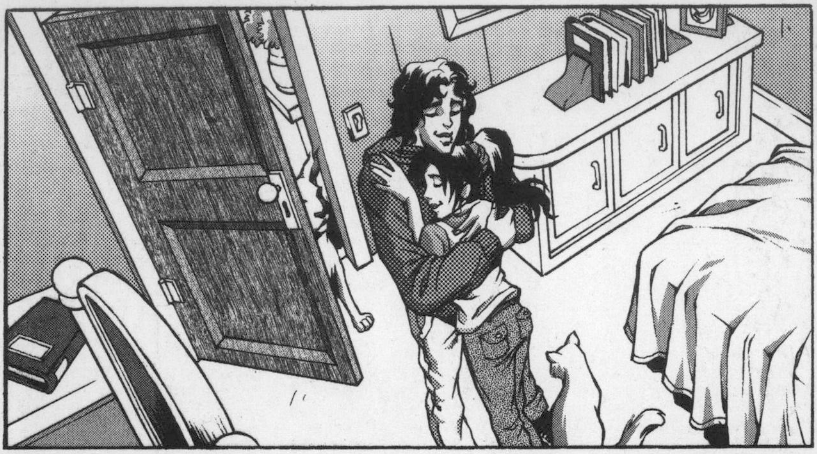

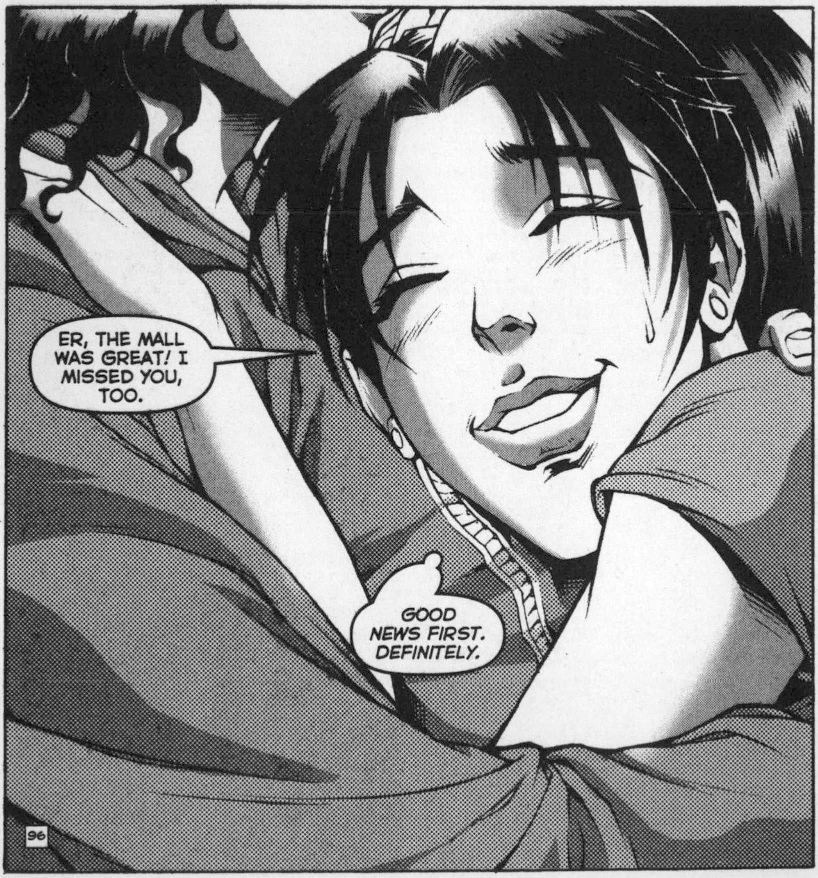
ER, THE MALL WAS GREAT! I MISSED YOU, TOO.
GOOD NEWS FIRST. DEFINITELY.

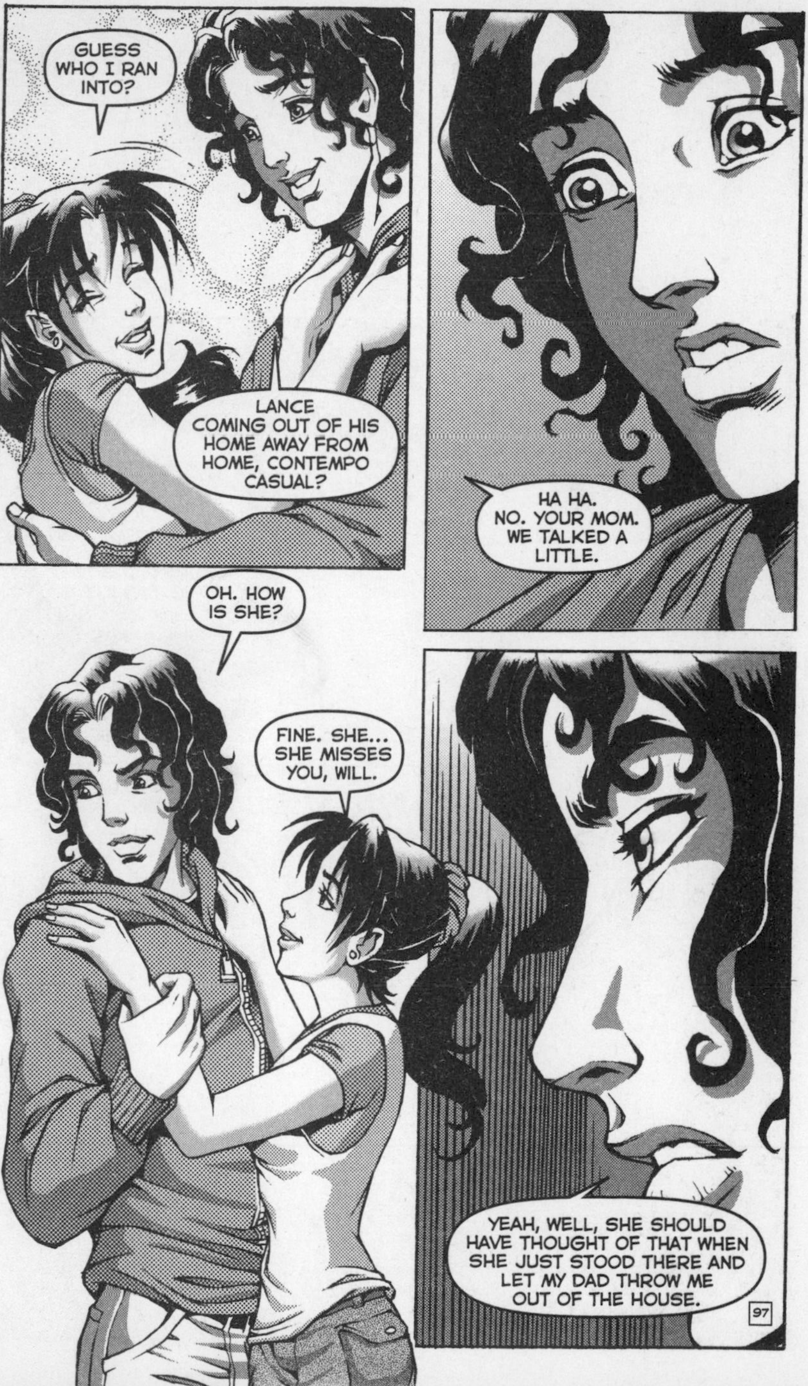
GUESS WHO I RAN INTO?
LANCE COMING OUT OF HIS HOME AWAY FROM HOME, CONTEMPO CASUAL?
HA HA. NO. YOUR MOM. WE TALKED A LITTLE.
OH. HOW IS SHE?
FINE. SHE... SHE MISSES YOU, WILL.
YEAH, WELL, SHE SHOULD HAVE THOUGHT OF THAT WHEN SHE JUST STOOD THERE AND LET MY DAD THROW ME OUT OF THE HOUSE.

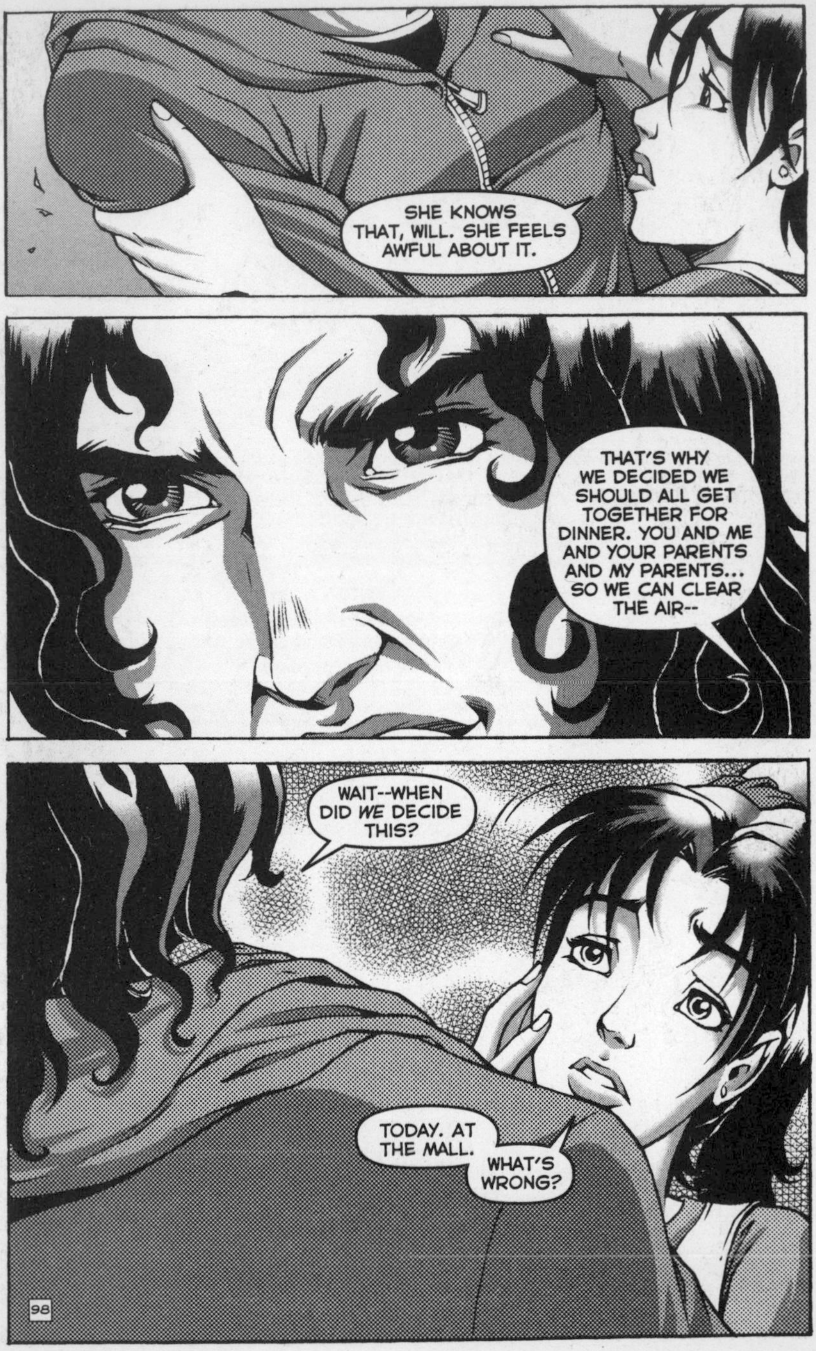
SHE KNOWS THAT, WILL. SHE FEELS AWFUL ABOUT IT.
THAT'S WHY WE DECIDED WE SHOULD ALL GET TOGETHER FOR DINNER. YOU AND ME AND YOUR PARENTS AND MY PARENTS... SO WE CAN CLEAR THE AIR--
WAIT--WHEN DID *WE* DECIDE THIS?
TODAY. AT THE MALL.
WHAT'S WRONG?

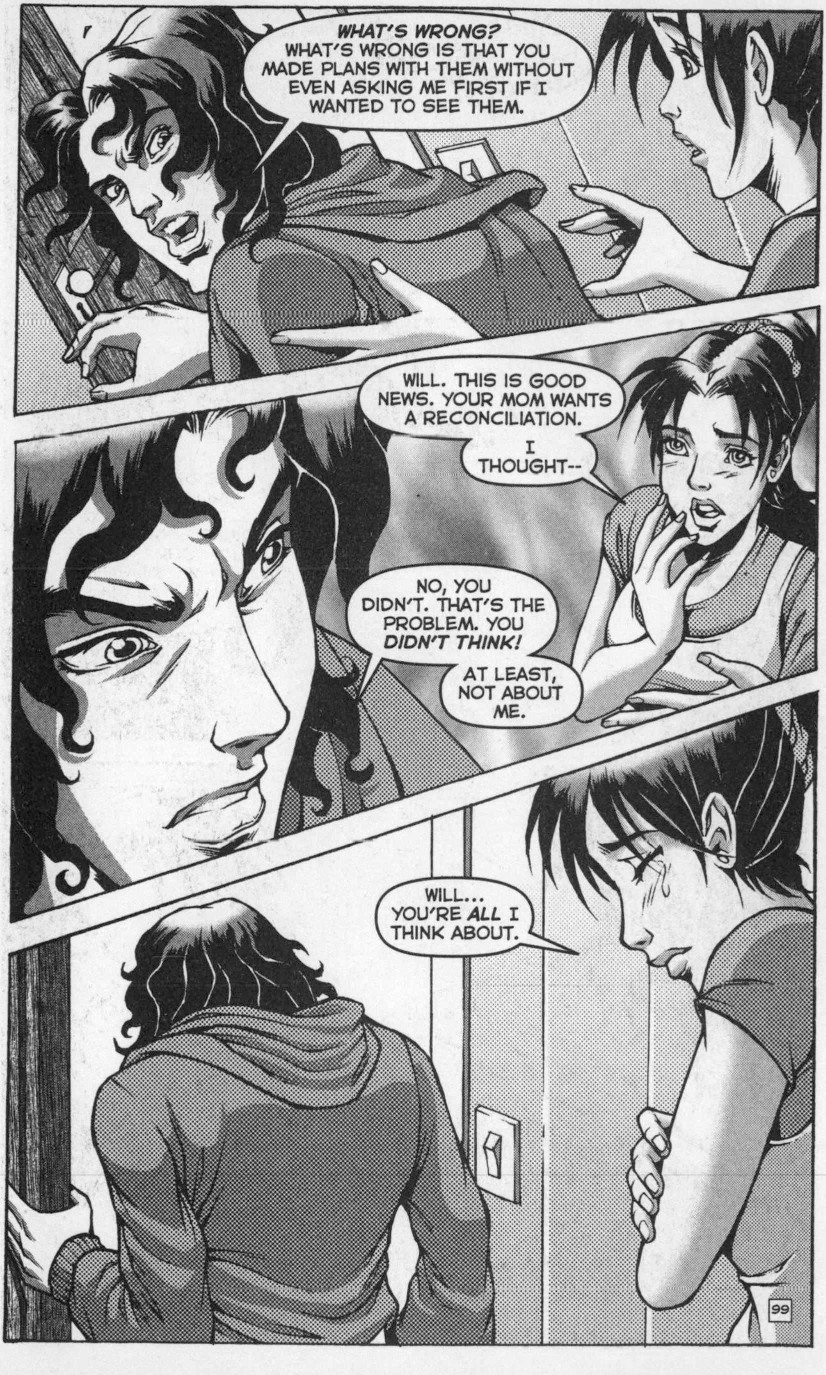
WHAT'S WRONG? WHAT'S WRONG IS THAT YOU MADE PLANS WITH THEM WITHOUT EVEN ASKING ME FIRST IF I WANTED TO SEE THEM.
WILL. THIS IS GOOD NEWS. YOUR MOM WANTS A RECONCILIATION.
I THOUGHT--
NO, YOU DIDN'T. THAT'S THE PROBLEM. YOU DIDN'T THINK!
AT LEAST, NOT ABOUT ME.
WILL... YOU'RE ALL I THINK ABOUT.

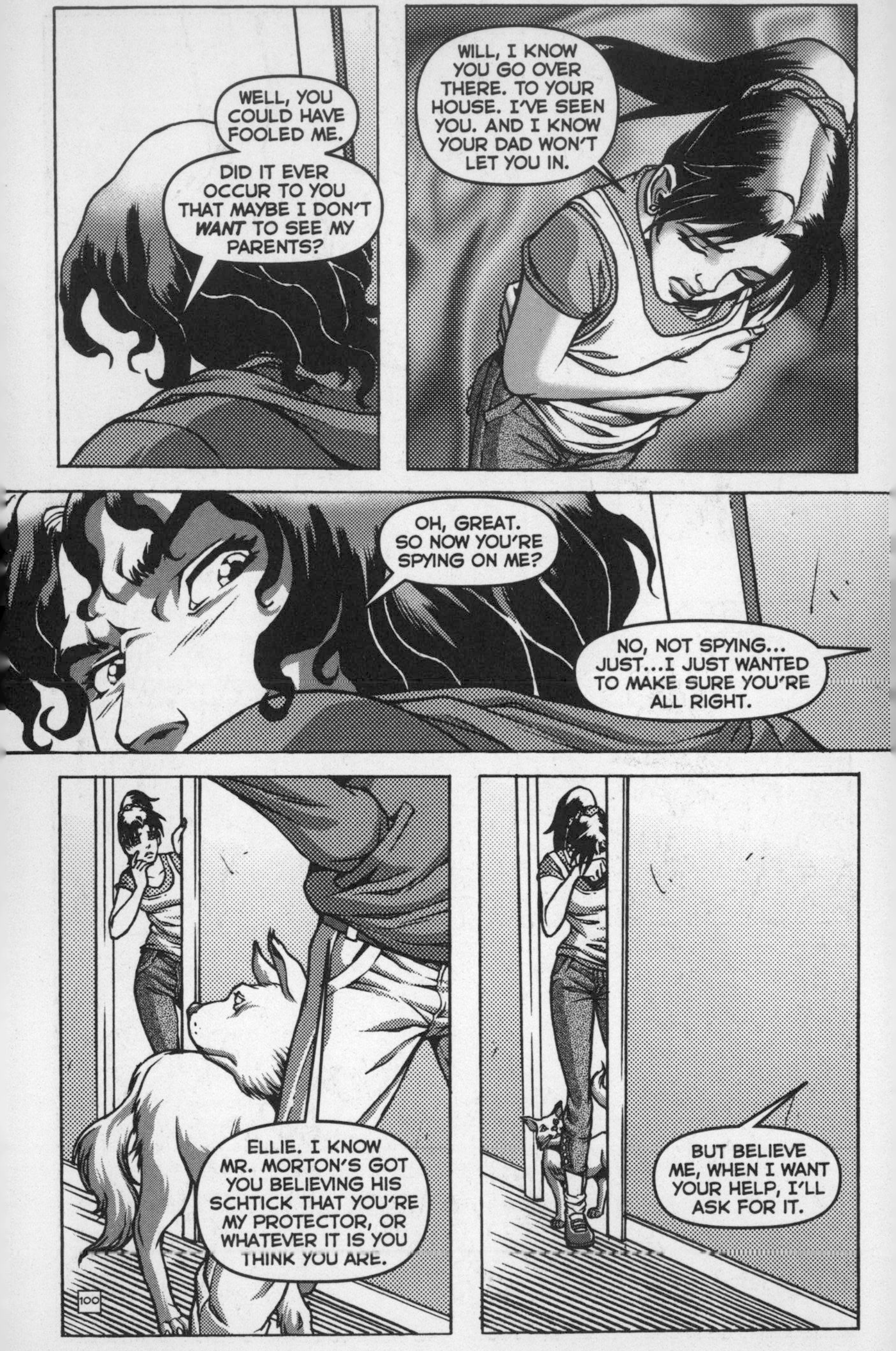
WELL, YOU COULD HAVE FOOLED ME.
DID IT EVER OCCUR TO YOU THAT MAYBE I DON'T *WANT* TO SEE MY PARENTS?
WILL, I KNOW YOU GO OVER THERE. TO YOUR HOUSE. I'VE SEEN YOU. AND I KNOW YOUR DAD WON'T LET YOU IN.
OH, GREAT. SO NOW YOU'RE SPYING ON ME?
NO, NOT SPYING... JUST...I JUST WANTED TO MAKE SURE YOU'RE ALL RIGHT.
ELLIE. I KNOW MR. MORTON'S GOT YOU BELIEVING HIS SCHTICK THAT YOU'RE MY PROTECTOR, OR WHATEVER IT IS YOU THINK YOU ARE.
BUT BELIEVE ME, WHEN I WANT YOUR HELP, I'LL ASK FOR IT.

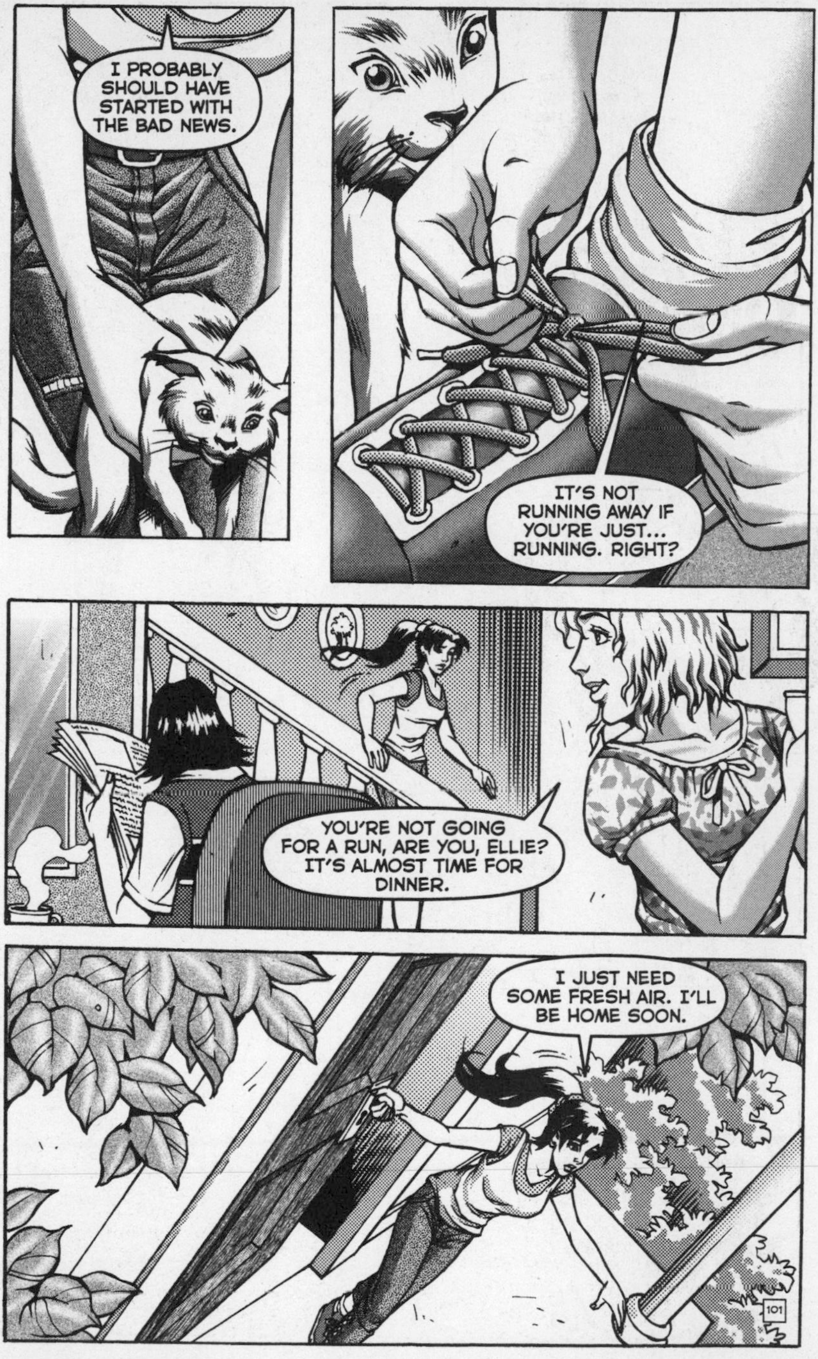
I PROBABLY SHOULD HAVE STARTED WITH THE BAD NEWS.
IT'S NOT RUNNING AWAY IF YOU'RE JUST... RUNNING. RIGHT?
YOU'RE NOT GOING FOR A RUN, ARE YOU, ELLIE? IT'S ALMOST TIME FOR DINNER.
I JUST NEED SOME FRESH AIR. I'LL BE HOME SOON.

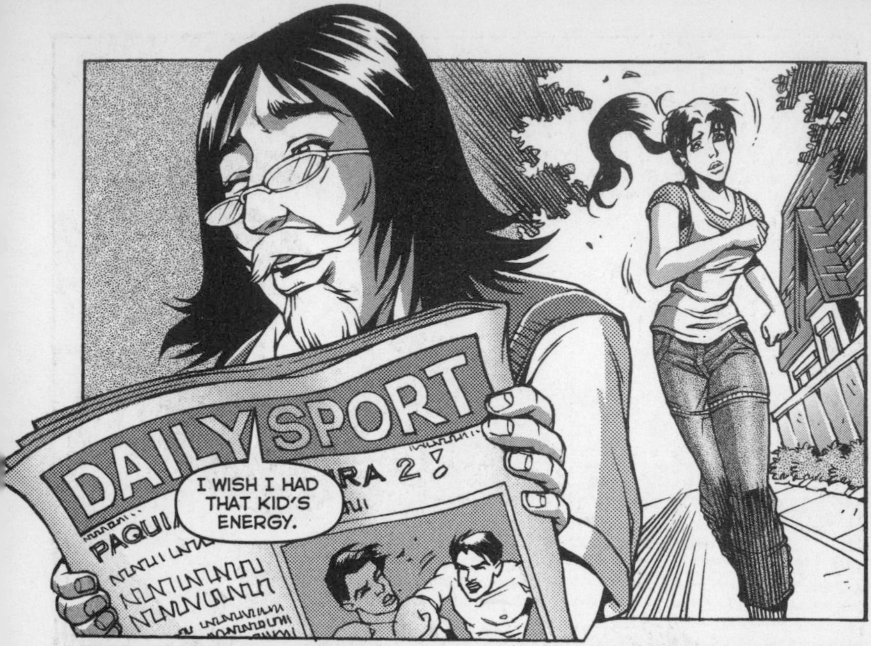
DAILY SPORT
I WISH I HAD THAT KID'S ENERGY.

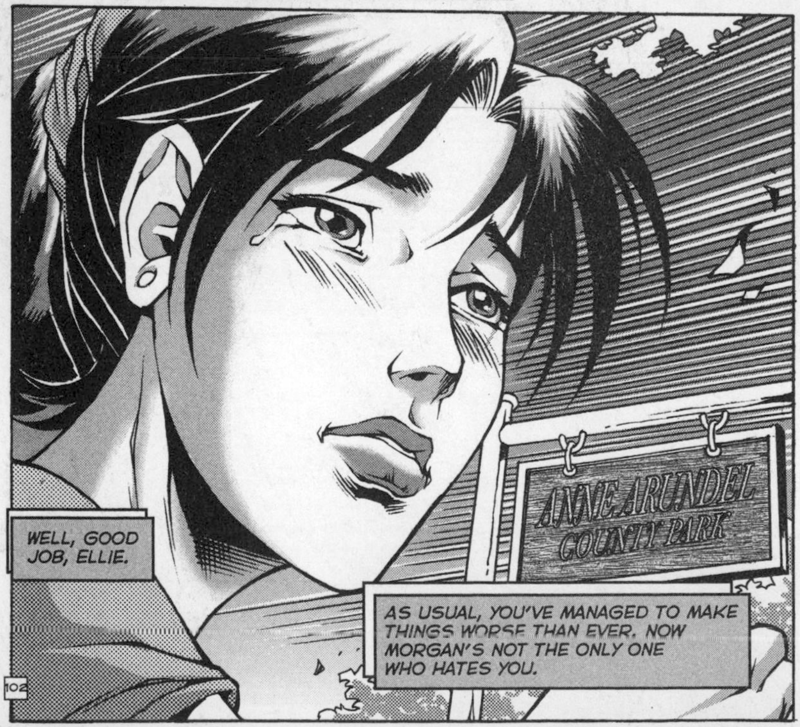
WELL, GOOD JOB, ELLIE.
ANNE ARUNDEL COUNTY PARK
AS USUAL, YOU'VE MANAGED TO MAKE THINGS WORSE THAN EVER. NOW MORGAN'S NOT THE ONLY ONE WHO HATES YOU.

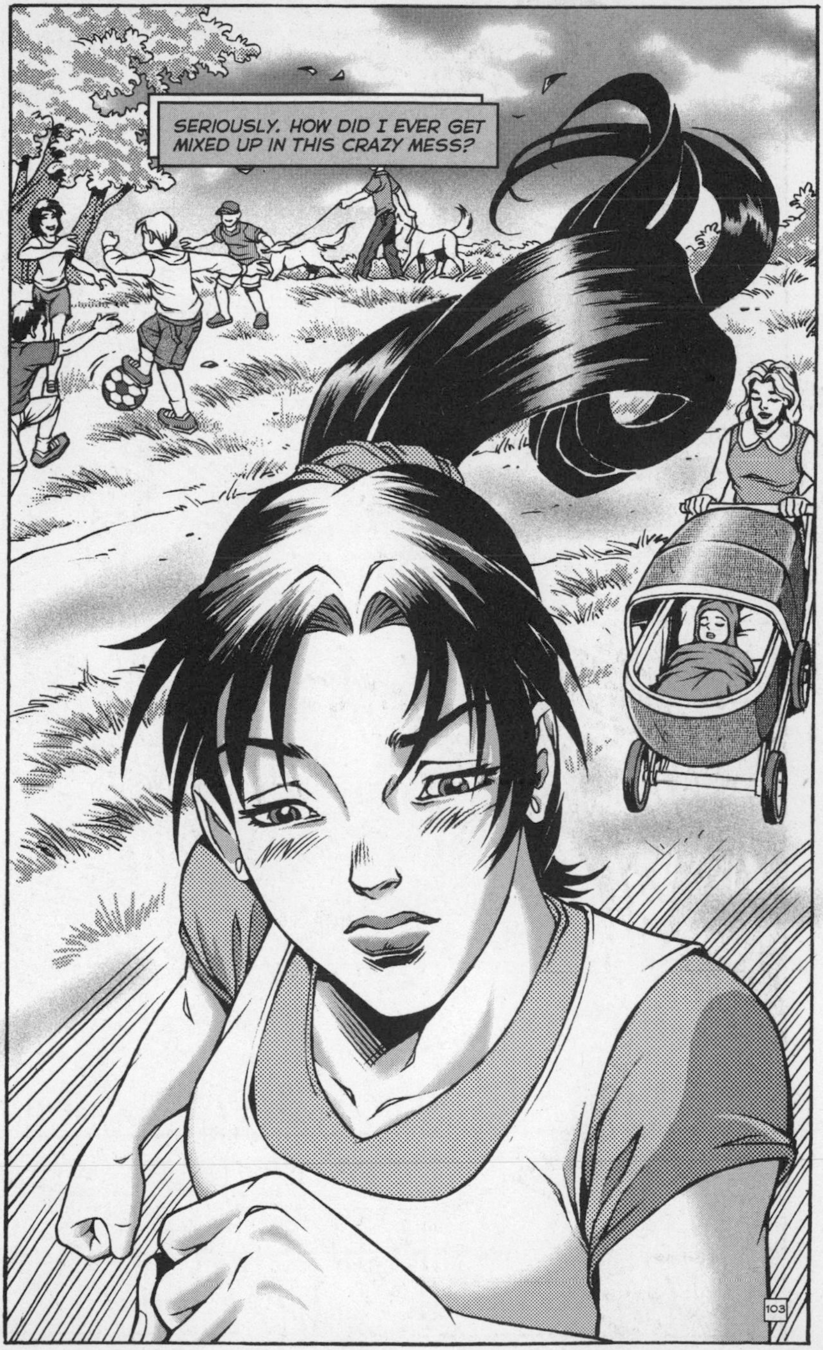
SERIOUSLY. HOW DID I EVER GET MIXED UP IN THIS CRAZY MESS?

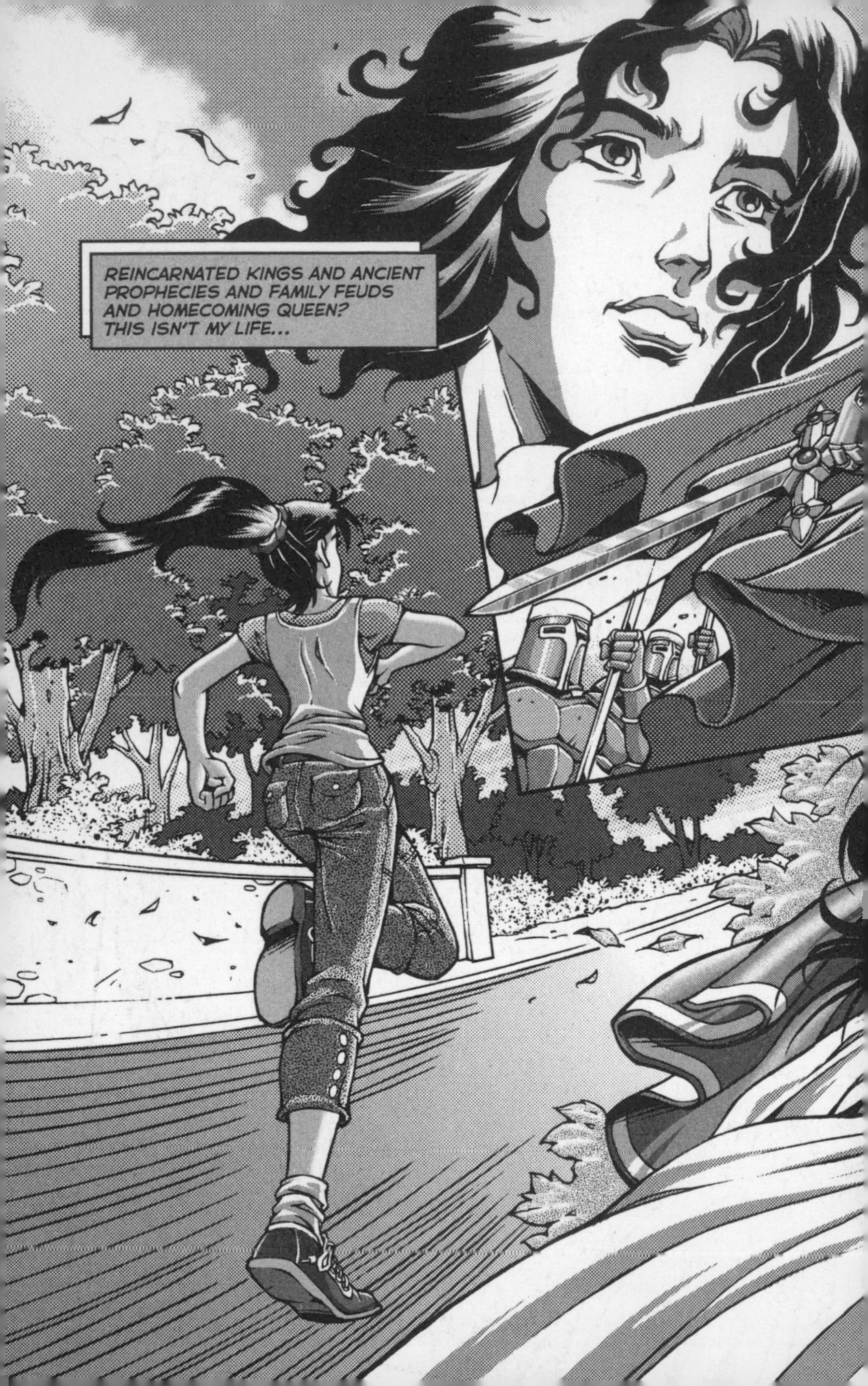
REINCARNATED KINGS AND ANCIENT PROPHECIES AND FAMILY FEUDS AND HOMECOMING QUEEN? THIS ISN'T MY LIFE...

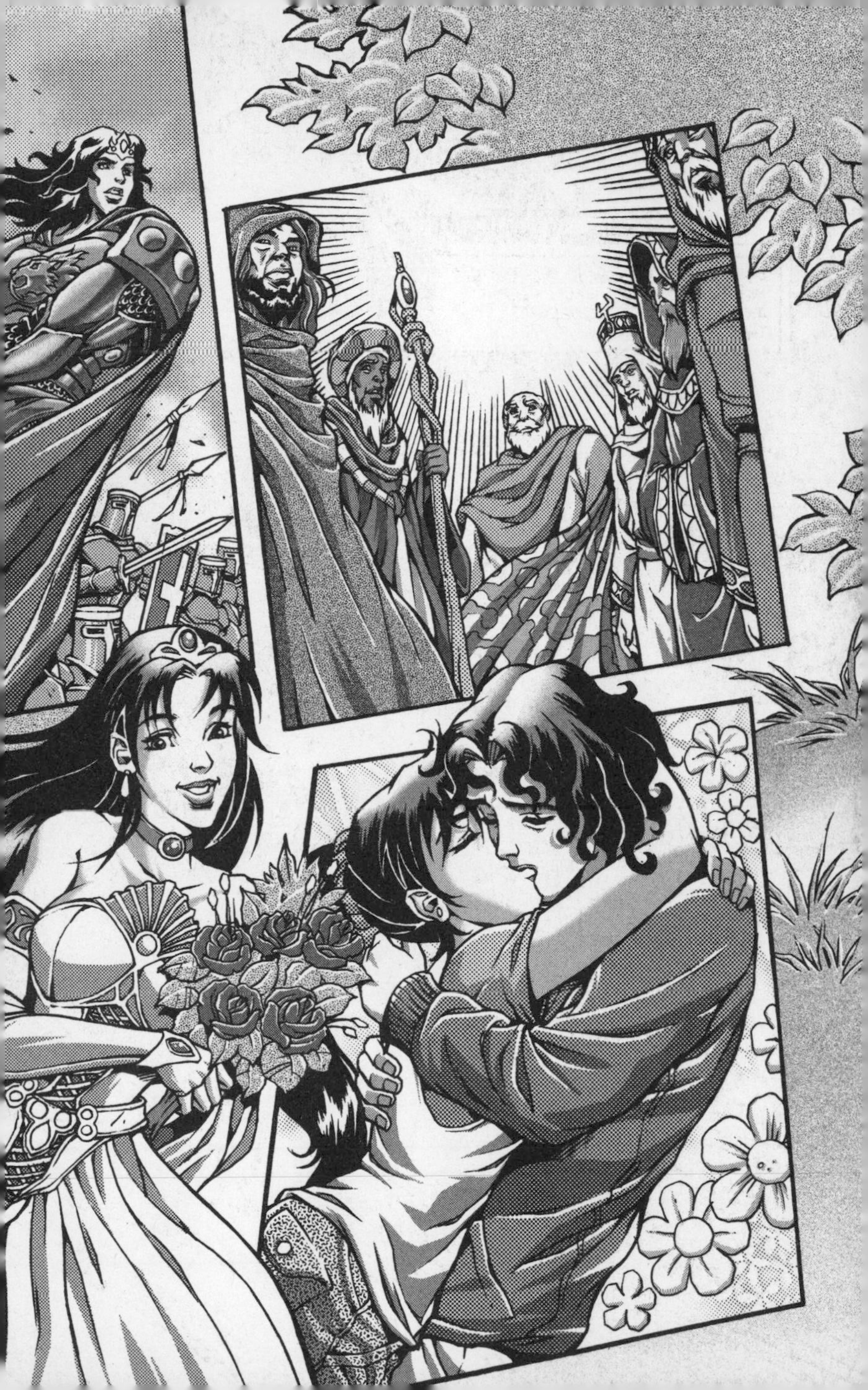

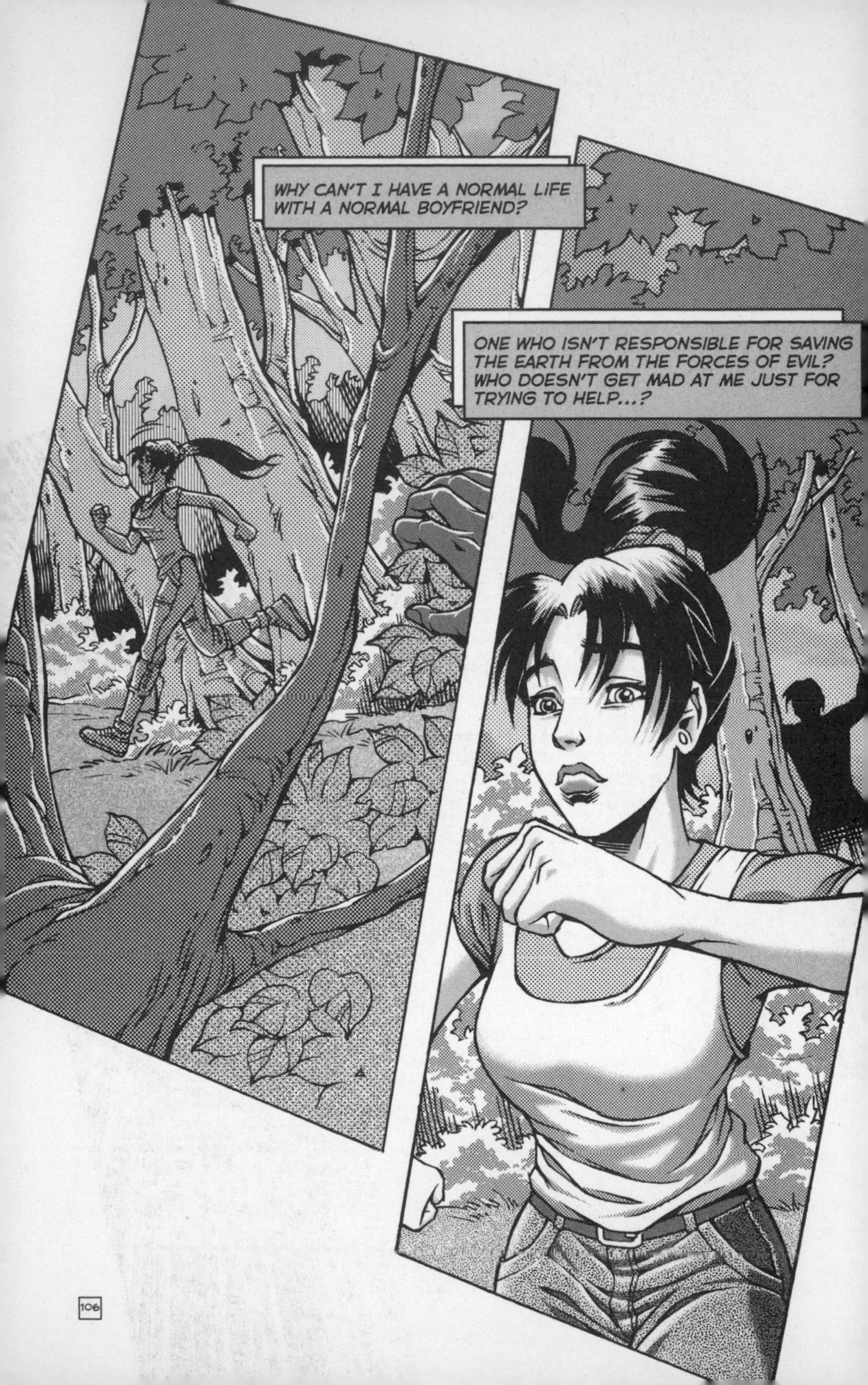
WHY CAN'T I HAVE A NORMAL LIFE WITH A NORMAL BOYFRIEND?
ONE WHO ISN'T RESPONSIBLE FOR SAVING THE EARTH FROM THE FORCES OF EVIL? WHO DOESN'T GET MAD AT ME JUST FOR TRYING TO HELP...?

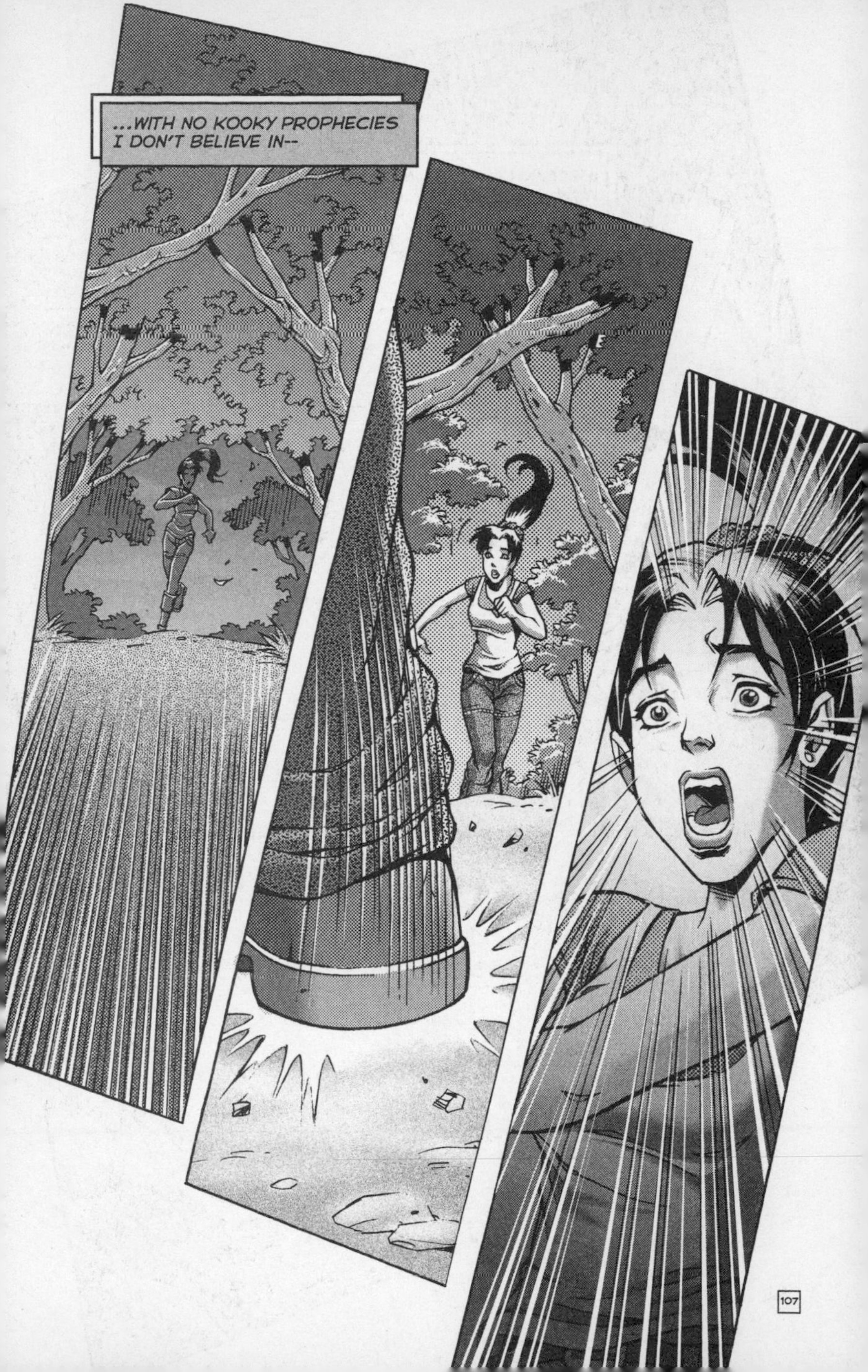
...WITH NO KOOKY PROPHECIES I DON'T BELIEVE IN--

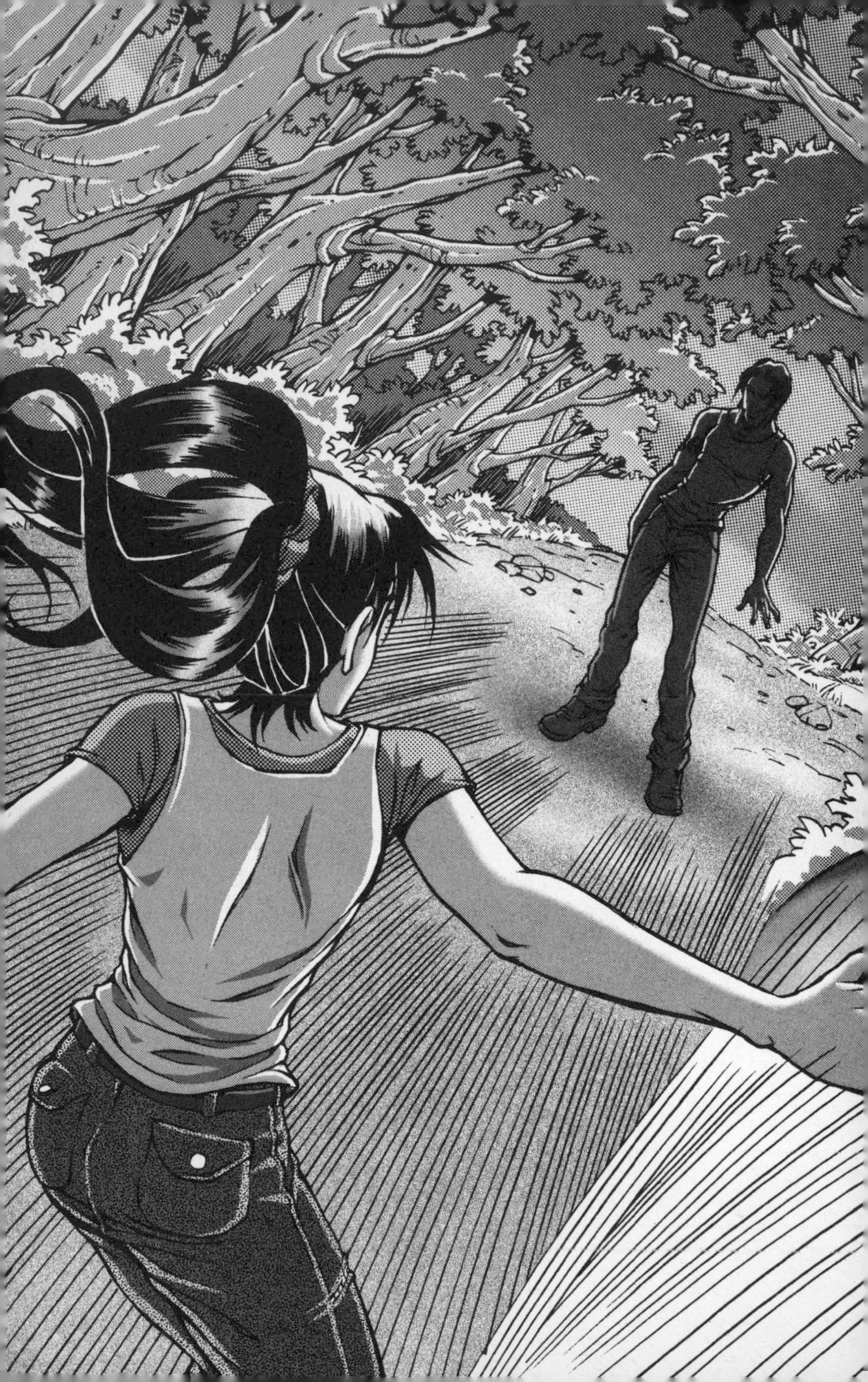

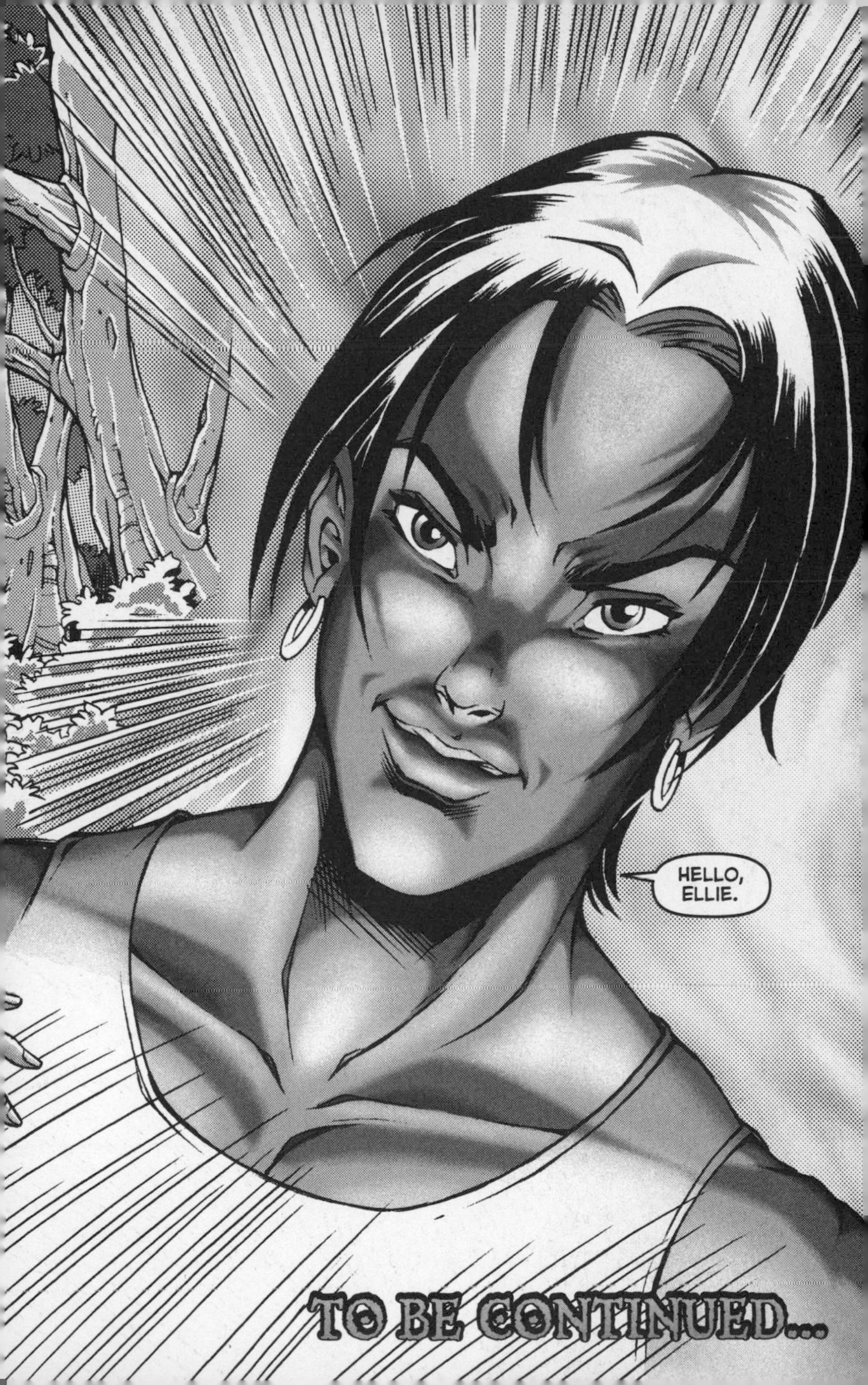
HELLO, ELLIE.
TO BE CONTINUED...

For all the books about Ellie and more by

MEG CABOT

check out the following pages!

You'll find:

- More about *Avalon High*, the novel!
- Blurbs about Meg's other exciting books
- Info about the Princess Diaries series

Still not enough?
For even more about Meg Cabot, go to

www.harperteen.com/megcabot

You can read Meg's online diary,
find the latest info on her books,
take quizzes, and win fabulous prizes!

Ellie has a hunch that nothing is as it seems in

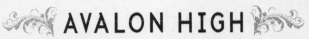

AVALON HIGH

Avalon High seems like a typical school, with typical students. There's Lance, the jock. Jennifer, the cheerleader. And Will, senior class president, quarterback, and all-around good guy. But not everyone at Avalon High is who they appear to be . . . not even, as new student Ellie is about to discover, herself. What part does she play in the drama that is unfolding? What if the chain of coincidences she has pieced together means—like the court of King Arthur—tragedy is fast approaching Avalon High? Worst of all, what if there's nothing she can do about it?

From

AVALON HIGH

I got out of the car and did a few stretches while I surreptitiously watched my dad prepare for his run. He'd put away his wire rims—he's blind as a bat without them. In fact, in medieval times, he'd probably have been dead by the age of three or four from falling down a well or whatever; I'd inherited my mom's twenty-twenty vision, so most likely I'd have lived a bit longer—and put on these thick plastic-rimmed glasses that have an elastic band he can snap behind his head to keep them from sliding off while he runs. Mom calls this his Dork Strap.

"This is a nice running path," my dad was saying, as he adjusted his Dork Strap. Unlike me, who'd spent hours in the pool, Dad wasn't a bit tan. His legs were the color of notebook paper. Only with hair. "It's exactly one mile per lap. It goes through some woods—a kind of arboretum—over there. See? So it's not all in the hot sun. There's some shade."

I slid my headphones on. I can't run without music, except during meets, when they won't let you. I find that rap is ideal for running. The angrier the rapper, the better. Eminem is ideal to listen to while running, because he's so mad at everyone. Except his daughter.

"Two laps?" I asked my dad.

"Sure," he said.

And so I turned on my iPod mini—I keep it on an arm strap when I run, which is different than a Dork Strap—and started running.

It was hard at first. It's more humid in Maryland than it is back home, I guess on account of the sea. The air is actually heavy. It's like running through soup.

But after a while, my joints seemed to loosen up. I started remembering how much I'd liked to run back home. It's hard and everything. Don't get me wrong. But I like how strong and powerful my legs feel underneath me while I run . . . like I can do anything. Anything at all.

There was hardly anyone else on the path—just old ladies, mostly, power-walking with their dogs—but I tore past them, leaving them in my wake. I didn't smile as I ran by. Back home, everybody smiles at strangers. Here, the only time people smile is if you smile first. It didn't take my parents very long to catch on to this. Now they make me smile—and even wave—at everyone we pass. Especially our new neighbors, when they're out in their yards mowing their lawns or whatever. Image, my mom calls it. It's important to keep up a good image, she says. So people won't think we're snobs.

Except that I'm not really sure I care what people around here think about me.

The running path started out like a normal track, with closely cut grass on either side of it, snaking between the baseball diamond and the lacrosse field, then curving past the dog runs and around the parking lot.

Then it left the grass behind, and disappeared into a surprisingly thick forest. Yeah, a real forest, right in the middle of nowhere, with a discreet little brown sign that said WELCOME TO THE ANNE ARUNDEL COUNTY ARBORETUM by the side of the path.

I was a little shocked, as I ran past the sign, at how wild the undergrowth on either side of the trail had been allowed to get. Plunging into the deep shade of the arboretum, I noticed that the leaves overhead were so thick, hardly any sunlight at all was allowed to get through.

Still, the vegetation on either side of me was lush and prickly looking. I was sure there was also a ton of poison ivy in there, too . . . something that, if you contracted it badly enough back in medieval times, could probably have killed you, since there wasn't any cortisone.

You could barely see two feet beyond the path, the brambles and trees were so close together. But it was at least ten degrees cooler in the arboretum than it was in the rest of the park. The shade cooled the sweat that was dripping down my face and chest. It was hard to believe, running through that thick wood, that I was still near civilization. But when I pulled out my headphones to listen, I could hear cars going by on the highway beyond the thick growth of trees.

Which was kind of a relief. You know, that I hadn't accidentally gotten lost in Jurassic Park, or whatever.

I plopped my earphones back into place and kept going. I was breathing really hard now, but I still felt good. I couldn't hear my feet striking the path—I could only hear the music in my ears—but it seemed to me for a minute that I was the only person in these woods . . . maybe the only person in the whole world.

Which was ridiculous, since I knew my dad wasn't that far behind me—probably not going much faster than the power-walking ladies, but behind me nonetheless.

Still, I had seen too many TV movies where the heroine was jogging innocently along and some random psychopath comes popping out of thick growth, just like the stuff on either side of me, and attacks her. I wasn't taking any chances. Who knew what kind of freaks were lurking? I mean, it was Annapolis, home of the U.S. Naval Academy and the capital of Maryland, and all—hardly an area known for harboring violent criminals.

But you never know.

Good thing my legs were so strong. If someone did jump out at me from the trees, I was pretty confident that I could deliver a good kick to his head. And keep stomping on him until help came.

It was right as I was thinking this that I saw him.

A hilarious new novel about getting in trouble, getting caught, and getting the guy!

#1 NATIONAL BESTSELLING AUTHOR

MEG CABOT

Pants on Fire

Katie Ellison has everything going for her senior year—a great job, two boyfriends, and a good shot at being crowned Quahog Princess of her small coastal town in Connecticut. So why does Tommy Sullivan have to come back into her life? Sure, they used to be friends, but that was before the huge screwup that turned their whole town against him. Now he's back, and making Katie's perfect life a total disaster. Can the Quahog Princess and the *freak* have anything in common? Could they even be falling for each other?

HARPER TEEN
An Imprint of HarperCollins Publishers

www.harperteen.com

the mediator

Suze can see ghosts. Which is kind of a pain most of the time, but when Suze moves to California and finds Jesse, the ghost of a nineteenth-century hottie haunting her bedroom, things begin to look up.

THE MEDIATOR 1:

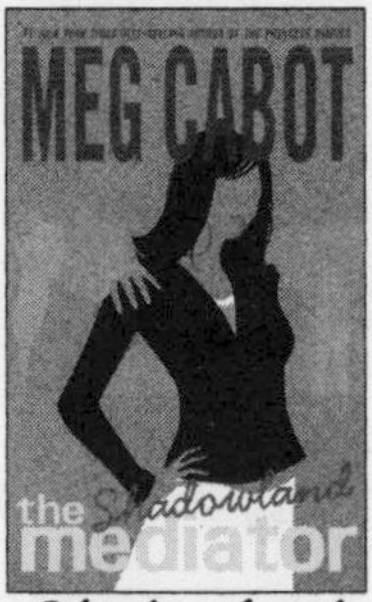
MEG CABOT
Shadowland
the mediator

Shadowland

THE MEDIATOR 2:

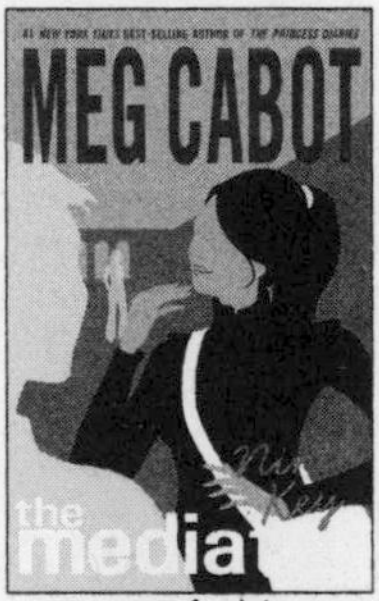
MEG CABOT

Ninth Key

THE MEDIATOR 3:

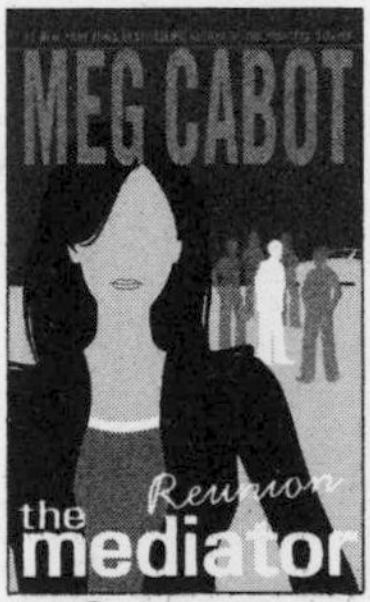
MEG CABOT
Reunion
the mediator

Reunion

THE MEDIATOR 4:

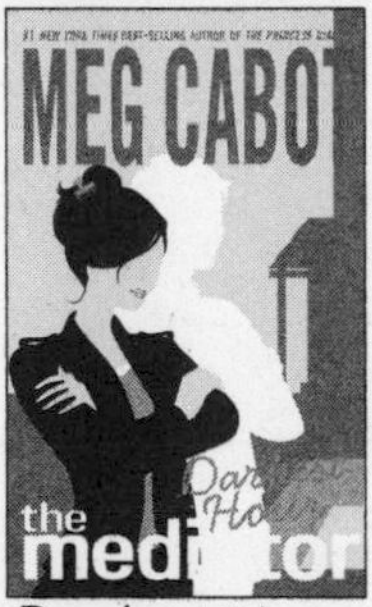
MEG CABOT

Darkest Hour

THE MEDIATOR 5:

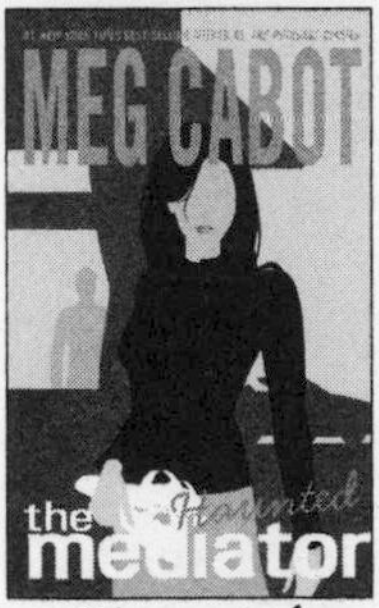
MEG CABOT
Haunted

Haunted

THE MEDIATOR 6:

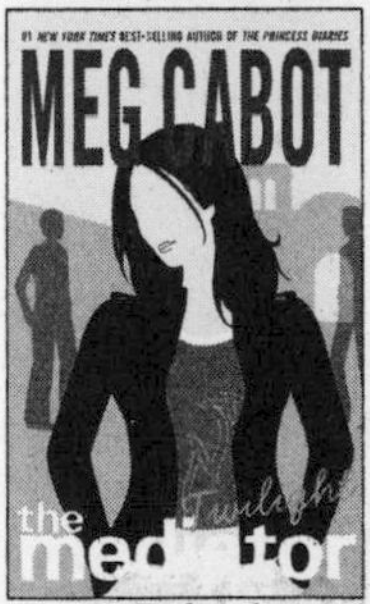
MEG CABOT

Twilight

ALL-AMERICAN *Girl*

What if you were going about your average life when all of a sudden, you accidentally saved the president's life? Oops! This is exactly what happens to Samantha Madison while she's busy eating cookies and rummaging through CDs. Suddenly her life as a sophomore in high school, usually spent pining after her older sister's boyfriend or living in the academic shadows of her younger sister's genius, is sent spinning. Now everyone at school—and in the country!—seems to think Sam is some kind of hero. Everyone, that is, except herself. But the number-one reason Samantha Madison's life has gone completely insane is that, on top of all this . . . the president's son just might be in love with her!

Ready OR *Not*

In this sequel to *All-American Girl*, everyone thinks Samantha Madison—who, yes, DID save the president's life—is ready: Her parents think she's ready to learn the value of a dollar by working part-time, her art teacher thinks she's ready for "life drawing" (who knew that would mean "naked people"?!), the president thinks she's ready to make a speech on live TV, and her boyfriend (who just happens to be David, the president's son) seems to think they're ready to take their relationship to the Next Level. . . .

The only person who's not sure Samantha Madison is ready for any of the above is Samantha herself!

Girl-next-door Jenny Greenley goes stir-crazy
(or star-crazy?) in Meg Cabot's

TEEN IDOL

Jenny Greenley's good at solving problems—so good she's the school paper's anonymous advice columnist. But when nineteen-year-old screen sensation Luke Striker comes to Jenny's small town to research a role, he creates havoc that even level-headed Jenny isn't sure she can repair . . . especially since she's right in the middle of all of it. Can Jenny, who always manages to be there for everybody else, learn to take her own advice, and find true love at last?

Does Steph have what it takes?

HOW TO BE *Popular*

Everyone wants to be popular—or at least, Stephanie Landry does. Steph's been the least popular girl in her class since a certain cherry Super Big Gulp catastrophe five years earlier. And she's determined to get in with the It Crowd this year—no matter what! After all, Steph's got a secret weapon: an old book called—what else?—*How to Be Popular.*

Turns out . . . it's easy to become popular. What isn't so easy? Staying that way!

Finally, don't miss these
two irresistible love stories!

Nicola *and the* Viscount

It's only her first London Season, but sixteen-year-old Nicola has made up her mind: Handsome, charming, poetry-reading Lord Sebastian is, simply, a god. So when the divine viscount starts paying special attention to her, Nicola is certain she's found her destiny.

Everything is perfect until the infuriating—and disturbingly handsome—Nathaniel Sheridan begins to cast doubt on the viscount's character . . . and on Nicola's feelings.

Victoria *and the* Rogue

Wealthy young heiress Lady Victoria Arbuthnot is accustomed to handling her own affairs—and everyone else's. So when she's suddenly sent to London to find a husband, Victoria quickly finds a perfect English gentleman.

Everything is just as she wants it—that is, if the raffish young ship captain Jacob Carstairs would stop meddling in her plans.

READ ALL OF THE BOOKS ABOUT MIA!

The Princess Diaries

THE PRINCESS DIARIES, VOLUME II:
Princess in the Spotlight

THE PRINCESS DIARIES, VOLUME III:
Princess in Love

THE PRINCESS DIARIES, VOLUME IV:
Princess in Waiting

Valentine Princess
A PRINCESS DIARIES BOOK (VOLUME IV AND A QUARTER)

THE PRINCESS DIARIES, VOLUME IV AND A HALF:
Project Princess

THE PRINCESS DIARIES, VOLUME V:
Princess in Pink

THE PRINCESS DIARIES, VOLUME VI:
Princess in Training

The Princess Present:
A PRINCESS DIARIES BOOK (VOLUME VI AND A HALF)

THE PRINCESS DIARIES, VOLUME VII:
Party Princess

Sweet Sixteen Princess:
A PRINCESS DIARIES BOOK (VOLUME VII AND A HALF)

THE PRINCESS DIARIES, VOLUME VIII:
Princess on the Brink

ILLUSTRATED BY CHESLEY McLAREN

Princess Lessons:
A PRINCESS DIARIES BOOK

Perfect Princess:
A PRINCESS DIARIES BOOK

Holiday Princess:
A PRINCESS DIARIES BOOK

But wait!
There's more by Meg:

THE BOY NEXT DOOR

BOY MEETS GIRL

EVERY BOY'S GOT ONE

SIZE 12 IS NOT FAT

SIZE 14 IS NOT FAT EITHER

QUEEN OF BABBLE

QUEEN OF BABBLE IN THE BIG CITY